THE PLACE CALLED DAGON

THE PLACE CALLED DAGON

Herbert Gorman

With an Introduction by Larry Creasy
and an Afterword by S. T. Joshi

Hippocampus Press

New York

Published by Hippocampus Press
P.O. Box 641, New York, NY 10156.
http://www.hippocampuspress.com

Cover design and Lovecraft series logo by Barbara Briggs Silbert.
Cover art and interior illustrations by Allen Koszowski © 2003 by Allen
Koszowski, and used by permission of Charon House.

Hippocampus Press logo designed by Anastasia Damianakos.

First Edition
Second Printing 2008
3 5 7 9 8 6 4 2

ISBN 9780972164436

TO

MARTHA

a mystery among mysteries

Introduction

by
Larry Creasy

Herbert Sherman Gorman was born on January 1, 1893, to Thomas and Mary Gorman of Springfield, Massachusetts. A new year baby, by all available records he appears to have been the couple's only child.

Gorman's father, Thomas Jerome Gorman, was born in Ireland in 1842. A horseman and racing driver, he came to the United States in the 1860s. Described by his son as "a hard-riding, hard-drinking, improvident cuss with a fiery temper,"[1] he may well have served as the model for the caustic seaman Uriah Carrier in *The Place Called Dagon*, at least in disposition. Having settled in New England, he presumably fought in the Civil War for the Union. By Gorman's own account, he was in every way a poor father. Thomas Gorman died in 1924, leaving a bitter son to write contemptuously of his father as having been "always broke . . . [he] gave me a Gawd-forsaken, poverty-stricken childhood."[2]

Gorman's mother was born Mary Longway in 1860 to Louis Longway and Lucinda Griswold. The Griswolds were a well-known, long-established family in New England dating back to the colonial era, and the mystique of such ancestral roots may have had some influence in the genealogical probing Gorman would include in the aforementioned novel. In any case, his mother was herself half-Gaelic, and with this background he was raised distinctly aware of his Old World heritage.

Herbert Gorman's literary predilection seems to have been instilled in him by his mother, whom he described as being "small, dark, talkative, [and] an inveterate bookworm."[3] Indeed, despite having suffered congenital cataracts in both eyes during early childhood, by the age of eight the future author was already an omnivorous reader—a skill that would later prove invaluable, as it would account completely for his higher education.

While Gorman attended public schools throughout childhood, and later technical high school in his teens, he was in no financial position to pursue formal academic ambitions at any college or university upon coming

---

1. *Current Biography: 1940*, ed. Maxine Block (New York: H. W. Wilson Co., 1940), p. 342.
2. Ibid.
3. Ibid.

of age. He filled this void by spending countless hours reading on a daily basis at the public library. Of this period he would claim: "I used to read about fifteen hours a day for months on end," adding with his typically cynical humor, "how could a penniless boy get 'eddycated' any other way?"[4]

For a time Gorman plied his hand at various trades, including bank clerk, assistant to a cobbler, and work in a rubber-stamp factory—a stint that almost cost him a finger. In 1912 he pursued a brief career as an actor in various stock company and vaudeville acts. Consistently stricken by stage-fright, the author would later sum up his thespian abilities with the succinct statement: "I simply stank."[5]

It was at about this time that Gorman began to submit poetry to various amateur publications, as well as the local newspapers. Taking notice of his literary bent through these efforts (and, no doubt, his reputation for being ever-present in the town library), Gorman was hired by the local newspaper, the *Springfield Republican*, as a book reviewer in 1915. It was a job he was obviously well-suited for, and would usher in a long career in journalism that would encompass reporting, editing, and writing in various capacities for a number of prestigious newspapers, most notably the *New York Times*.

In 1916, at the height of World War I, Gorman was called upon as a propaganda writer for the Liberty Loan Publicity Bureau, Second Federal Reserve, in New York. He would return to his hometown to work for the *Springfield Union*, but his taste of the big city had forever changed him, and in 1918 he made his first full move to Manhattan, where he began work at the *New York Sun*.

While he continued to publish poetry in such periodicals as the *Outlook, Current Opinion,* and *Red Cross Magazine,* in 1920 he made his first major breakthrough with the publication of *The Fool of Love,* a collection of his poetry. With his work now between hardcovers, Gorman began to take the first steps made toward a career as a full-time writer. That same year, while still at the *Sun*, his book reviews began to appear in the *Times*, and *Reedy's Mirror* published "The Barcarole of James Smith," the poem that would lend its title to his second collection of verse.

In 1921, Gorman married Jean Wright, of Cleveland, Ohio. She also harbored literary ambitions, and the two of them attended the celebrated "MacDowell Colony" for artists in Peterborough, New Hampshire. Founded in 1907 by the composer Edward MacDowell, the colony still

---

4. Ibid.
5. Ibid.

functions to this day as a sylvan refuge for artists seeking to cultivate their skills in a creative environment free from distractions. The result of the Gormans' stay was *The Peterborough Anthology* (1923), which they coedited, and which served as a showcase for the various poets who had visited the retreat. Among the poems found in the collection, at least one is deserving of special attention for its weird content. "Black Roses," by Hervey Allen—author of the Poe biography *Israfel*—is powerfully imaginative in its macabre imagery.

The years 1922–24 saw the publication of Gorman's second book of poetry and his first biocritical sketch of James Joyce. It was also during these years that Gorman and his wife cultivated their presence in the New York arts scene. Among members of their literary circle were such notables as Stephen Vincent Benét, Elinor Wylie, Theodore Dreiser, Ford Madox Ford, Carl Van Doren (whom Jean Gorman would later marry after the dissolution of her marriage with Herbert in 1932), Sinclair Lewis, Floyd Dell, and Thomas Wolfe. The majority of these writers had also attended the MacDowell colony, and it is possible that many of them first met there.

The group would often meet at the Gormans' Greenwich Village apartment. While not scandalous, the parties did gain notoriety wherein high-minded talks of literature not infrequently deteriorated over many drinks, despite the efforts of Prohibition. Gorman's ability to imbibe shamed that of his guests, and he would go on record as saying: "[I] love my liquor and love it strong, but can drink beer all night."[6] Such indulgences did not, however, interfere with Gorman's productivity, and the law does not appear to have ever caught on to his wife's and his domestic speakeasy. He continued a steady output of poems, critiques, and essays for numerous magazines and newspapers, including the *Saturday Review,* the *North American Review,* and the *Literary Review (New York Evening Post).*

In 1925, at age thirty-two, Gorman published his first novel, *Gold by Gold.* The author readily admitted the work as being "a slavish imitation"[7] of James Joyce's style, as employed in *Ulysses,* and utilized many of that author's experimental innovations. However, from a critical standpoint, the work offered a more telling insight into the author than merely his literary influences at the time. Harry R. Warfel, in *American Novelists of Today* (1951), described *Gold by Gold* as being "about a poor widow's son . . . whose poetic temperament leads him from a New England manufacturing town to Greenwich

6. Herschel Brickell, "The Cry of Dolores," *Saturday Review of Literature* 31, No. 6 (7 February 1948): 9.
7. Ibid.

Village, where his lack of ability shows up in his descent into a life of frustration and futility."[8] Obviously based in part on the author's personal background, it stands as a remarkably frank statement of Gorman's own deeply felt insecurities and anxiety regarding his talent. He would immediately abandon any further attempts at recreating Joyce's style, but, as would be seen, Gorman would never be free of that author's shadow.

In 1926 would follow his second novel, *The Two Virginities*, and his first full-length biography, *A Victorian American: Henry Wadsworth Longfellow*. It seems a logical conclusion that through Longfellow, Gorman became equally interested in the life of Nathaniel Hawthorne. The two men had been friends, and in researching Longfellow the correspondence trail might have led Gorman to contemplate the interior world of that considerably darker genius of American letters. Whatever the case, *Nathaniel Hawthorne: A Study in Solitude* appeared the following year, 1927, as did his first and only foray into supernatural fiction, *The Place Called Dagon*, to which we will return later for a closer look.

In 1928, at age thirty-five, Gorman, after a decade of working for New York newspapers (the *Sun* [1918–21], the *Evening Post* [1921–23], the *Times* [1923–27], and the *Herald-Tribune* [1927–28]), gave up journalism and began traveling abroad. His destination was Europe. In France he met and befriended James Joyce, four years after the publication of his short biography. It was the time between the World Wars, and the Irish Joyce thoroughly warmed to the American, whom he recognized as a fellow countryman in spirit. The two men found much in common, in literature and appetite for drink.

He traveled back and forth across the Continent and the British Isles several times, living in London for a year, as well as Ireland, and Scotland, with an interval spent in Switzerland. These trips provided the subjects for both his novels and biographies. In 1929 he published *The Incredible Marquis*, a biography of Dumas.

Throughout this eleven-year period, Gorman also made many trips back to America, and on May 9, 1932, he married Claire O. Crawford of New York. That year he published *Scottish Queen*, a biography of Mary, Queen of Scots. The following year on April 23, Claire gave birth to a daughter, Patricia. She was their only child, and the proud father always liked to point out that she shared the same birthday as William Shakespeare.

---

8. Harry R. Warfel, *American Novelists of Today* (New York: American Book Co., 1951), p. 180.

Three years after the appearance of the historical novel *Jonathan Bishop* (1933), a unique point in Gorman's career arose when *Suzy* (1934)—a contemporary romance—was made into a film with Jean Harlow and Cary Grant. Oddly enough, the author does not seem to have left any public statement of his opinion on the film. The written word seldom translates over to film in a manner that satisfies the story's author, and it may be that Gorman, like many writers whose novels have been filmed, chose to disown Hollywood's interpretation of his work. Despite the film's two heavyweight stars, the film *Suzy* (1936) apparently did not bring the author any appreciable rise in public recognition as enjoyed by some writers whose work was adapted to the big screen.

Undaunted, Gorman published one more historical novel, *The Mountain and the Plain*, in 1936. A three-year period of silence followed, and in 1939, with the outbreak of World War II, Gorman and his family returned to the States. Detached as he was from his friendships made overseas, his return allowed him the mental space he needed to piece together the massive wealth of information and personal insight he had been gathering on his friend James Joyce. In 1940, with that author's blessings, the monumental *James Joyce: A Biography* appeared. The book was widely regarded as the definitive work on the man, his life, and his art prior to the emergence of Richard Ellmann's biography in 1959. It would also prove to be the last great milestone in Gorman's life.

Unable to return to Europe, the author settled in Mexico. Throughout the mid to late '40s that country would provide the inspiration and background for a critically hailed "Mexican trilogy," consisting of *The Wine of San Lorenzo* (1945), *The Cry of Dolores* (1948), and *The Breast of the Dove* (1949). Critical praise, however, is by no means a yardstick of lasting (or even contemporary) popularity, and all his novels have long since disappeared into obscurity, *The Place Called Dagon* certainly being no exception. Only his nonfiction books, immune as such utilitarian volumes frequently are from fickle public taste, remain marginally available, having found safe havens from oblivion among the dusty shelves of university and high school libraries. The one exception is the Joyce biography, which is still regarded as having significant value. Thus, if Gorman's legacy survives at all in any real sense, it is almost wholly by way of his famous friend's life story.

On October 28, 1954, at age sixty-one, Herbert Gorman died at his home in Hughsonville, New York after five long years battling an illness the family did not make public. He left behind his wife and twenty-one-year-old daughter Patricia and an unfinished semi-autobiographical novel, *The Piper's Son*. He was laid to rest in Woodlawn Cemetery.

*   *   *

So how did this one work of supernatural fiction, so completely at odds with everything else the author produced, come into being? Within the context of Gorman's life a direct line can be drawn from the place he was living at the time to the works he produced. This is, of course, no major revelation; all artists must draw from experience. However, had Gorman never left New England there would be little to discern about the man himself from what he produced. His time at the MacDowell Colony would clearly indicate a genuine interest in being a writer, but it would not reveal the extent of his commitment. Few artists are willing or able to support themselves solely by their art.

During 1927, Gorman's thoughts were still very much on New England. He had written and published *Nathaniel Hawthorne: A Study in Solitude.* The background work done for the biography had led Gorman's imagination back to that dark period of persecution that stained the history of both men's native soil. He was under a witch's spell, and knew it . . . and had his notebook ready to take down the inspiration as it came.

Nathaniel Hawthorne, a native of Salem, was well-versed in the legends associated with his hometown, and he employed the supernatural frequently in one form or another throughout his work. However, like the spectral intrusions in Shakespeare's works, Hawthorne's world—both in fiction and reality—was one in which belief in the supernatural was still widely held throughout most of the population. Thus the material was by no means shrugged off by his readers as strictly fantasy fare, as it would be today. Indeed, as Gorman would find out, the man himself was not free of such beliefs. Hawthorne's ancestor, John Hathorne (spelled as such at the time), had sent several accused "witches" to the gallows, having presided as a judge at the trials. The guilt from this association was the cause behind the family's change in spelling their name. But particularly troubling to Hawthorne was the belief that a genuine curse followed the family bloodline leading back to Judge Hathorne.

The theme of ancestral guilt, like that of the supernatural, is frequently an element in much of Hawthorne's work, and both are present in the story "Young Goodman Brown," which originally appeared in the collection *Mosses from an Old Manse* in 1846. We find in this tale the basis for *The Place Called Dagon.* The parallels are numerous and obvious, and to probe too deeply herein will do a disservice to those about to read the novel. Suffice to say that Gorman's Dr. Dreeme is an extension of the impetuous Goodman Brown, as both are inexorably drawn into satanic confrontations through their own meddling—meddling that places both of them amidst the notorious Black Mass celebrations of witch-lore. Both characters must weigh their infernal temptations against the love of an innocent woman, and both are forced to make desperate journeys through primeval haunted woods, as they speed toward their respective destinies.

Also of interest is the use by both Hawthorne and Gorman of the historical figure of Martha Carrier. The so-called "Queen of Hell," she was one of the many unfortunates persecuted in the trials. However, her fiery tongue and defiant posturing continue to leave such an impression among those studying the events that some to this day seem prepared to believe she was the genuine article. Hawthorne merely includes her by name as being among the celebrants at the Black Mass, but she figures much more prominently in Gorman's novel. The *femme fatale* character Martha Westcott is the direct descendant of Martha Carrier in *Dagon*, and the spectre of the ancestor witch makes an appearance in a flashback scene, complete with rope marks burned into her neck.

But why the place called "Dagon"?

The author's decision to use the ancient Phoenician deity's name for the accursed gathering place of the witches in his novel is unclear. To his original devotees, Dagon was a god of agriculture and fertility, associated with corn harvests to those who dwelt inland, and symbolized as a fish by those who lived near the coast and whose livelihoods depended upon the sea. In one passage in the book Dr. Henry Lathrop relates vaguely the origin of the place-name, but not the reason behind the choice of the name itself. History teaches us that the gods of one civilization often become the demons of another when that civilization is conquered and assimilated. Such is the lot of both Dagon and Baal (among numerous others) in the Bible as the Hebrews overtook the lands where they were worshipped. As such, Dagon is referred to in Scripture as being yet another "devil" worshipped by heathens. It seems likely that out of the many pagan gods mentioned in the Bible, Dagon may very well have been pulled out of a hat by Gorman, serving for as suitable a "blasphemous" name from antiquity as any.

Yet, beyond the obvious parallels between the story and the novel, it is the entire *essence* of Hawthorne's witch-haunted world that served to inspire Gorman to create his own town of dark conspirators. A world where the sins of the fathers come down to succeeding generations as very real and terrible curses, where one has only to look into a warlock's black book to see his own name written within, where houses themselves keep memories of the deeds committed within their walls—these collective themes as a whole, so closely associated with Hawthorne, are what fueled Gorman's conception for his novel. In doing so, he seems to have exorcised his own demons. He would never return to the dark shores of Hawthorne's world, those ghosts being most thoroughly laid to rest.

And so, long before Stephen King's *Salem's Lot*, Thomas Tryon's *Harvest Home*, Charles L. Grant's Oxrun Station, or any of the myriad other haunted towns, beleaguered villages, and conspiratorial communities that have become standard stomping grounds in modern horror fiction, Herbert S. Gorman's Marlborough (with its unique titular country club) has existed as an unjustly neglected landmark. Just like the "ancient evils" kept under wraps in those other hot spots, Marlborough has been biding its time, waiting for the newcomers who will surely come. It has been off the map for a long time, but it's now open for visitors. We hope you enjoy the stay!

THE PLACE CALLED DAGON

Chapter One

I

Doctor Dreeme, turning sleepily on his pillow, heard the clatter of a horse's hoofs coming down the steep Leeminster Road. The steely clash on the rock-path tore abruptly through his semi-trance and he opened his eyes, scowling vaguely at the milky blur of ceiling. The horse stopped with a rough grating of hoofs below the window and the doctor sighed. Marlborough was like that. It was undoubtedly another farmer with a pain in his back who might just as well wait until morning. It was at night that his taciturn neighbors were most obsessed with the somber consequences of their lonely ailments. In daylight they would bear them with the dumb equanimity of animals, sitting behind drawn curtains or plodding painfully over their stony fields. But they were horribly afraid of dying at night. The bell clanked feebly. The doctor threw back his quilted coverlet of great square patches, rose in the darkness of the room, and strode over to the window. He leaned out, straining his eyes to see who stood in the gray mist of the moon outside his door.

"Who is it?" he called sharply. "Who, in the name of Heaven . . . at this time of night . . ."

A boyish treble answered him.

"Doctor Dreeme? I'm Miles, Jeffrey Westcott's hired boy. Mr. Westcott's taken something awful. He wants for you to come and help him right away. He's shot himself and . . ."

"I'll be right down," snapped the doctor.

He fumbled about the room, lit a kerosene oil lamp, and hastily dressed himself, drawing his trousers on over his rumpled pyjamas. Pausing an instant before the cracked mirror he smoothed back his tousled hair and dashed some cold water from the china bowl upon his sleep-warm face. It was a square-cut visage, young, thin-lipped, and with long narrow eyes that stared back briefly at him. Two years' arduous practice in Marlborough, a relentless precision of deaths and births and ailments, had etched tiny lines about his mouth and eyes and forehead, lines of watchfulness and concentration, but he was still surprisingly youthful in appearance and alert in action. He grasped his black bag and hurried down the stairs, slipping the bolt and stepping into the dim lane where the huge farmhorse pawed impatiently at the ground. The blank windows of the Slater house stared down at him gloomily as he turned to the boy, Miles, who perched like a small monkey on his mount.

"Are you sure that Jeffrey Westcott wants me to come?" asked Dreeme as he climbed to a seat on the blanket that served for a saddle. There was a minor note of amazement in his voice.

The boy said nothing but chirped to his horse and the huge beast swung in the lane and mounted the hill, slowly at first and then at a smart canter as the ascent eased its sharp angle. The blurred moon flew with them, trailing long bat-like wings of milky opacity across the crumbling stone walls and the buildings with their lurching outhouses. Beside them swept their broad shadow, a two-torsoed centaur, indistinct and formidable in outline. Looking back Dreeme could see the little town of Marlborough stretched out like a conglomeration of dark tombs. A cool air tingling with the freshness of impending rain flowed by his face. Low trees flung chunky green arms across the twisting fences at him. They were black in the dimmed moonlight. The shaggy hoofs of the horse thudded heavily on the sand-road. Suddenly the boy answered Dreeme's question.

"He told me to fetch you, anyway," he remarked to the darkness before him.

The doctor said nothing and the boy, turning his head, observed him fleetingly. Dreeme caught the flash of a small, dark, imp-like face and two dull-green eyes.

So far as the doctor knew nobody ever called at the Westcott farm. It was avoided territory, forbidden to children wandering through the byways between Marlborough and Leeminster and skirted hastily by the taciturn farmers who dwelt in its vicinity. Dreeme had observed the rambling white-washed buildings from the road often enough as he had passed on his way to various patients and occasionally he had seen Jeffrey Westcott ride into town for supplies, but that was all. The Westcotts took no part in the life of Marlborough. Indeed, they seemed frankly to court an ostracism that had long ago been willingly granted them by the unusual breed of natives who dwelt in this part of New England. Dreeme, curious and observant when he first arrived in Marlborough and took up the practice of his father's old friend, Humphrey Lathrop, had asked questions about the

Westcotts, as, indeed, he had about all the farmers in the neighborhood, for he believed in mixing as much psychological insight as possible with his medicinal treatments, but he soon discovered that questions were not welcome in the town. An excessive reticence possessed these leather-skinned delvers in the soil, these small-shopkeepers, and even the brief scattering of professional men who conducted the affairs of Marlborough. Therefore, as Dreeme was an astute and adaptable young man, he speedily learned to keep his mouth shut and, at least outwardly, to suppress his curiosity. It was enough to serve as well as he could when he was called upon and to expend whatever mental energies he might have in the study of various profound books on medicine and psychology. Although time passed slowly it passed agreeably for loneliness did not obsess Dreeme. He was New England enough himself to slip naturally into a rut of reticence and to occupy himself with his own thoughts. Still there were many times when of all the curious folk in his environment he let his cogitations wander to the Westcotts.

They were unusual in their abandonment of the common intercourse of daily life. Apparently they had no friends, not even those cursory friends who met in the Post Office and General Store and discussed in brief bursts of monosyllables the politics and phenomena of the day. They were decidedly sufficient unto themselves. Dreeme always thought of the Westcotts as a plural number although he had never laid eyes on Mrs. Westcott. He knew that she existed and that was all. This, of course, was extraordinary in a small New England town where every individual might be supposed to know intimately the smallest details of a neighbor's life; where, as a rule, the women, at least, maintained a sharp and malicious watch on one another. But this, after all, was an unusual New England town as Humphrey Lathrop had insisted to the young man when Dreeme first ventured upon Marlborough.

"You have seen New Englanders all your life," the older doctor had said, "and you know their usual characteristics, reticence tinged with curiosity, religious fervor jaundiced with personal hypocrisy, an old pride bolstered by a stony soil, a nasal twang possibly induced by generations of psalm-singing through the nose, a stubborn zeal in labor and an inborn stinginess. You have seen that type of New Englander and I do not go so far as to say that you will not find it here; but there is a type of New Englander in this place that you have never seen before and of which I knew nothing until I came here. Marlborough and, to a lesser degree, Leeminster are cul-de-sacs into which an ancient backwash of old blood has flowed. It has been unrelieved by any new influx for two hundred years or more. It is not easy to get up here, you know, and once here there is little to hold an ambitious man. That is why you will go away some day. These people have dwelt here in this valley so opportunely surrounded by the Florida mountains and have intermarried for generations. Some day, perhaps the day when you leave for ever, I will tell you what curious breed of Puritan drifted into this valley and established these communities. You will be amazed, for they are a breed of which you catch but furtive glances and hints in Pilgrim and Puritan chronicles. A curious intermixture of ethical and Dionysiac madness produced the forefathers of these people to whom you must administer as wisely as you can and with a minimum of words and questions." The old doctor cleared his throat with a tremendous harrumph, his elephantine body quivering like a great jelly-fish, and Dreeme decided that he had been told nothing at all. If he was to solve the mystery of Marlborough—and there *was* a mystery, for he felt it like two huge dark wings hovering over the entire community—he must do it all by himself.

For two years now the mystery had stood just outside his door, a dark and disquieting impalpability that teased him into fruitless suppositions, that revealed itself fleetingly in the swift sidelong glitter of cautious eyes, that threaded the valley and the town with a dim muffled sense of something unearthly. And yet the sun shone brightly enough, the farmers went about their business with the usual grim doggedness of men who scrape a difficult living from miserly soil, and the thin-faced women, scrawny-armed and bowed in the shoulders, existed as women do in a small world of ceaseless irritating tasks. There were moments when Dreeme decided that there was no mystery at all, that his imagination was playing tricks with him, and that his intuitions were the idle outgrowths of a mind too much concerned with itself and revolving inwardly and creating vague bogies for lack of other occupations. But after such moments of doubt would come still days when the lurching houses seemed to watch him maliciously and when the still trees, flinging their black shadows across the yellow glitter of deserted roads, would stand as symbols of some invisible prowling specter that patrolled the valley and observed him with blank lidless eyes. His flesh crawled on his bones and it was only by an effort that he put the obsession from him. He would say to himself that it was ennui, that it was a morbid reaction to his existence in a small world where, in spite of his ministrations, he was an outsider, that it was nerves, but, considering the matter deliberately, he knew that it was none of these likely causes. He possessed no nerves; he was not weary of his loneliness; his mind was not too idle. It was something outside of him pushing gently against his mind.

II

The horse thudded ponderously up the road.

"How did Westcott shoot himself?" asked Dreeme suddenly.

The boy turned his thin face and green eyes over his small hunched shoulder, opened his mouth to speak, and then closed it firmly. "I calculate that he'll tell you that," he finally answered. He kicked ferociously at the horse's ribs with his small bare feet.

A few drops of rain dashed against Dreeme's face. It was extraordinarily dark now for the moon had disappeared, swallowed up in the soundless rain-cloud that stretched across the sky like a monstrous sable circus-tent. More by sense than anything else the young doctor knew that he had passed the old burned mill and an instant later the horse clattered across the small wooden bridge which spanned the narrow Saccarac River. He was now on the final stretch of dirt-road leading to the Westcott farm. This route was exceedingly familiar to Dreeme for he traversed it often, going either to some farm or to the larger town of Leeminster where there was a bank, a stone schoolhouse, a deserted gin-distillery crumbling to ruin, and a small court-house. The road turned in a great slow arc and was bordered by low stone fences, dejected and wrecked by weather into wide breaches at intervals. Between the roadway and the feeble barriers grew occasional clumps of birch trees and beneath them in season bloomed the dusty black-eyed Susans and asthma-compelling golden-rod. Behind the fences stretched the ploughed fields and grass meadows of the various small farms, all of them sloping downward for the Marlborough-Leeminster road progressed along a ridge. A faint mingled smell of piled dung, rotting hay and skinny poultry permeated the air. Dreeme knew the territory well enough by day. The white-washed houses, set well back from the road and a story more in the rear than they were in front because of the ground slope, lifted tilted smoking chimneys. Dogs, cursed with legions of perpetually active fleas, barked from sagging porches and blear-eyed cocks crowed in the wire-enclosures behind the long lurching kitchens that seemed to have been added as afterthoughts to the dispirited houses. Some of these dwellings were astonishingly old and even the white-wash failed to conceal their dejected venerability. The doors and windows, sunken by the years as though Time had leaned on the lintels and sills with a heavy elbow, leered like the features of a twisted face. All this was in the daytime. At night a profound darkness enveloped these staggering structures. There were no lights in the small opaque windows, nothing but the blank glow of the moon and stars. The farmers of Marlborough sought their beds at an early hour, and the candles and kerosene oil which still sufficed for illumination cost money. Only when the moon was at its brightest did the houses step somewhat out of their brooding night shadow and turn the incurious eyes of their windows toward the curving road. Then they seemed to squat like an unfriendly array of old crones in soiled white wrappers, watching the highway along which so many strange figures had passed since the first mysterious settlers arrived in the valley and found it a likely place wherein to raise their hewn log houses and their solitary mill.

The horse stopped suddenly and Dreeme, surmising that he had reached his journey's end, slipped to the ground, his feet clattering on loose pebbles as he maintained his balance. A long ominous growl immediately before him greeted his footsteps and he drew back with some trepidation. He knew all about the half-savage dogs that patrolled the farmyards at night. The boy hurried by him and there was a sound of poles being pulled out of their sockets at a gateway. A cold damp snout thrust itself against Dreeme's hand just as the boy hissed an unintelligible phrase and an instant later there was the sound of a heavy body forcing its way through the bushes which lined the road. Dreeme knew that the dog was watching him from a distance with savage curiosity. The boy came back and grasped the rope that served for bridle on the horse. "This is the way, doctor," he said. "Don't be afraid of the dog." They stumbled through what was apparently an aperture in the fence and followed a twisted and hummocky path. Dreeme tripped over unsuspected hollows and small jutting boulders until they circled the dark bulk of the house and were at a rear door. A few drops of rain pattered against his face as he looked up at the rear windows. It was curious that he could perceive no least vestige of light emanating from the blank panes. The building stood morosely in a pool of high trees and this intensified the darkness about it. At the door the boy knocked delicately, his thin knuckles playing upon the splintered woodwork, and, after a moment, while Dreeme felt very foolish and slightly startled, there were a few whispered words with some invisible personage who had shot back a series of bolts. The brief beam of a candle leaped across the doctor's face and he felt himself urged forward and into a room where the shadows fled sluggishly before the feeble whiplash of light from the cylinder of wax. There was a rattling sound as the bolts were shot and Dreeme knew that he was locked in the Westcott farm-house.

Clutching his black bag, he stared curiously about him but all that he could perceive was a simply furnished room, the usual "sitting room" of a farm-house with its few stuffed chairs, its wax-flowers under glass on a side table, its faded family pictures, a framed silver plate from a coffin, and an antiquated spinning wheel that squatted forlornly in a corner. Before him stood a stocky figure holding a fat candle in one hand and directing him toward an opposite door with the other. The meager flame from the candle slanted back and illuminated a deep red beard and two glassy eyes. Dreeme, his vision clearing in the feeble glow, noted that his companion was evidently the hired man, a burly figure absurdly short for his girth and garmented in dejected looking blue overalls and a faded woolen shirt. This apparition was in his stocking feet and he made no sound as he padded across the floor. The hired man said nothing but cleared his throat with a choking sound as though he were endeavoring to loosen unused vocal chords, and then, apparently giving it up as something beyond his powers, proceeded toward the door which he had indicated with an awkward flourish of a square hairy hand. He rapped timidly at the door.

"Wagner?" cried a sharp voice from within.

Wagner opened the door a trifle, thrust in his shaggy red head, and seemed to croak hoarsely.

"All right! All right!" the voice snapped immediately, and Wagner stood back and motioned Doctor Dreeme toward the patch of yellow light that poured through the half-opened door.

III

It was a small room into which Dreeme ventured and one in which the walls seemed to push forward, an aspect intensified, perhaps, by the tall lurching cases of books which surrounded the square table at which Jeffrey Westcott sat. There were books everywhere, in the cases, scattered over the table, and piled in slumping heaps on the floor. The greater portion of them were huge tomes, bound in old buckrams, in worm-eaten moroccos, or in yellow vellum. The dull gold lettering, subdued in the glow of Westcott's kerosene lamp, seemed like the sleepy half-shut eyes of somnolent beasts waiting patiently for the word of the master who should bring them to life. But there was no word now. They rested, these mysterious beasts of ancient knowledge, holding their secrets close to their muted hearts. Dreeme paused just inside the door staring about him in amazement.

An impatient exclamation roused him to his professional duties and he turned toward Jeffrey Westcott, observing him closely for the first time.

"Good evening or good morning," remarked the man seated by the table. "I have lost count of the hours, doctor."

"It is a very fine library, I assure you," continued the farmer.

Westcott was a heavily-built man, smooth-faced, and with a shaven head.. This round skull, blue with an incipient growth of dark hair, reminded Dreeme irresistibly of the tonsured cranium of some medieval friar. It was curiously ridged in the center, as though the two sides of the skull had been pressed together while molten and so joined, leaving a cloven line where the bone had bulged upward on either side. The ears were long and rose thin and prominent on either side of this curious head. The broad brow slanted back at an obvious angle and the chin, blue also with incipient hair, thrust forward aggressively, the ensemble giving the impression of semi-malignant imperiousness. Westcott's nose was broken and this accident accentuated the curious profile which he presented when he turned his head, a profile almost ape-like but redeemed by a certain vitality of knowledge. His eyes, large, coal-black and motionless, glittered dully, but it was not the dull glitter of stupidity. Rather was it a repressed but unceasing watchfulness that was somehow mocking in its semblance of indifference. Dreeme was reminded of the eyes of a cat when it permits a bird to flutter within a few feet of its curved claws.

"It is a very fine library, I assure you," continued the farmer with a casual flutter of one sun-burned hand toward the lurching cases. Dreeme sensed a purring irony in the man's voice. "I should like to show it to you but just now I am somewhat inconvenienced by this cursed bullet wound."

Dreeme, with a muttered apology, hurried forward fumbling at the catch to his black bag.

"It is not often—at least in this part of the world—that one sees so many books," he said. "You must excuse me."

His amazement was frank and he made no attempt to conceal it.

"You are freely pardoned," replied the ironic voice.

The doctor knelt and began to remove the blood-stained bandage that swathed the plump calf of the farmer.

"How did this happen?" he inquired as the wrapping slipped away and he saw the black bullet-hole surrounded by a crusted clot of blood.

"Experiment," returned Westcott shortly.

"Experiment?" echoed Dreeme questioningly, glancing up into the still black eyes. Westcott reached deliberately for a cigar, drawing one from the large box that stood on the table at his elbow. He said nothing but stared blandly at the doctor as he lighted the long dark weed. Dreeme, flushed and feeling foolish, turned back to his labor. He decided that Westcott was an offensive brute.

"I want a pan of hot water," he said, after inspecting the wound. "I shall have to probe for the bullet. It may pain you a bit."

He felt a moment's elation at the idea of giving Westcott pain.

The farmer turned his head and shouted toward the door.

"Wagner!" he cried. "Wagner!"

In the short pause that ensued, Dreeme, still kneeling before the stocky Westcott, studied the worn backs of the books in the case opposite him. They seemed to emanate an atmosphere that was ominous. There was something dark and forbidding about them, an intangible suggestion of an evil culture. The crowding walls advanced stealthily bringing an aura of suffocation with them.

The farmer cursed softly and pleasantly to himself.

"My dear doctor," he began, "I am afraid you will have to . . ."

"What is it, Jeff?" inquired a feminine voice, low and husky, behind them.

Both men turned at this unexpected sound. Westcott was plainly put out and for a moment his large eyes glittered angrily. Dreeme gazed upward at the woman who had so quietly entered the room with a curiosity which almost instantly merged into amazement. There are women who at a first glance arrest the attention not so much by any ulterior beauty or unique qualities of bearing as by an inward spirit which seems to beat fiercely against the thin walls of flesh and strive vehemently to liberate itself from its entangling disguises. These women may not be beautiful in the fleshy sense of the word, but somehow they achieve more than the semblance of beauty in the eyes of the sensitive observer. Dreeme saw such a woman before him and knew instantly and instinctively that it was not alone the comeliness of her features that so casually and indifferently subdued and betrayed the deliberate impartiality of his reason. He saw immediately an extraordinary inward impulse that climbed in her bosom and all but trembled on her blood-red mouth. It was her eyes and mouth that first seized his imagination. These eyes were dark and they glowed beneath large white lids that drooped somewhat as with the ennui of identical days. They seemed endless in depth like half-concealed forest springs and yet a quickening spark glimmered in these unfathomable lakes of hushed amber fire. The mouth was full with curling lips almost archaic in their contour, and Dreeme was vaguely reminded of his adolescent ideas of the snaky-haired Medusa. There was a subtle cruelty in this mouth.

"I told you to stay in your own room, my dear helpful Martha," said Westcott, his chin thrusting forward, "but since you are here, permit me to present my invaluable friend, Doctor—er—Dreeme, I think. This is my wife, doctor."

She did not glance toward Dreeme.

"Wagner has gone to the—" She left the sentence unfinished. "I thought you would need hot water."

"Your mind is always acute, Martha," remarked Westcott, giving her a malicious look. "And who sent Wagner to the—"

"I did," she responded coolly, placing the basin of hot water on the floor close by Dreeme who still remained on one knee gazing at her. Westcott smiled sourly and turned to the doctor.

"Come, doctor," he said. "You must be wanting to get back to your comfortable bed."

Dreeme flushed and turned confusedly to his labors.

For a moment there was silence.

"The age of amazement," said Westcott softly to the air, "is worthy of a study in itself. There are so many ways of considering it."

He winced as the probe touched the raw flesh.

"Softly, doctor, softly," he begged. "Now take the age of amazement as it affects the individual. Is it not true, my dear doctor, that if we knew why a man was amazed and each time that he was amazed we should know a great deal about him?"

Dreeme, intent on his work, said nothing.

"The question is merely theoretical," proceeded Westcott. "I do not expect an answer. I, for my own part, mingle so seldom in the world of men that I have but small opportunity to put my theory in practice but whenever I do see a man I strive to observe his surprised reactions to things. It tells me something about him."

The bullet slipped from the wound and Dreeme busied himself for a moment in washing the torn flesh. At length he looked up for the silence seemed to invite him to speak, to carry on a conversation that was rather meaningless. He stared into Westcott's dark expressionless eyes.

"And me?" he said, smiling. "What have you learned about me in the few minutes that I have been here?"

Westcott was obviously waiting for the question.

"Your reactions of surprise were obvious," he answered, cocking his head on one side. He began to count the points off on his fingers.

"Number one. You were amazed at finding so excellent and unexpected a library here. I gather from that that your idea of the literacy of this part of the world is not high. I agree with you in the main—but there are exceptions everywhere, doctor. You were also amazed at finding in me a man not wholly a stranger to the subtleties of the mind. I may be flattering myself in this assumption but I do not think so. In other words, you had thought of me as a mysterious, surly, country clodhopper."

There was a soft snarl in his voice. Before Dreeme could expostulate he went on with his enumeration.

"Number two. You were amazed to hear that my little wound was the result of an experiment. It piqued a curiosity which, unfortunately for you, I shall not satisfy."

"I assure you, I—" began Dreeme stiffly, but the soft voice proceeded.

"Number three. You were amazed to see my wife. Well, I hardly blame you. She amazes me at times."

Again the soft snarl permeated his voice.

Dreeme instinctively glanced at Mrs. Westcott. She was standing by a small window gazing out on the darkness and he could see no more than the cool oval of her face. She seemed to be looking upward toward the rainy sky with a strained attentiveness that suggested the listener. It was, perhaps, the rain to which she was listening, for Dreeme could hear the soft gurgle and suck of the water as it dripped outside the window. With a final skillful twist he fastened the new bandage about Westcott's calf and stood upright. The farmer looked at him calmly, his lips slightly apart, and Dreeme could see the man's long yellow teeth.

"I should say from the casual glimpse I have had of you," remarked Westcott, "that you are a capable doctor, a painstaking man, a sensitive person perhaps a little stiff in reactions to unexpected things, and an individual who must fight against the impulse of being—well, not a busybody but one who is driven too far sometimes by the itch of curiosity."

Dreeme laughed aloud and picked up his bag. Absurdly enough, he could feel the presence of Mrs. Westcott behind him, a presence like the soft invisible approach of some great feline through the impenetrable darkness of a forest.

"Your analysis is amusing," he said. "But must I take it too seriously?"

"You must take it for what it is worth," replied Westcott, fastening his yellow teeth upon his cigar and puffing meditatively. "Be good enough, my dear doctor, to send your little bill by mail. I can dress the wound myself or have it done for me by . . . Wagner."

He looked up sharply, removing his cigar as the hint of a smile died from his face.

"Doctor Dreeme," he said. "I am a peculiar man. I am a student who has found a secluded harborage. I do not care to make acquaintances. They are unpleasant responsibilities and they deprive me of that leisure which I owe to my researches. I live my own life in my own way. I do not want to be disturbed by the curiosity of—er—neighbors."

Dreeme bowed silently, his face flushed, and turned to the door. Yes, he decided, Westcott was an offensive brute. The farmer smiled faintly, his cloven head bending forward in the lamplight.

"You must pardon my abruptness," he remarked. "I am a solitary anchorite except for my little circle and am not, perhaps, as courteous as I should be."

Dreeme said nothing. He could sense the faint mockery in the farmer's stiff speech.

"Will you show the doctor to the door?" said Westcott gently to his wife.

She started from her attitude of rapt listening and turned toward Dreeme, her heavy-lidded casual eyes flitting coolly across his face. Then she moved slowly toward the door. Dreeme's last picture of Westcott was of a curiously cloven head suddenly bowed above a huge tome. He could hear the soft rustling of Mrs. Westcott's skirt as she crossed the sitting room floor. His heart pounded rapidly as he moved through the closeness of the room after her. It was as though a strange drug that affected his breathing filled the air. He heard her unbar the door, and, as it opened, a rush of cool rain-washed air swept across his face bringing instant relief from the choked sensation that had overpowered him in the room. It was still raining, a desultory and gloomy patter that rattled on the trees and the tiny roof of the back porch. The wet air was filled with the fresh scent of water and soaked grass. Dreeme drew in long breaths of it as he stepped bareheaded into the rain, wondering somewhat vaguely how he was to be conducted back to town. Just as he was about to bid Mrs. Westcott goodby and was turning toward her he felt her arm fall sharply against his shoulder.

"Do you hear anything?" she asked in her low husky voice.

He strained his ears in some surprise and for a moment in the patter of rain he seemed to hear a thin rushing overhead as though a flock of heavy-winged birds were beating through the night air. The sound swept into nothingness so suddenly that he decided it was no more than the blood beating in his own ears or the upper whir of the rain. It was as though a door had been suddenly closed.

"No," he answered. "I don't hear anything but the rain."

Her hand pressed against him and he could sense in the darkness the soft rise and fall of her bosom. The blood started to race through his pulses again and the choked feeling that had persisted during the short space of time while they had crossed the dark room to the door filled him. He felt his lips trembling as though with a faint palsy. As he strained his eyes violently toward her he could dimly note the outline of her face turned toward his and he knew that her heavy-lidded eyes were wide open and fixed with a disturbing intensity upon him. Her full blood-red lips moved slowly. Then her hand dropped from his arm, and it was as though a strange power had been removed from him.

"Good night," she said in her low muffled tones.

The door closed softly and he heard the bolts being shot into place. Still he stood there, knowing that she, too, was standing just on the other side of the bolted door. After a moment's pause he heard her footsteps passing slowly and evenly through the room. Dreeme turned to the rain, a bewildered smile at his own impressionability creeping to his lips. At the same moment he heard Miles clucking to the horse. Blundering through the dark, he stumbled toward the road. Before he reached the gate it began to rain furiously, a heavy roaring downpour that soaked him to the skin.

Chapter Two

I

A rainy night abdicated to a warm sun-shot day. Dreeme, who had slept late after his disturbed rest, rose to a world that moved calmly and soberly toward midday. From his window he could see the weather-beaten sides of houses basking in the tranquil light and hear the deliberate and heavy footsteps of occasional pedestrians drifting down to the post-office or the general store. This was his Marlborough as he knew it best, a sober and silent community that clustered about the narrow Saccarac River and occupied itself with the daily functions of a somewhat abstemious living. Superficially Marlborough was uninteresting although it was not without a certain suggested placidity that might appeal strongly to the man in search of quietness, rest, and an escape from the febrile business of that greater world of cities where life was such a strenuous matter. There was little to see here and still less to beguile one. It is true that occasional youngsters ventured into the river but they did not make a habit of it. There were no halls of entertainment, no motion pictures, no wandering tent shows to raise their canvas on one of the surrounding meadows. Social intercourse was limited to casual greetings and infrequent meals. Each Sunday witnessed the crowding of the small white Congregational church and a dry and unimpressive religious service. Thus for one day in the week the space before the church was crowded with horses and small buggies and even one or two rattling Fords which disappeared as swiftly as ghosts after the service was completed. The reticent church-goers eddied from the door of the house of worship, mumbled a few words to one another, and then sped away toward their separate farms or strolled gloomily to their houses in town, their new Sunday shoes creaking woefully under the strain of unexpected use. Their voices seemed dry and rusty as though with long disuse and an absurd self-consciousness emphasized the natural awkwardness of their bearing. They plucked gingerly at unaccustomed collars and viewed one another with dumbly diffident eyes. Yet they possessed some bond in common, some link of connected life that bound them together into a whole, something that arrayed them against strangers and "furriners" although it was not evidenced in any obvious camaraderie.

It was not alone the bond of environment although that was evident enough. Men could not live year in and year out in the same tiny circumscribed area, scraping at the same granite-pitted soil, walking through the same tree-bordered streets, turning in at doors that were white-washed or green-painted replicas of one another, enduring the same biting winters when the surface of the river was a white plate of steel and the same scorching summers when the locusts shrilled in the brown stubble, witnessing the birth and death of the same flowers and trees, talking the same monosyllabic language and praying in the same manner to a far-away stone-faced God, without becoming infinitesimal portions of something that was unified and progressing in a solitary direction. Therefore the superficial characteristics of the men of Marlborough were the same just as their harsh voices sounded the same unlovely crow-like chord. But their similarity extended beyond this outer covering of manners, gestures, and appearances. Their humorlessness, their extraordinary seriousness, their unimpeachable reticence, their thinly-disguised surliness, all these deplorable and hermit-like traits seemed to point (at least in the young doctor's mind) toward an unhappy and despairing consciousness. It might be that they were tired of living. They might be a weary race of ghostly fatalists expressing tacitly their disapprobation of existence. It was true, the young doctor realized, that a portion (and a goodly portion, too,) of this desolate aspect of Marlborough might well be the mirage of his own brooding nature. He was imaginative enough, he knew, to see things in a colored guise. His own feelings rushed into his eyes and his mind and shifted his perspective. And his feelings were naturally morbid. Still, he was sure that the subterranean strangeness of Marlborough was not alone due to his gloomy fancy. He might play upon it and enlarge it far beyond its actual proportions but there must be something there to begin with, something that was the core, so to speak, about which the community had grown, covering it with layer after layer of taciturn generations until it disappeared completely. He strove to fix his mind upon these people in a rigidly impartial historical survey. Perhaps in this way he might reach light, might, through a series of logical and psychological deductions, define the spirit of Marlborough to his own satisfaction, but he discovered, after an intensive trial at such cerebration, that the results were meager and dissatisfying. He was not an inspired analyst. He was only a curious young man.

Here is a forgotten valley, he thought, a cul-de-sac in the hills of western New England. Into this sequestered place came the sons of Pilgrims and the Puritans and here they raised their first log-houses, their mills, their trading stations with the Indians, and their fortified church. They had no time for the lighter pleasures of living, and, indeed, their ethical conception of existence forbade them. They eschewed the colored ribbands of life. They were grim, therefore, long-faced and unsmiling and their days were taken up with clearing away virgin forests, struggling with the hordes of painted Indians, raising houses and churches and mills and forts and armories. The dark soil, spotted with boulders, fought with the Indians against them and they subdued it by the might of their tenacious minds and unresting arms. They had no time for love or laughter but they had plenty of time for labor and a taciturn doggedness not always unbroken by sighs. Surely the women must have sighed. Life was not a career but an onerous duty. It was a profound struggle against formidable and illimitable foes. What could such a people do but grow into a fierce, silent, unsmiling, and unimaginative race? What became of their animal natures in such a land of travail as this? Would they be diverted into a fanatical zeal for their God who bore always in His right hand a drawn sword? Or would the Dionysiac passions, the ancient inward pagan urges, break forth at odd and unsuspected moments in bright flares of malignant color? It was difficult to conceive of a complete suppression of all the old zests of living and Dreeme could see no way out for them but by a dark perversion that twisted them into sudden outbreaks or secret and terrible channels.

Well, these were the ancestors of the farmers of Marlborough. They had lived their drab lives and passed away and been buried in the forgotten graveyards and their sons, carrying in their hearts and brains this sullen heritage, had come after them and these sons had been equally reticent, taciturn, somber, and forbidding. With the years a slight leaven might have introduced itself, a gradual lightening of the colors of living, but it had not been enough to erase the ancient characteristics. Elsewhere in New England, in the busy manufacturing districts now dotted with cities and towns where the clacking looms and roaring machinery were never still, it was different. There the old urges were indelibly dead, perished for want of an iron breed to carry them on, overwhelmed by the great floods of foreign immigrations, devoured by a materialistic lust that knew no bounds. And in other places, in the agricultural corners of the land, a kindlier albeit somewhat threadbare tradition manifested itself. Dreeme knew for he had lived in those other portions of the old New England and had seen how drastically the land had changed. An occasional Puritan strain, a brief old-world courtesy—a trifle grim, to be sure, and a propped-up pride still persisted, but for the most part it was as Humphrey Lathrop had said—a land of curiosity, hypocrisy, labor, and stinginess. It was true that in certain secluded corners, in sun-dappled village streets, in twisted roads bordered by crumbling stone fences, in thinned woodlands flashing with the slim-white trunks of swaying birches, a hint of the old New England lingered for the pilgrim imaginative enough to sense it, a hint of mellow days and grave silences. It glowed at its brightest in the red cheeks of the apples and the gold and crimson of the sumach. It was there like a wistful ghost roaming through deserted roads. But it was not in Marlborough and no historical perspective could satisfy Dreeme as to why the community emanated the atmosphere which it undoubtedly did.

He might say that these farmers were the successors of the iron-willed pioneers who had darkened the soil with their blood and sweat, but that was not saying enough. They were all this, and they were something more beside. Behind them was something secret and profound. Under the layers of generations. Although they might be no more than vaguely conscious of it, Dreeme was almost satisfied in his mind that the nature of these natives was colored and subdued by a breed of ancestors who had possessed some inexplicable outlet for their suppressed madnesses. The young doctor could give no logical reasons for his conviction, but there it was. Perhaps Humphrey Lathrop had hinted it to him. These people differed from the other New Englanders, argued Dreeme to himself, in that they had been diverted in some mysterious manner from the obvious development of the New England temperament. Fortune had strangely enough sequestered this community and kept it intact through so many years and generations that the ancient characteristics had persisted on. No influx of foreigners with their European schemes of living had muddied it, for foreigners did not come here. No manufacturing boom had smashed it to pieces and founded a new world upon it. Marlborough stretched out beneath the summer sun and awaited the investigation of the close student of ethnology. Although its doors and windows might be open it seemed as though invisible skeins of mystery swayed before these apertures and defeated the eyes of the brain and intuitions. Dreeme seemed more conscious of this than ever as he perfected his toilet and prepared for what the day might offer. His dormant curiosity, which he had stilled so well, lifted a sluggish head and peered curiously about.

The young doctor descended the stairs slowly for the breakfast which had been prepared for him by his next-door neighbor, Mrs. Slater.

II

Mrs. Slater was methodical. It was her duty to run in during the morning with Dreeme's breakfast and the mail which she collected at the

post-office when she did her early morning buying. She never called it
"shopping." For his dinner (served at noon in Marlborough) and supper
Dreeme crossed over to Mrs. Slater's house where he sat in the midst of
five pop-eyed children, speechless Walden Slater, the Reverend George
Burroughs—invariably called "Preacher" by the community, and Mrs. Slater herself, a small, plump, dumpy woman, originally from Leeminster,
who was rather more officious than practical. Not being "born Marlborough" she did not affect the complete reticence of her neighbors. Still, she
had lived in the community long enough to learn to refrain from displaying
curiosity about things. It was only by a fluttering of her eyes and a somewhat cross-eyed inspection of things in general that she revealed the fact
that she was aware of matters which puzzled her. It was this fluttering of
the eyes that greeted Dreeme as he entered the room back of his office on
the ground-floor, a room which served as a breakfast chamber and a study.
He immediately understood that she had heard the arrival of the horse in
the night, and he waited, a trifle maliciously, to see if she would refer to it.
He had never looked at her intently, and he did not intend to do so now.
Indeed, he had never looked at any of the Slater ménage with enough curiosity to fix their features in his mind. He had a general idea, of course, of
Slater and the "Preacher," one was slouchy and the other was dark, but he
could not tell the children apart. Indeed, he was uncertain as to their sex.
Were three of them boys and two girls, or was it the other way around? He
sat down at the table smiling to himself.

Mrs. Slater scurried about the table, removing the blue china cover
from the platter of fried eggs and ham and pushing the three letters closer
to Dreeme's plate. There was a highly symbolic dolphin on the blue china
cover. It served as a handle. It was a bad handle now for its tail had been
smashed off during some disastrous washing.

"It seems as though I would work myself to death," Mrs. Slater said in
her peculiarly breathless voice. "I was out of bed at five-thirty this morning
getting Walden off to the field. That man sleeps like a log. You have to
shake him and shake him. And now it's you. And then it will be the boys."

"You don't have to shake me, anyway, Mrs. Slater," said Dreeme, his
mouth full of toast.

A small woman shaking a huge man. Get up! Get up! A poodle snapping at a somnolent St. Bernard. Mrs. Slater sighed, fluttered her eyes, and
gazed in a very cross-eyed manner at the design on the wall-paper. She
caught a wisp of her straw-colored hair and tucked it into the tight knob
on the back of her head. Her arms were covered with freckles and her nails
were blunted and broken. Dreeme slit his letters open and looked at them

briefly, letting them flutter to the floor. One was a catalogue for medical goods. "Use our electric frictioneer; it enlivens the blood." Another was a subscription blank for an agricultural magazine. How to mix a cheap fertilizer. The third announced a new supply of seeds and bulbs at Williams' Grain Shop, Main Street, Leeminster.

"Did you sleep well last night, Mrs. Slater?" inquired Dreeme. This was malice aforethought.

"If you worked as hard as I do *you'd* sleep well," she replied. The design on the wall-paper enchanted her.

"Well," said Dreeme, smiling broadly. "You'd better hurry along and get the boys ready for school. It is later than usual, you know."

Mrs. Slater walked slowly toward the door, small, plump, a bantam of a woman, her eyes fluttering fiercely. When she reached the threshold she paused and turned back.

"I hope you won't be late for dinner," she declared. "There's corn-beef and new cabbage."

"I'll be early, then," announced Dreeme.

She hovered for a moment with fluttering eyes and then walked out, slapping the door to behind her.

Dreeme smiled happily. He was getting to be quite a denizen of Marlborough himself. He could keep his mouth shut and perhaps, after all, it was a good thing. There was strength in silence. There was an advantage in it, too. It was nobody's business that he had been called to the Westcott farm and he knew in his soul that the natives were all banded together so far as he was concerned. They would tell *him* nothing. He was a stranger. Although he might live there for fifty years he would still be a stranger. He could open his heart as generously as he might, still he knew that there would be no reciprocity from Marlborough. Even Mrs. Slater (and his daily presence in her house created a sort of inescapable intimacy) kept her own counsels. He was not on the "inside" with anybody.

Finishing his breakfast he rose to his feet and wandered about the small room in a desultory fashion. There was nothing much to see there except his shelves of books and nothing seemed farther away from him at this moment than books or study. He was too restless to read and yet he could hardly define his restlessness. Something spoke to him in the back of his brain but it spoke with a small muffled voice, and he could not understand the words. Without being conscious of it he was brooding about some tangled mystery and he would have to wait until the secret lifted boldly out of the dark waves of his subconsciousness and he could see it in the bright sunshine of understanding. He sensed something. Like a lean dog with dilated nostrils he was aware of a dim carefully-concealed trail that led into the tenebrous gloom of Marlborough. He would have to go to Humphrey Lathrop, he reflected, and force that ancient intellect to divulge the secrets of the community. Humphrey might not know all, but at least he could indicate the right trail, a trail that could be followed to the very end, and at the end of that trail would not be a pot of gold, perhaps, but assuredly a pot of sulphur. It was true that Humphrey had warned him against curiosity, but there were times when curiosity ceased to be a mere impertinence and translated itself into a malady of the soul that could only be cured by the frankest revelation. Dreeme smiled a bit at putting the thought so solemnly to himself, but there it was, and he was forced to admit that his curiosity was steadily developing into a huge monster that would certainly devour him. It was no longer a titillation of the mind, but an agony of the spirit. He had lived in Marlborough for two years now, and he had rigorously caged this curiosity concerning the community, but he had never killed it. It had been drugged by books and the casual meditations of a New England mind, but it had never been put out of the way entirely. There were moments when it had stirred sluggishly behind its bars, rising slowly to its dark feet and peering out into the light with vague green eyes. Now Dreeme felt the fragile bars being snapped one after the other, and he knew that sooner or later the beast would step forth and either destroy him or be destroyed by him. All this, he imagined, was the result of a loneliness that had not preyed too much upon him at first, but which had been there all the time, gathering strength and biding its time. He had not been satisfied all these quiet months. He had been drugged by his own weariness of spirit. And now, at the touch of a hand, he was awake and conscious of a problem looming before him that seemed as high as the Himalayas.

The touch of a hand! Dreeme had been forcing his mind away from the thought that tugged at him, but now he gave way to it as he picked up his hat and walked out of the house and up the lane toward the old burned mill and the bridge over the Saccarac River. His feet fell pleasantly on the dark soil as he strode along. He had been curious before, but he could date the fierce restlessness of his curiosity to that moment the night before when Mrs. Westcott had pressed against him in the rain and listened to noises that were no noises, after all, in the black clouds. As he walked along the narrow rising street bordered with the unblinking windows of the clapboard houses, his thoughts revolved about the Westcotts. He had seen the surly type of New England farmer, the secret drunkard, the illiterate misogynist, but none of them had been like Jeffrey Westcott. There was a cu-

rious finish to Westcott, the evident marks of a culture that extended far
beyond Marlborough and which possessed something European in its
fleeting polish. It had not been manifested in words so much as in an easy
insolence of demeanor, a sureness of self that emanated from an ugly but
intelligent face. This man might have been reared among these hills, but he
had certainly not received his knowledge of the world here. He had gone
beyond the hills and the seas and into the most curious places. And having
done so it was all the more remarkable that he should choose to settle in
the intellectually-arid valley that could boast no better civilization than the
taciturn towns of Leeminster and Marlborough. To think about the Westcotts at all meant to creep upon them logically and deliberately. Dreeme
realized that he would have to adjust his thoughts in a precise manner if he
was to arrive at any reasonable deductions regarding them.

As he sauntered along the road and nodded vaguely to the few tanned
expressionless faces which passed him he sought to place his thoughts in
order and achieve a sort of deductive acumen so far as the Westcotts were
concerned. He would consider Jeffrey Westcott first of all. Or, no, he
would take the farm first and its occupants last. What had he known about
Westcott before he had been called to the farm the preceding night? Practically nothing at all. He had been aware of a farm, however, because he
had passed it numberless times. It was a large farm for it ran all the way to
the profitless soil of Briony Wood. And Dreeme sought to fix the farm
firmly in his mind, for, after all, the soil played its part in the development
of any man. It was the soil that counted, the soil that colored the mind.
Well, the farm faced on the Leeminster Road and it boasted the usual
sprawling building with a number of ells built on like afterthoughts. There
were several out-houses that faced the reddish dirt of the road and the untidy yard. Then there were the fields in back of the white-washed structures. Dreeme had never walked through them, but he imagined they were,
for the most part, uncultivated. Except for occasional patches of ploughed
land, small squares of fecundity in a neglected expanse, they stretched sere
and yellow in the parching sun or green and unkempt through the heavy
rains to the slightly elevated territory upon which grew the acre or so of
closely set trees which were called Briony Wood. This wood was a gloomy
and deserted place, deserted, perhaps, because one could not reach it without first passing through Westcott's land, and there were good reasons for
not taking this weed-choked road. Behind Briony Wood was Nigger
Swamp or perhaps it would be better to say that Briony Wood degenerated
into Nigger Swamp. Dreeme had never been near Nigger Swamp, but he
had heard of it as a miasmic stretch of sunken land into which the Saccarac

River seeped through subterranean channels. It was an unhealthy spot, the home of buzzing insects and slimy reptiles. As to why it was called Nigger Swamp, Dreeme possessed no idea. Perhaps negroes had been secreted there during the pre-Civil War days of the Underground Railroad, those feverish times when the escaped slaves were rushed through to the Canadian border. Anyway, it was obvious that black men had had something to do with the swamp in the past. Or, perhaps again, it was merely the darkness and desolation of the place that occasioned the cognomen. These things, however, threw no light on Jeffrey Westcott. He could hardly be connected with Nigger Swamp. Indeed, it was difficult to associate him with the farm. It was true that he lived there constantly and that he cultivated a corner of his extensive holding, but that was all. He was not primarily a farmer.

Having disposed of the land and having reached no conclusions whatsoever, Dreeme, who had reached the ruins of the old burned mill, a black gaping maw of crumbling bricks and beams, paused to look back and down at Marlborough. It seemed a pleasant enough town in the bright sunlight with its white and yellow houses, its gonfalons of thin smoke waving from the chimneys, and its shade trees rising in the narrow streets. From this distance it was New England to the backbone, marked by that sweet austerity and pleasant simplicity that is the aspect of the older communities. There was nothing gothic or strained or unearthly about it, and yet, looking back so, Dreeme was more than ever convinced of the mystery that hovered over the town. It was an obsession with him now. The houses were masks and their true features were never turned to the light of the day. Beside him the destroyed mill gloomed, and gazing into its gutted walls through the wide square of doorway he could see the black cell of the interior and the broken embrasure of a crumbling window that over-looked the mill-pond. Proceeding on his way to the faint music of crunching footsteps, Dreeme reached the small wooden bridge that crossed the Saccarac River, and here he paused to lean on the worn railing and gaze down on the sparkling stream that wandered on at so sedate and silent a pace. It was pleasant to watch the water while the warm sun caressed the back of his head. The river ran like a dream, like something seen in a trance. He must go on with his surmises now, for his unquiet mind pricked him constantly forward and along the Leeminster Road. Well, he had disposed of the land and learned nothing from it. There remained the human beings who occupied that land. He would take them in order, considering the less important first.

There was the boy Miles. What was there about Miles that was unusual? He was small, warped in body, large-headed, and obviously older than his size suggested. His face was twisted, his eyes were of a greenish hue, and he had a disconcerting way of answering questions. That was all. The queerness of Miles might be attributed to incipient epilepsy. And then Dreeme recalled Humphrey Lathrop's remark about these people inter-marrying from generation to generation. Did he mean incest? Dreeme had heard of such practices in the lonelier quarters of New England where the deserted farms were far from communal centers and a savage ingrowth, physical and spiritual, persisted. But Marlborough was a fairly good-sized community and it was difficult to imagine that Lathrop really meant that. What he undoubtedly meant was that the original families (and there might have been dozens of them to start with) intermarried and did not welcome unions with strangers who wandered by chance into the valley. Miles was possibly of an old breed that had worn thin. He was just an eccentric and stupid boy who knew no more than the loneliness of hard labor on an avoided farm and who, therefore, was a stranger in a strange land when he discoursed with strangers. Dreeme decided that there was nothing to be gotten out of an analysis of Miles. Well, there was Wagner, the shaggy, red-bearded hired-man. Wagner was obviously the hard-worker on the West-cott farm. It was he who developed the soil and raised the few crops and tore the boulders up and did all the excessive heart-breaking manual labor that warped the shoulders, lengthened the arms, bowed the legs, and tanned the red leathery skin. He was the pack-horse, the human brute in action. He could be dismissed, after all, as a grown-up Miles, a laboring animal of excessive stupidity who talked so seldom that his voice had rusted in his throat. There was little to glean from these lesser figures and Dreeme's thoughts, held rigorously back, now turned to the Westcotts themselves.

Of course there was Jeffrey Westcott to start with. Dreeme drew a long breath as he turned from his inspection of the water and proceeded along the bridge to the Leeminster Road, walking slowly and gazing casu-ally at the flickering glimpses of houses through the trees on either side of him. It was not enough to say that Westcott avoided and was avoided. That was merely the beginning. Now that Dreeme had seen the farmer in his house and heard his voice he suspected that there was much more be-hind this, much, perhaps, that might be explained easily if the answers were forthcoming but much again for which there was no answer. Westcott, first of all, was a cultured man, apparently a scholar. He spent less time tilling the soil than he did poring through his huge books. He was an un-likeable person. There was no doubt of that in Dreeme's mind. There was an oily menace in him, a soft snarl in his speech, a barely-concealed cruelty of demeanor that was emphasized by the superficial polish of the man. His whole being was dominated by an unclean spirit. As Dreeme thought of Westcott's appearance, his cloven head and black sparkless eyes, a slow wave of fear, impossible to restrain, crept up his flesh. Yet there was nothing that the young doctor could actually adduce as evidence of any evil on the farmer's part. Considered logically Westcott was no more than a man who desired to be left alone with his books. He troubled no one and he wanted no one to trouble him. That was reasonable enough. But logic meant little so far as Westcott was concerned. There are bodies out of which souls speak without words and Dreeme had seen one of them in Westcott. He had sensed an unclean atmosphere about the farmer just as he had sensed an atmosphere of evil emanating from the huge volumes that lined the farmer's room. These things were matters of instinct and intuition and Dreeme could not dismiss them by any logical explanations or deductions. Something fierce and fanatic and commanding lurked inside Westcott's sturdy body and watched the world with a slow maliciousness. What this spirit was could not be deduced by any casual study of the man. It had a purpose, Dreeme was sure, and that purpose was monstrous in its intent and merciless in the steps which it took toward its ordained objective. So much bespoke a fanatic and Dreeme was sure that if he could ferret out the reason for this fanaticism he would be well on the way toward solving the mystery of Marlborough. The young doctor was not conscious of any logical chain of reasoning by which he tied the secret purpose of Jeffrey Westcott up with Marlborough but was convinced that the tie between the community and the man was close and unbreakable. There were moments when all this seemed like the wildest reasoning of an imaginative boy to him and he strove, even in the midst of his revery, to laugh at his assumptions but something stifled the ridicule in his throat. Though he might brood about secret objectives and fanatical purposes and buried evils and unclean spirits without the slightest proof to bolster them up he found himself incapable of raising his head and scattering all these thoughts as the misgivings of a neurotic romanticism that was the result of a too lonely living among dour people. No, there *was* something there. And Dreeme, unable to restrain himself, proceeded with his thoughts even as he proceeded with his stroll up the Leeminster Road.

There was Martha Westcott to be considered. Even as her name thrust itself into Dreeme's consciousness a slight giddiness took him and he experienced a brief choking sensation in his throat. It was as though a thin vapor had suddenly risen in the air beside him and drifted across his face. At least, *she* was unexplainable. She was a walking mystery, a veiled being whose veil was flesh, a detached spirit wandering in a commonplace world. Dreeme thought of her as he saw her standing at the window and listening and it seemed to him now that she was like a person standing at a door she hesitated to open and yet must open. It was impossible to analyze her in any way, to say that her heavy-lidded eyes were the result of too-much sunlight or too much snow, that her blood-red mouth had grown so weary from an endless loneliness, that her quietness was the quietness of a shunned person. She existed beyond her flesh and yet her flesh, too, so cool and yet so stirred with a still life, existed beyond the flesh of other people. How she had become Jeffrey Westcott's wife and who she was, from what family in the valley she had sprung, were mysteries as yet, mysteries that, perhaps, Humphrey Lathrop, if he were goaded hard enough, might solve, but even the solution of these temporal gestures would hardly clarify her. Dreeme was amazed at his reactions to Martha Westcott and a small voice of reason kept thrusting into his thoughts and arguing a sudden fascination. But Dreeme knew that this fascination was not the usual type of blind worship. He had not fallen in love at first sight and there was no question of his ever falling in love with Martha Westcott. It was something else altogether that compelled him to surmise in such mystical terms about the farmer's wife. There was a power in her mere presence that unsettled him and he did not strive too arduously to make it clear to himself for he knew that it would be impossible.

His mind was growing into a hungry octopus now and it stretched out a dozen and one tentacles that grasped feebly to right and left, adventuring weakly in search of enlightenment. But the clear illumination for which he sought was not to be found. Vague lights like indistinct marsh-lights glittered wanly for a moment and then were enveloped by the tenebrosities of a sheer ignorance that was maddening in itself. He was seeking for something that was hardly to be found without the most obvious clews. And there were no clews. Nothing but endless speculation, surmises, unreasonable intuitions, objectless guesses. Though he might ponder on the Westcotts and the life they followed it all led to nothing. For a moment he doubted his own rationality, pointing out to himself with a mocking elaboration of mental gesture that he was spinning mysteries out of the imbroglio of his disconcerted mind. There was really nothing to go on, no abrupt transitions from the normalities of existence, no vindictive flashes of evil lighting up this valley as lightning might illuminate it, no ominous gestures revealing the unsuspected. There was nothing about the Westcotts to suggest the uncleanness of being which he associated with them. It was all in his own mind, in his restless intuitions. He *felt* these things and feeling them he could do no more than give full vent to his morbid fancies. He might be a fool . . . it was very possible that he was . . . but even this humiliating reflection failed to subdue that uneasiness of spirit that shook him when he brooded upon Marlborough and the Westcotts. It was as though a far-off and forgotten voice was speaking somewhere in the jungle of his intelligence, telling him the most terrible things in the most deliberate manner. He could not gather the sense of the message. He could not even hear the voice. But somehow he knew that it was there and speaking. It was like a small obsession making itself more and more evident as he brooded more and more about it. There was no escape from it now. He would have to make up his mind to *that*, at least. No escape . . .

Dreeme lifted his head, rising like a swimmer from the turbid waters of his thoughts, and saw half-concealed in the trees ahead of him the shapeless mass of the Westcott farm-house. He stopped instantly and stood indecisively in the road meditating whether to go on or to turn in his tracks and retrace his steps to Marlborough. Even as he meditated he knew that he had wandered along this road with only one purpose and that he would not achieve any ease of mind, if, indeed, he did then, until he had fulfilled it. Turning aside he left the road and strode through the bushes into the field, Bidwell's meadow, that bordered on Westcott's property. The dry grass crackled beneath his feet and great grasshoppers leaped industriously about the crushed growth. He could hear a locust grinding its rasping note. Otherwise it was still . . . a hot windless stillness that caused him to pant slightly as he forced his way toward the twisting stone-fence that guarded Westcott's land. Reaching it he sank in the tall dry grass by a crumbling breach where the stone had pitched forward into the farmer's yard. From this vantage point he could see the blank side of the house, once a dirty white but now a streaked colorlessness. A thin curl of smoke rose from the chimney of the built-on kitchen. The curtains of the windows were drawn against the sun. A solitary rooster crooked sleepily as he turned a glassy side-long eye at the stone-fence and the man concealed behind it. Dreeme could see the uneven rocky path by which he had circled the house the night before. He was surprised to discover that it was much shorter than he had thought it to be in the darkness. Darkness was like that. It lengthened things and translated them. For fifteen minutes or so the young doctor squatted in the grass and spied upon the house and the empty yard. He could feel the hot press of the sun on the back of his head and the sharp thrusts of the dry stalks beneath him. He would wait now. Until . . .

The door at the rear of the house opened slowly and Martha Westcott walked down the steps, a white china pitcher in her hand.

Dreeme lowered his head quickly and peered between the uneven stones of the fence. He saw her traverse the yard slowly and pause by the wooden square of the well. She lowered the bucket, running it downward with long even thrusts of her arm. As she turned her head the sun glistened upon her blue-black hair and the dead white nape of her neck. The curving sweep of her broad shoulders and arm was a beautiful thing to watch. She was like some fatal goddess in action, in sleepy action. Astarte Syriaca. The name sprang suddenly into Dreeme's mind. He had not sought for it. It came of its own volition. Well . . . Astarte Syriaca, then . . . an evil goddess. She drew the brimming bucket up to the shelf of the well, and, tipping it, filled the white china pitcher with a curving arc of water that glittered like silver in the sun. Then she hooked the bucket and turned toward the house. As she did so her eyes swept along the stone wall and the expanse of sun-parched field beyond. They traveled steadily, large and still and dark under the heavy lids. Dreeme, crouched in the grass, felt his heart beat furiously and a slow color crept up his face. It would be ridiculous to . . . Her eyes hesitated an instant at the very spot through which the young doctor was peering at her. He could see the great motionless pupils as fixed as the stare of some huge cat and the tiny scarlet blood-sacs in the inner corners of her eyes. There was absolutely no expression in these eyes that seemed to look through stone walls. They were frozen pools of stillness that seemed to take the world as they found it without any surprise and with a knowledge that was as ancient as the browned stones upon which the sleepy green slivers of lizards dozed. Dreeme, pressed abjectly against the stone wall, experienced an agitation through all his limbs. A choking sensation welled up in his dry throat and his hands, clinging fiercely to the parched stalks by his knees, shook as though with a palsy. It was only for an instant. Her eyes continued their blank survey and reached the house. Turning, she walked slowly back to the door, the white china pitcher outlined against her black dress, and slipped silently in. The door shut behind her without a sound. Dreeme remained for several minutes against the stone wall fearing to test the strength of his legs. Then he rose to his feet and tramped back through the burnt and brittle grass, crashing through the bushes to the road. He walked swiftly along the Leeminster Road to Marlborough without looking back.

III

The girl's eyes were like wet violets, a soaked blue so deep as to be astonishing. Mrs. Slater had said: "Deborah. . . . This is Doctor Dreeme . .

." and then she had added in a grudging tone: "My niece . . . Deborah is my niece . . ." Dreeme remembered that he had bowed and mumbled vaguely in his throat. It did not surprise him that Mrs. Slater had a niece. She looked as though she had nieces. Besides, all New Englanders had nieces. It was the penalty of the country. That . . . or . . . well, perhaps, no nieces. It was all a question of family, of children, of course. Grandfathers were at a premium in New England now but nieces and nephews and cousins were the common coinage of pride. It was impossible to go into a musty Back Bay parlor, for instance, without hearing something about: "He's a cousin of . . ." or "She's the niece of . . ." It was like that. Being reduced to mop up one's lesser relatives, so to speak. Or to reach out through a dubious cousinal (*could* there be such a word?) connection and so getting a foot *in*. Families scattered and broke up; the main stem shattered; there was nothing but twigs left. "I am a twig of the Winthrops." A wind-blown twig without any leaves. Mrs. Slater scraped his chair back and he sank into it. She was staring at him with fluttering eyes. There were snapping eyes all around the table. He was getting choppy in his thoughts. Choppy . . . choppy.

He assumed a bland indifference and waited for the smoking bowl of cabbage to be pushed his way. The long red slices of corned beef lay like so many tongues at his elbow. He forked one neatly and slapped it onto his plate.

Physiognomy, they said, was a science in itself. The twist of a man's mind from the twist of his mouth. *His* slant from the slant of his nose. But what about a man with a cloven head? What about a woman with . . . oh, wonderful! The cabbage, a pale browny-green glistening with tiny jewels of grease, reached him and he speared an efficient mound of it. A long walk induced hunger. Take faces now. The sly student ran his eyes over a face and solved it as easily as a rebus is solved, a rebus put together for infantile intellects. One assumed that the student was right but one did not really know. Still . . . there must be a lot in it. If the proper perspective was achieved the face fell into an approximate map of the mind. Easy. Like pulling a rabbit out of a silk hat. But you had to catch your rabbit first. Dreeme put his knife and fork down softly. He was light-headed. Giddy. Too much sun. But if he was going to get anywhere he would have to study faces, covertly, tracking out half-obliterated urges, deciphering. . . . Mrs. Slater asked him if he would like some vinegar on his cabbage. Good God, no! "Thank you," he said and shook his head. He picked up the fork and thrust it into his smoking mound of cabbage. The little jewels of grease dripped from the raised portion. He gazed about him, stifling an intensity of stare behind an assumed nonchalance.

He was surrounded by masticating jaws. Walden Slater, the Reverend George Burroughs, five little Slaters with pop eyes and glistening chins down which cabbage-grease ran. And . . . that girl. Mrs. Slater, having placed everything on the table, sank with a sigh of relief into her seat. Her eyes fluttered as one brown, freckled hand reached for the corned beef platter. She, at least, was patent. Her plumpness bulged at the caught-in house-wrapper. Her face was a small moon with a turned-up nose, a wide mouth that inclined downwards at the corners, and round eyes that thrust forward from the puffed circles that contained them. Her wispy straw-colored hair was drawn back in a sort of door-knob and the heads of three metal hairpins stood up from it like tiny croquet arches. She *was* an aunt, after all. It was quite reasonable. Opposite her Walden Slater's long upper lip snapped feverishly at a dangling bit of cabbage. The lip of a camel. The cocks-comb of hair stood upright on his head and the thousand and one wrinkles in his red weather-beaten neck rippled as he leaned forward over his plate. The tuft of ragged hair beneath his lower lip glistened with cabbage grease. There were marks of perspiration about the arm-pits of his blue denim shirt. His broken nails carried a fair share of the dark soil of Marlborough. Now and then he would raise his watery gray eyes and look swiftly about the table. The heavy brows above them, bristling with a non-descript brush of hair, rose and fell as his long jaw moved up and down. Jabbing his fork into a long tongue of corned beef he tossed it dexterously upward and caught it with a lip that seemed, rubber-like, to stretch down to meet it. It was a triumph of coordination and Dreeme watched it with a pleased and sleepy satisfaction. Now if he could catch corned beef like that . . . on the wing, so to speak. . . . The five little Slaters cracked their iron-shod heels against the legs of their chairs as they dribbled food. Give them time. They would grow as dexterous as Walden. They were a regimented quintet. They rushed out to school with a great clattering of feet and rushed back again to dinner with the same infernal racket. Their immature minds were small muddy circles into which the schoolmaster flung flawed pearls. The jewels sank to the bottom and were seen no more.

Dreeme's mind revolved, for an instant, about educational processes. Tomorrow this community of Marlborough would be changed. It would be renewed by the five little Slaters and their companions in age. What would they make of the valley and the dour town? Would things remain the same? Would that persistent shadow of mystery that hovered over the place be lifted or would its darkness, like the impalpable darkness of invisible wings, deepen and remain? Who could prophesy what would be the state of affairs at that not-so-distant time? There was no reason why the outer world should impinge too strongly on Marlborough, for, after all, the valley was a cul-de-sac, a cache into which the Past had thrust an untidy bundle of urges and traditions and left them there to rot in the sunlight. And Dreeme seemed to see the Marlborough of the future stretching out like a corpse in the bright sunlight of the valley and striving . . . striving. . . . He shuddered at the picture so suddenly brought up before his mind, a picture of a white leprous mass struggling to live, dead and yet never dying, with closed eyes that continually quivered, with blue lips rolling back over yellow decayed teeth, with long skeleton fingers opening and shutting and fighting against the *rigor mortis* of Time. He slowly put down the . . .

"If you *please!*"

The Reverend George Burroughs' sallow face was thrust appealingly at him and the mechanical portion of Dreeme's brain slowly grasped the request.

"Cabbage? What cabbage? Oh, yes," he said hurriedly and pushed the decimated platter of curdling grease along the table.

Mr. Burroughs, his face drawn into a severe and disapproving recognition of wool-gathering in general, accepted the glistening remnants with some degree of asperity. Like a little horse. Like a little yellow withered horse. Mr. Burroughs certainly had an equine appearance. Dreeme permitted his eyes to survey the preacher with a faint degree of curiosity. Though he had sat at the same table with him for two years he had never developed enough curiosity about the skinny man of God to observe him closely. Now he would do it. He would fix him in his mind as a butterfly is fixed in a box. He would thrust the sharp pin of his comprehension through the withered thorax of the Reverend George Burroughs. The preacher dropped his face and successfully eluded his silent inquisitor. Dreeme almost called out, "Hey, there!" The preacher's bald forehead bent above his second helping of cabbage. Dark hair, starting from the ridge of that high forehead, grew downward and lost itself in the musty black coat that huddled over the dingy collar. The man's skin was as sallow as a Chinaman with the jaundice. Though partially concealed by the amusing foreshortening attendant to a lowered head Dreeme could see a fairly long face with high cheek-bones, eyes set far apart, and a good-sized mouth. "He will raise his head and neigh at me in a minute," thought Dreeme. The preacher did raise his head but he did not neigh. Instead of that he looked fixedly at the young doctor for an instant with horribly still eyes and then transferred his attention to his cabbage. For no reason at all Dreeme was embarrassed at this expressionless study and he hastily diverted his eyes elsewhere.

Dreeme seemed to see the Marlborough of the future stretching out like a corpse in the bright sunlight of the valley and striving . . . striving. . . .

The girl's eyes were like wet violets, a soaked blue so deep as to be astonishing.

Mrs. Slater had said. . . . Why yes, she was a niece. . . . A New England niece. Now that was funny for she did not look like a niece at all. Nieces were . . . oh, *nieces!* She was a slender pliant wisp in a matter-of-fact gray dress and with a tiny white collar and cuffs. She ate daintily, nibbling at the bits of corned beef which she raised on the tip of a fork held in the smallest hand for an adult that Dreeme had ever seen. Her absurdly miniature mouth was slightly pursed as though an infant bee had stung it, the smallest of stings, so to speak. Her hair was a bright soft bronze, the sort of hair that . . . well, thought Dreeme, it probably feels like warm mist. Now that he was fairly looking at her he could see how porcelain-like she was, how small in bones and fastidious in gestures. Such a niece for Mrs. Slater! It was almost impossible and Dreeme's glance flitted swiftly over the five children kicking their heels and gulping their food and Walden Slater conducting a successful foray against a chunk of corned beef that had desperately striven to elude his remorseless fork. The young doctor's eyes returned to the girl. Deborah. Her name was Deborah. Mrs. Slater had said. . . . The girl looked up and caught Dreeme's glance with a bright flash of her absurdly blue eyes. The smallest hint of a smile touched her pursed lips and she turned back to her food. Dreeme suddenly felt quite elated. It was not that he *cared*. He was not a lady's man in any sense of the word. Just a hard-working doctor who, at this moment, was neglecting his work because of certain silly obsessions that were driving him to distraction, obsessions that Humphrey Lathrop would have to clear away. He would see Humphrey that afternoon, drop in late and smoke a pipe with him, perhaps. Anyway. . . . Deborah looked up again. Her eyes seemed to say, "We have a joke together, haven't we? Niece? How absurd!" Dreeme pushed his plate back and waited for somebody to speak.

Nobody did. Marlborough meals were like this. A greedy silence lowered over the table.

Walden Slater, overcoming the resistance of the last bit of corned beef on his plate, rose awkwardly to his feet, scraped once or twice, belched forth a triumphant elegy of wind over the meal, and turned toward the door. He shambled out, long arms dangling. His exit was a signal for a general clattering of chairs. The five children avalanched toward the front yard for their fifteen minutes of surly play before the warning bell of the little one-room school house across the way made them still surlier. Mr. Burroughs walked softly to the window and stood there humming "Rock of Ages." He was atrociously out of key, a droning whine that clung

tenaciously to one note. His still eyes wandered absently toward Deborah
as he lulled his dinner to sleep. Dreeme said:

"So you're Mrs. Slater's niece?"

The girl looked up brightly.

"Her poor relation," she replied. "She is very kind to me. Since father
died she . . ."

"You might bring out some dishes," broke in Mrs. Slater vigorously.

She was a small girl and she carried the stack of greasy plates with an
instinctive grace that pleased Dreeme. When she came back she renewed
her bright attention toward the young doctor.

"We lived in Leeminster, you know," she said.

Dreeme did not know but he nodded understandingly.

"Perhaps you read about father," went on the girl, as she piled saucers
in a high heap. "It was in the county paper. The bag of cement fell on him,
you know."

"Of course," said Dreeme politely.

"The Lord gives and the Lord takes," insinuated the neighing voice of
Mr. Burroughs, who broke off his humming for this shaft of divine wisdom and then instantly resumed it.

"He died in half an hour," added the girl.

"Really?" exclaimed Dreeme.

He watched her go out with interested eyes. Mr. Burroughs' humming
got on his nerves and he writhed uneasily at the dreary drone. The
preacher was like an old bumble bee with bronchitis. He stood in the window, his large mouth pursed, his horsey forehead slightly lowered, and intimated sadly that the Rock had been cleft especially for *him*. In the flattest
of whines he announced his burning desire to fly to Its bosom. "May it fall
upon you and crush you!" thought Dreeme somewhat vindictively, the unending whine scraping along his nerves. He waited, in some expectancy,
for the reappearance of the girl. But it was not she who came through the
door and gathered up the remaining débris of the meal. It was Mrs. Slater,
a Mrs. Slater with fluttering eyes and quick lumbering movements. Dreeme
felt like smiling but instead of giving way to any such impulse he rose to
his feet and sauntered toward the door. A lugubrious whine followed him,
creeping up his back and gently pushing him toward the hot early afternoon sunlight. At the lintel he paused and looked back. A musty expanse
of black coat and an oblong of black hair. Behind it a shapeless hum that
drearily mangled a helpless hymn. A dumpy woman folding a red and
white checked table-cloth. She was expressionless now. A big clock ticking.
Also expressionless. A waterfall design in pink wall-paper. Curved pink

water falling indecently into black base-boards. Scattered chairs to be placed discreetly against the wall until supper. They stood about dejectedly, awaiting the touch of a hand . . . what was it? He stepped through the hall and into the street. The heat was oppressive. It rose at him on scarlet haunches and panted against his face. He stood looking up and down the thoroughfare at nothing before he returned to his next-door office in the little cottage. At nothing. Absolutely nothing. That was it. That was where *he* stood. That was where they put *him.* A niece, eh? Well, why not? Mrs. Stater probably had a dozen nephews and nieces living within a radius of ten miles and the fact that *he* had seen none of them in two years really meant nothing. Mrs. Slater was like that. Marlborough was like that. She didn't want the girl to grow too friendly with him. To tell him things. Not even obvious things. Ridiculous. He would ply the girl with questions at supper-time and shock, astound, disconcert, and upset the whole table. Well. . . . He stood smiling at his own thoughts. Let them, then. . . . Now what did that mean? He was growing reckless as well as nervously excitable. It was time to see Humphrey Lathrop. Decidedly, Marlborough was getting . . . He progressed slowly to his own door and placed a hand upon the polished knob.

Chapter Three

I

Doctor Humphrey Lathrop was so huge that it was difficult for him to move about even with the aid of the two gnarled canes that flanked either side of his gargantuan reinforced chair, a throne that creaked ominously as his shifting bulk, a bulk that seemed to roll slowly like cooling lava, swayed forward in wheezing conversation. He sat like an enormous and kindly jellyfish, his stomach resting on his great round thighs and straining fiercely against the bulging vest spangled with fobs and seals, his triple chins trembling beneath his wrinkled face, his broad flat feet encased in comfortable slippers that suggested a pair of medium-sized Gladstone bags. His black velvet smoking jacket, odorous with a villainous tobacco, spread over him like a voluminous cape. The polished baldness of his round cranium was thrust into a skull-cap that fitted as snugly as a skin. On the back of his neck the rolls of fat rippled as he stretched a plump arm out and lifted the tiny green tea-cup in a massive hand. He wheezed softly as he moved, a pleasant sibilant sound that chimed with the remonstrative creaking of his overloaded chair. Dreeme, perched opposite him on the end of his chair, observed the ancient friend of his father with an approving and respectful eye. He saw the moon-face and sagging jowls tanned by many suns and eaten by an intricate net-work of wrinkles (which Lathrop called "my map to eternity") and the large blue intelligent eyes gazing out of the gold circles of precariously balanced spectacles, and experienced, as always, a curious sense of inferiority and complete trust in the wisdom of the old doctor. Humphrey Lathrop was more than an ancient friend. He was a monument of probity and wisdom, a great quivering idol from whose lips issued counsel and the finalities of an achieved experience. He was a Mahomet transformed into a mountain. For fifty years he had been the solitary medical adviser to Marlborough and it had only been after his bulk had reached such proportions as to render it impossible for him to get about or climb in or out of his rusty old buggy that he had turned over a meager and thankless practice to the son of his boyhood friend. He had done so with misgiving and regret for he distrusted the vagaries of the young in the profession which he had honored for half a century. He was old-fashioned, deucedly so, believing that a doctor's prime concoction was common-sense mixed with a little peppermint. It had been enough for him to supply the simplest of remedies to the ailing and he possessed an undying suspicion of what he denominated as "applied book-learning" in so far as the practical treatment of sickness was concerned. He pointed out time and again that there were no rare diseases in Marlborough. Children were born in the usual way and men and women died as they had always died. Between these two important dates were the ailments of the young, mumps, diphtheria, scarlet fever, and measles. After that there were accidents, cuts and bruises and broken limbs, and then such major ailments as typhoid fever, chronic stomach trouble (which, so far as Doctor Lathrop was concerned, included stomach, kidneys, and liver), and pneumonia. He scoffed at appendicitis, calling it "an aristocratic belly-ache." In spite of his limitations as a doctor, and, perhaps, because of the wiry health of his patients he had been accounted an unusually successful practitioner. The thunderous approach of his great flat feet and thumping canes were the immediate prophecies of relief. What impressed Dreeme most strongly about him was the excellence and keenness of his mind when taken apart from his dogged attitude toward medicine. Though he might be a narrow-minded old fogey of a doctor, he was, as a thinking man on general topics and life in general, far-sighted, deliberative in judgment, ratiocinative, and exceedingly shrewd. He mixed a certain amount of imagination with his observations and limited it with a complacent fatalism that was less abrupt than dimly wistful. Therefore, whenever Dreeme was perplexed he visited Lathrop, finding in him a genial fount of encouragement and pertinent comment. At this moment he was fumbling toward an utterance of the problem weighing upon his puzzled mind and the old doctor, fully aware of the purpose of the visit, studied him with some amusement, his blue eyes twinkling behind the gold spectacles.

"I was called out to the Westcott farm last night," said Dreeme finally, pushing his cup from the edge of the little table.

Lathrop's blue eyes opened wide and then closed. He wheezed gently and drank his tea, pausing to blow at the scalding mixture, and then put the cup down. It tinkled sharply in the silence of the room. Dreeme heard the monotonous buzzing of a fly in the curtains by the window.

"So?" said Lathrop at last. Then he seemed to dismiss the subject, reaching for his blackened corncob pipe and stuffing it from the can of shag on the table.

"You don't come to see me often, Daniel," said the old doctor as he lit a match, applied it to the pipe, and puffed wheezily. The pipe wouldn't draw. "Drat it!" he exclaimed, putting down the charred corncob, and gazing about the room with a calm benevolent smile.

"I don't see anyone often," remarked Dreeme somewhat dejectedly.

Lathrop looked at him quickly, pursing his large lips.

"I warned you that this was no place for a young man," he said. "You can't go about here. There is nothing to see and still less to do. I don't mind it but I am an old man and I couldn't get about if I wanted to. I have to sit in this chair like an old rheumatic hippopotamus and look out the window."

"And nobody goes by," added Dreeme gloomily.

A faint chuckle irrupted from the huge body before him.

"Nothing but the sun and the rain and the clouds and the snow and the night," checked off Lathrop on his pudgy fingers. "But I don't mind. It isn't so bad to have the chair placed out in the sun and to doze in it. It warms me up."

"I haven't minded it either," said Dreeme, "that is, until a day or so ago. Then my mind got working again and I began to grow curious. I want to know the 'why' of things. I want to know about people and why communities are what they are."

"That's simple," declared Lathrop. "Environment . . . blood . . . breeding."

Dreeme flung out an impatient hand.

"Oh, I know," he said. "I know all that. But there is something in back of those things, something that creeps in the soil and climbs in the trees and looks out of empty window-panes and circulates about you when you walk in the street, and . . ." He broke off abruptly. "Do you believe in magic, Humphrey?" he inquired suddenly.

Lathrop chuckled and wheezed, fumbling for the handkerchief in the side pocket of his smoking jacket. The blowing of his nose was like the sounding of a trumpet.

"So that's it," he said. "So that's it. Lordy, Lordy."

He picked up his pipe again and sought for the penknife in his trousers pocket and began to clean out the stubborn bowl.

"Daniel," he said, "I'll tell you what I believe. Perhaps it will help you and perhaps it won't."

He paused and maintained a silence until the pipe was cleaned, filled, lighted, and drawing comfortably. Then he settled his huge bulk back in the creaking chair and observed Dreeme with bland blue eyes through the gold spectacles.

"You'll have to forgive the inconsistencies, Daniel," he began. "I've never worked out a system of things. I've been too lazy and too conscious of my own ignorance to do that. But I have certain instinctive beliefs and I imagine they are unalloyed with the new-fangled notions that are called modern psychology. I think that we have two ways of classifying what is strange and mysterious to us—the supernormal and the supernatural. I do not say 'no' to any of the supernormal things. Against the supernatural I turn my face. It isn't reasonable. It isn't even spiritually reasonable. For instance, the most ordinary inventions today would have seemed supernatural three hundred years ago, whereas, at that time, they were merely supernormal, existing in that unexplored terrain outside of the comprehension and investigation of the day. So today we have faith that the things which seem supernatural are merely in *our* unexplored terrain and that tomorrow or next year or next century they will be made ordinary to us. There is a great difference between the radio and Jonah in the whale's belly. One is supernormal and the other is supernatural. A man cannot be heard from San Francisco to New York, as people loosely state, but a mechanical invention carries the sound of his voice. That is supernormal but conceivable. But Jonah in the whale's belly is not represented by any kind of mechanical contrivance. He is not carried there and represented by any kind of ultra-wave. He is just there, his physical self. That is supernatural. A man putting his head in a pail of water and holding it there for three hours and then coming out unaffected by the immersion is supernatural. But a man in a diver's suit with oxygen tanks attached who goes beneath the sea for three hours is merely supernormal. I believe in the supernormal—in the vast and still unexplored terrain that stretches before us—but I do not believe in the supernatural."

"You believe in the scientific explanation of everything," said Dreeme.

"I wouldn't say that," replied Lathrop, pursing his lips. "No, sir, I wouldn't say that. I would even go so far as to say that there are things which I conceive to be supernormal that cannot be explained by any scientific theory whatsoever. I do not believe in the levitation of tables by spirit-hands although I do not say that tables are not levitated. I do not believe that an ectoplasm is a materialization of the dead but I do not say that there is nothing unexplainable there for the eye to see. I do not believe that the dead talk through the lips of the living although I do not affirm that the words issuing from the medium's mouth are always her own."

Doctor Lathrop waved his pipe at Dreeme.

"I believe in mysteries," he insisted. "I believe these mysteries to be intellectually suspected at rare moments but never actually solved. I do not believe that we will ever solve them. So far as I know they move on another circle of time or in another dimension or anything you choose. But I demand that they be called supernormal and not supernatural."

"Do you believe that there is a supernormal aspect to Marlborough, then?" asked Dreeme, seeing at last a short-cut to the thoughts that boiled so inchoately in his mind.

Lathrop nodded his head and Dreeme laughed triumphantly.

"Then you know what I mean," he said, "when I say there is some-thing in back of all this, something in the soil and the air and the very houses," and he waved his hand toward the window.

"Yes, yes," agreed Lathrop, "I haven't denied it, have I? Every com-munity has its supernormal aspects, its twisted web of mysteries floating like a fine skein in the air above it. We're all tangled up with supernormal things. I admit it. You cannot go anywhere without finding yourself pushed against a dark wall of impenetrable silence that speaks without words and always speaks in a foreign tongue."

Dreeme's lean face grew solemn as he hitched his chair closer to the little table and extended his hand, palm upward, toward Lathrop.

"That may be true enough," he said. "But the sensation I experience in Marlborough is different. Every community has its own strange aura rising from it. Even the veriest over-night town thrown together beside oil-wells or gold-mines speaks in what you might call a foreign tongue. But it says brave or bright or progressive things. It lifts itself toward some sparkle in the adventurous sky above it. I have been in New York and raised my eyes to the heavens and seen, in my mind's eye, at least, a thousand glittering spires which were the reflection not of the monstrous shafts of granite about me but of the City behind the city, the great, mad, impressive, un-resting urge upon which the infinite foundations of this finite metropolis are built. It was awesome but it was not fearful. Marlborough, I tell you, is different."

Lathrop stirred uneasily, his enormous bulk swaying forward to a stri-dent creaking of the chair.

"I told you when you first came here that Marlborough was different," he said. The shadow of a growing perplexity was in his eyes.

"I know you did," responded Dreeme, "and telling me so much you told me nothing. You told me there was a breed of New Englanders here that I had never seen before. I admit it now. But why is this breed differ-ent? You did not tell me that. You told me that a mixture of ethical and Dionysiac madnesses produced the fore-fathers of these people, of the Bidwells and Barnsons and Westcotts and Slaters. Well, what does that mean? You opened the door of a dark room to me, a door which I should have pushed open myself sooner or later, but you did not give me any lamp. Do you know what the sensation is that I have when I think of Marlborough?"

Lathrop shook his head slowly, the loose chins beneath his round face wagging like the wattles on a cock.

"I think constantly of a horrible dead body, a white leprous mass of flesh, that is striving to live," answered Dreeme in a low voice. "The dark circles of the closed eyes quiver, the blue lips roll back, and the long fingers, struggling against *rigor mortis*, slowly open. There are only shadows in the palms of the hands."

"Good God!" exclaimed Lathrop, reaching hastily for his cup of cold tea. After a moment he laughed in his wheezing way.

"You have the imagination of a penny-dreadful," he remarked.

"Have I?" asked Dreeme. "Do you really think so, doctor?"

Lathrop drank the last swallow of his chilled beverage and then put the cup back and turned to his corncob pipe.

"Look here, Daniel," he commanded. "Do you want me to prescribe for you? You're suffering from nerves. Your digestion is bad. Do you sleep well? How about a nice vacation? Eh, what?"

Dreeme shook his head.

"I'm all right, Humphrey," he said. "You can't get rid of me in that way. You've got to tell me things."

Lathrop sighed loudly.

"I was telling you things," he remarked. "I was telling you what I believed. Let me go on. Perhaps there will be a clew in it for you."

He paused for an instant and whistled loudly as his blue eyes roamed about the room.

"Let me give you some of my detached thoughts," he said at last. "I believe in the sense of the past. I believe it to be a living urge in itself but I also believe that it may be explained. Any place that has been lived in long enough will rear a fine fabric of associated ideas stretching back through the centuries. I believe that a philosophy of living may be developed from this sense of the past. I believe that a philosophy of living may unhinge the brain if it is based on vague enough historical urges and cause a man to mistake supernormal phenomena for supernatural things. I believe in the power of the fanatic and so many things may be regarded as fanaticisms— the fanaticism of ego, of evil, of good, of superstition, of a displaced historical sense. This last one alone is worth a treatise in itself. I believe in the suggestion of the more powerful will and its might in causing lesser wills to pervert the realities into mysteries. I believe in the concerted suggestion of the crowd to formulate a seeming atmosphere in any community. Do these thoughts tell you anything about Marlborough?"

"In a way," answered Dreeme. "But not enough. Give me the key to all this, Humphrey, for you must know it. You've lived here for half a century and you have had opportunities to observe."

"No more than you have," replied Lathrop quickly. "Haven't I intimated to you that an idle curiosity was the worst of all evils? Daniel, you
must not try to pry into things too closely. I could, perhaps, tell you
enough to quicken your curiosity into an intolerable sneakiness. You would
go about peering at people, watching their movements, spying upon their
activities, surmising their thoughts and reactions and springs of being. And,
sooner or later, you would be known for the Paul Pry you would be and
your practice would be lost and it would be impossible for you to live in
Marlborough. I tell you," and the doctor slapped his fat knee loudly, "these
people *will* not be watched and analyzed. Let well enough alone."

Dreeme raised his eyebrows.

"I'm not a Paul Pry," he said finally. Lathrop seemed to take this remark as a dismissal of the subject and his joviality, which had been somewhat dampened by Dreeme's insistence, reasserted itself. He hammered
the floor lustily with his cane and after a moment a long vinegary countenance thrust itself through the door.

"Lucinda," ordered Lathrop, "bring a bottle of apple-jack, and two
tumblers."

The vinegary face grew still longer. A thin mouth, a mere slit in the
wrinkled face, shrivelled in severe disapproval.

"You had some apple-jack this mornin'," announced a high nasal
voice.

"I'm going to have some more now," answered Lathrop blandly.

The visage swayed for a moment in the doorway and then disappeared
to the sound of a loud sigh.

Lathrop winked at Dreeme.

"The old fool," he said. "Lucinda's been with me for forty years and
she still considers me a giddy dissipated youth."

"Do you believe in God?" asked Dreeme suddenly, apparently giving
utterance to some train of thought in his mind. It was now Lathrop's turn
to sigh as loudly as Lucinda had sighed.

"Daniel, Daniel," he said, shaking his head. "Can you tell me what you
mean by God?"

"That's the old way of evasion," said Dreeme impatiently. "Do you
believe we exist as individuals after we die?"

"I believe we exist as individuals in a thousand and one ways and eyes
and minds and words spoken or written," answered the old doctor.

"Do you believe that we exist in the consciousness of ourselves as individuals after we die?" persisted Dreeme.

"I do not," answered Lathrop wearily.

Dreeme slipped back into his train of thought and a moment or so sped by while the stillness of the room was broken only by the buzzing of the fly still entangled in the window-curtain. It shrilled loudly as it darted blindly from the soft folds of cloth to the hard surface of the transparent pane of glass.

"Even in life," added Lathrop, "I do not believe that we exist as individuals in ourselves, although, of course, our consciousnesses, being what they are, can tell us nothing else."

The door swung open and Lucinda's vinegary face appeared over the tray upon which perched the amber-hued apple-jack bottle and two greenish tumblers. She stalked silently to the table and deposited her burden upon it. Lucinda was tall and spare and her arms were extraordinarily thin. Her long face, small black eyes, and pursed mouth registered a deep disapproval beneath the thin graying hair, tied in a back-knot, that covered her narrow head.

"I should think one glass might be enough for you, Humphrey," she complained, backing from the table like a tall and awkward colt. At the door she turned to add a final word.

"And young men might do better than sit drinkin' alcohol when there's plenty of sick people about needin' attention."

The door closed noisily behind her. Lathrop's wheezing chuckle followed her to the kitchen.

"The old fool," he said softly and tenderly as he poured out the amber liquor.

Dreeme accepted the tumbler that was offered him in an absent-minded manner, placing it on the edge of the table. He sighed loudly and Lathrop, gazing over the top of his glass, scowled pleasantly but said nothing.

"Why do you side-track me, Humphrey, whenever I mention the Westcotts?" inquired the young man at length with asperity in his voice.

"Did I?" asked Lathrop mildly.

Dreeme did not answer but took a brief swallow of apple-jack.

"Good, isn't it?" questioned the old doctor with a fair degree of enthusiasm. "The national tipple of New England," he went on. "Eve's brew," he concluded, draining off the tumbler.

"What do you know about Eve?" taunted Dreeme with a wan smile.

Lathrop wheezed for a full minute, and then, reaching over with a great effort, dug at Dreeme's ribs. Then his face sobered.

"Oh dear!" he said. And then: "I didn't side-track you, Daniel. I merely ignore you."

Dreeme finished his drink slowly and put the tumbler down. He said:

"I shall find out about the Westcotts. I have been in the farm-house and I can go again."

"Did they invite you back?" inquired Lathrop.

The young man stared moodily across the table. Lathrop smiled blithely and poured himself a second tumbler of apple-jack.

"You'll get tipsy," remarked Dreeme.

"No such luck!" wheezed the old doctor. "I was brought up on this drink. I sucked it in at my mother's knee."

"That's a lie," answered Dreeme. "You were not permitted to drink anything stronger than milk at home."

"How did you know that, Daniel?" asked Lathrop with mild surprise. He drained half the tumbler and wiped his mouth. Dreeme sat doggedly in his chair.

"Very well," said the old doctor with a sigh of defeat. "I give up. What do you want to know about the Westcotts?"

"Everything," announced Dreeme. He did not change his position but a brief light of excitement danced in his eyes.

Lathrop shook his head. "I can't tell you that," he said, "because I don't know everything. But I'll tell you what I do know and you may make the most of it. With this preamble . . ." He cleared his throat. "You just wear a man down, Daniel. I'm departing from the rule of a life-time. Much good may it do you or me!"

He filled his ubiquitous pipe and lighted it. A piratical odor assailed the air.

"I came to Marlborough in '57," he said. "New England in '57 was a strange place. The old world was breaking into pieces and there were faint, very faint glimmers of a new order of things. It was the days shortly after Dan Webster had thrown his party. Charles Sumner was being assaulted in his seat in the Senate and the Abolitionists were roaring their heads off. It was a curious time because the Republic was rushing straight to perdition. It was State's Rights and 'nigger, nigger, who's got the nigger' all the time. There was always a nigger in *somebody's* wood-pile. Up popped a woolly head and the farmers who had no use for nigger-labor grunted like hedge-hogs for Abolition. I was pretty young and careless about the destiny of our revered Republic so I did not cogitate *too* much about things (you'd call them phenomena, Daniel) that were for me no more than theoretical problems. It was my business to explore the highways and byways of Marlborough, fish the streams, go fowling for bats, pick blueberries, and sleep in the sun. I don't imagine I thought much about the people whom I met. Most of them were funny. One of them rather impressed himself upon me for I used to enjoy snooping about the Leeminster Road and there I would meet him stomping along and smacking at the stones with his stick. That was old Captain Uriah Carrier. He had been a ship-mate of Hathorne of Salem, the one who died of fever at Surinam and whose son wrote books."

He paused and reached for his can of shag. Then he said:

"Is there anything crazier than writing books, Daniel? It is the ultimate idiocy, the last gasp of the lunatic."

"All this is getting somewhere?" asked Dreeme.

Lathrop wheezed. He said:

"More or less."

He settled back and proceeded with his rambling story.

"Let us, my impatient young friend, pause and consider Captain Uriah Carrier. He was the type of man that distinctly does not exist any more. He had hunted whales in the Pacific, had terrorized and robbed the natives of Tahiti, had blackbirded off the African Gold Coast, had carried a Manchu woman about with him for mistress, had retired, returned to Marlborough—for he was born here, joined the Congregational Church, married, raised children, and become the usual pillar of New England. He was a pillar of smoke by day, for his tobacco was vile, and a pillar of fire by night, for his cellar was full of Jamaica rum. He was a tall man with bristling white hair and stained whiskers (a lovely rust-color about his mouth) and an evil eye. He had an invariable greeting for me. 'Younker,' he'd say. 'Look out for the devil.' I'd say, 'Where is he, Capt'n?' 'In my 'bacca pouch,' he'd growl, and shake it at me. I was too old for that, though, and would laugh at him, whereupon he'd show his yellow fangs, smack another stone with his stick—it was big and knobby enough to kill Goliath with—and stomp along muttering to himself. A great man, Daniel, but I'm glad that I did not follow in his wicked footsteps."

He wheezed a soft sigh. Dreeme stirred impatiently in his chair.

"Well, now," went on Lathrop. "Captain Uriah Carrier had several children, all of whom died young except one and that was Peleg Carrier. I went away to college and came back after the Civil War. The old captain was dead. I heard that he sat up in his huge four-poster after Gettysburg sucking at a rum-bottle and singing some foul old sailor song full of the most terrific obscenities. Then he had fallen back, said 'What ho, now!' in faint surprise, and passed out. Peleg Carrier was a quiet sort of boy as I remember him but it is not so much the boy I remember as the man who returned from Germany to Marlborough after I had slipped into the saddle as doctor here. That must have been in the early seventies when Jesse James was shooting up Missouri and Kansas and old Sitting Bull was preparing his revenge and the buildings for the Philadelphia Centennial were being raised. Peleg Carrier was rather different from his blasphemous old scoundrel of a father. He was a melancholiac."

Lathrop brooded for a moment, one great hand raised to his round face. Dreeme could see the hairy ring of fat about the old doctor's wrist.

"My memory of Peleg Carrier is revised and aided and abetted by my later analysis of him," proceeded Lathrop. "I got to thinking about him early in life and for some years he was a pet study of mine. A sort of unusual specimen, you know. He lived all alone in the Carrier house on the Leeminster Road, a house that burned down long before your time. I imagine that leading a lonely rigorous life in a desolate country community induces melancholy. Don't you, Daniel? Peleg, however, was born a melancholiac. Melancholia, I take it, is not a malady so much as a matter of temperament. It renders its victims austere and dour. They dissimulate violent passions that are exhibited only through tempestuous outbreaks of weeping and nerves. By their nature they are exposed to a continual perturbation of the vital organs, to spasms and obstructions, for instance. These physical disorders induce an unquietness of mind without respite just as bad eating brings horrible dreams. Therefore in their waking hours these unfortunate people are the victims of disordered stomachs, spleens and livers. Their minds as well as their bodies are attacked and such a thing as constitutional anxiety sets in and predisposes them to sombre fancies. These pathological conditions favor an over-development of the interior life and melancholiacs become disposed to the depravities of the imagination. Errors of sense ensue and their enfeebled normalities become the slaves of phantoms. It is but a short step to frenzies and fanaticisms. Peleg Carrier was such a man. Tall, cadaverous, with a face as yellow as old parchment, and a continual twitch of the hands, he passed like a morose ghost through the life of Marlborough. Who knows what preyed upon his perverted mind? Perhaps it was the sins of his father, Uriah. Perhaps the inclination toward those sins was reborn in Peleg and strangled by him through a supreme effort of will. I don't know. If there was an ethical impulse in him it must have run against a stone wall in Uriah. Perhaps half the dourness of life is in living down the sins of our fathers. This seems to be getting nowhere, Daniel, but I want you to remember both of these Carriers, the first an old ferocious rascal and the second a nervous melancholiac. Peleg married late in life the woman who was his housekeeper and she had one child. The father died the day that Martha was born."

Dreeme pricked up his ears at the name.

"Well, there you are," said Lathrop placidly. "There you have Martha Westcott."

"I can't see . . ." began Dreeme.

"Of course you can't," broke in the old doctor, "and neither can I. But we can both guess. Westcott himself I know little about. I have heard that he was the son of one of Peleg Carrier's German friends, born in those days when Peleg was studying in Germany. I have also heard that he was a grandson of old Uriah Carrier. The first I saw of him was when he suddenly appeared in the valley to take charge of Peleg's funeral. Who sent for him and from where he came are mysteries to me."

"Is he so much older than his wife?" asked Dreeme with some surprise.

"Twenty years or so," remarked Lathrop. "Martha is only twenty-five."

"What!" exclaimed Dreeme.

Lathrop nodded.

"She's always looked sort of ageless," he said. "Westcott brought her up. They lived in the old Carrier house until it burned down. Then they went to Germany. When they came back seven or eight years ago they were married."

The old doctor yawned and stretched his huge arms. He looked quizzically at Dreeme from beneath his eyebrows.

"So there you are, Daniel," he said. "It is no story at all, you see."

"Who do you think Westcott is?" inquired Dreeme.

"Well," said Lathrop meditatively, "they say that old Uriah had a sort of cloven head. Perhaps he's the man in the moon, Daniel."

The soft chime of a clock broke in upon them and Dreeme counted six beats. It was time to go.

"You're not telling me much about Jeffrey Westcott and his wife," remarked the young doctor.

Lathrop shook his head despondently.

"I don't know anything about them, I tell you," he complained, a faint note of irritation in his voice. "I've never been inside their house. I haven't talked to them for five years. I haven't seen them. What do you want me to say, Daniel? Do you want me to invent a fine theory concerning them?"

"If you must," said Dreeme. "But why not tell me the fine theory you have already invented?"

For an instant Lathrop nearly exploded. Then he said softly:

"Darn it!"

He looked at Dreeme in a woeful manner. He said:

"You *will* have something, won't you?"

Leaning forward he grasped Dreeme's hand in his huge soft paw.

"Good-night, Daniel," he articulated heartily. "Good-night."

Dreeme disengaged his hand and sat tightly in his chair.

"I have my supper early," remarked Lathrop in a mildly protesting voice.

His chair creaked as he leaned back in it.

"I hate to talk about people," he said in a loud voice. "It means no good, I tell you."

There was a loud crash in the room and both men sat upright suddenly and stared about them. Lathrop's can of shag had slipped from the table to the floor. The dark curling tobacco lay in an untidy heap between them. The can rocked on its round side for a moment and then ceased.

"Humphrey," said Dreeme, "you have thought a lot about the Westcotts. You've even studied their hereditary strain. You describe a villain and a madman to me and then you introduce a man who has studied in Germany. God knows what he studied. The Black Arts, perhaps."

"There aren't any Black Arts," interjected Lathrop, gazing woefully at his tobacco.

"He studied something, anyway," went on Dreeme, ignoring the interruption, "and I will venture to assert that it was neither differential calculus nor Emmanuel Kant. He is still studying it. He's an abnormal creature and so is his wife. Why have you kept hinting at some sort of a fanaticism and pointing out the difference between supernormal and supernatural and insisting on the melancholia of Peleg Carrier?"

Lathrop made a motion as though washing and wiping his hands.

"I refuse to be led into wild theories, Daniel," he said. "I base my opinions on facts. Any other process means eventual madness. Good Lord, how do you suppose I have lived here for half a century without turning into a sheer lunatic? Principally by minding my own business, which I advise you to do. And by treating a fact as a fact and letting it carry me no farther."

The twilight, shot with the spent gold of the afternoon, curdled about the corners of the room. It dusted in through the windows and rolled in wispy vapors over the heads of the two men. It crept along the floor and eddied beneath the tables and chairs. Dreeme felt the slow tide rising about his feet and curling about his hands. He made an impatient movement as though to brush it from him. He started to feel Lathrop's hand suddenly placed on his knee.

"Daniel," said the old doctor, "thought is a terrible thing. You are too young to grow morbid. Your nerves are on edge. Let them rest. Forget the Westcotts and forget your mystery of Marlborough. It is only by new thought, by bright strenuous acceptances that this sad land may be translated from the barren graveyard of Puritan traditions to the New World that is our heritage. I will not give you half-baked notions to feed on for then you would grow as somber as the people you see about you. I've told you what I know about the Westcotts and if I have certain personal reactions to them and to the people in this community it is far better that I keep them to myself. I, at least, can cage my thoughts and let them grumble there and hurt no one. You are too young to keep your opinions to yourself and they would escape and end by devouring you. Eat, sleep, read, do your work, my boy. That is all that you need do."

"You've not kept a single thing from me, have you, Humphrey?" said the young doctor accusingly.

Lathrop pursed his great lips and refused to meet Dreeme's eyes.

The twilight edged the young man toward the door and he rose reluctantly. Humphrey Lathrop's huge bulk eased back in his chair to a noisy creaking. He smiled agreeably. Dreeme picked up his hat and held out his hand to the old doctor.

"I'll drop in and see you soon, Humphrey," he said.

"That's the boy," wheezed Lathrop, patting the back of his hand. "That's the boy."

Chapter Four

I

Mrs. Slater moved, a black silhouette, across the yellow glow of the kerosene-lamp, bearing in chubby hands the last of the supper dishes. She kicked the kitchen door open with a grunt and disappeared. It was silent in the room. Walden Slater, having removed his boots with the elastic sides, drifted almost surreptitiously to the back porch, his gray woollen socks touching the floor soundlessly. Reaching his haven he sank with a hoarse sigh of relief into the broken rocker. Dreeme could see his bent form against the misty light of evening whenever the door to the kitchen flapped open. He sat there and rocked to the faint creak-creak of the chair; his talon-like hands grasping the arms of the rocker. He was a personification of a certain aspect of this New England. He was the tired man reeking with dried sweat, earth, and barn-yard odors sitting in the quiet evening and drawing in hoarse and throbbing lung-fulls of fresh air. His bones were tired. His flesh crawled sluggishly with an old weariness. The hinges of his knees were stiff. He was a finality in himself, a period put to a long sentence of history. The kitchen door swung to and fro and Dreeme ceased to look at the farmer. He looked out of the window instead, into the dark side-yard where the Slater children sat huddled together on a broken barrow and talked soberly in low tones. Their voices sounded thin and far away, pinched sounds, words rolled between huge fists. The low light of the evening fell across the sides of their faces. Small impish profiles turned to the brooding night. A dark form passed between Dreeme's eyes and the children's faces and the young doctor saw the figure of the reverend George Burroughs, skinny hands clasped behind the frayed skirts of his musty coat, stalk off into the darkness. It was like a brief eclipse, an instant's impenetrable blackness, and then it was gone. Light footsteps died almost instantaneously in the direction of the Leeminster Road.

Dreeme looked back into the room . . . well . . . he progressed slowly toward the kitchen door.

"Where is your niece?" he asked Mrs. Slater with a directness that was unusual in Marlborough where people talked by inference. The woman's eyes fluttered wildly at this unexpected question.

"Deborah . . . well, Deborah . . ." She hurried toward the kitchen door

with a massed pillar of plates, a sort of leaning tower of Pisa that threatened
to dissolve, into fragments at every step. At the door she turned. She said:
"Helping out. . . . They needed somebody to help out. . . ."
Her voice drifted back through the door.
"Mrs. Westcott . . . sent for her. . . ."
Dreeme brooded upon this for an instant, fumbled in his pocket for
his pipe, and then sauntered slowly toward the kitchen. Mrs. Slater, at the
sink, her sleeves rolled back over her short plump arms, observed him with
a suspicious concern, her head cocked on one side, an eye turned back. It
was like the eye of a querulous parrot. Dreeme leaned against the wall, and,
watching her, filled his pipe.
"Has Mrs. Westcott been here?" he asked.
Mrs. Slater turned to her dishes. She said:
"Oh, no!"
It was inconceivable, of course.
Dreeme waited for a moment as he lighted his pipe.
"Who has?" he inquired.
Mrs. Slater looked reproachfully at him as she fumbled for certain
words in her throat.
"We thought we'd have Deborah with us . . . especially since . . ." A
clashing of dishes drowned a few words. "But the preacher said . . . he saw
Mrs. Westcott. . . ."
"You mean Burroughs had your niece sent over to the Westcott farm
as hired girl?" broke in Dreeme.
Mrs. Slater did not like the word.
"She's going to help out . . . until Mr. Westcott is better. . . ."
She actually glowered at Dreeme.
"In that lonely hole," thought Dreeme aloud.
"It's hard enough to live . . ." began Mrs. Slater.
"It *is,*" said the doctor strongly.
Well, it was none of his business. The poor relation. Go where you are
sent. All the same . . . it was a shame. Cloven head and his malignant eyes.
Eyes like wet violets. "Rock of Ages." Now why had he thought of that? He
opened his mouth to speak again to Mrs. Slater, thought better of it, and
turned back into the lamp-lit room. He had wanted to talk to the girl, to
find out what she thought of things and how this valley had affected her
young mind. But now . . . Why she might as well be in Timbuktoo. The
Westcott farm-gate opened into . . . "All hope abandon. . . ." He picked up
his hat from the little side-table and walked slowly through the hall and into
the yard. The hushed voices of the Slater children sounded like a faint

drone. He could hear the rocker on the back-porch. Creak-creak. The dew was heavy. It was better to keep to the gravel path. Creak-creak. He reached the street and turned toward his own house. Creak-creak. Shine, moon. He looked up at a murky sky. No moon. It was too early for the moon. Creak. "Stars of the summer night." Longfellow. "Far in yon azure . . ." Creak. He fumbled (creak) at the knob to his door, pushed it open, and entered the small hall. To go up-stairs. Bed. But he was not sleepy. He would go into the back study and read for a while. Or mull over Humphrey Lathrop's conversation. Humphrey knew. . . . He felt his way along the dark hall and pushed the door open into the study. The minute he entered the room he knew that there was somebody there. He was not frightened. He leaned back against the door and said softly: "Who is it?"

A throat cleared noisily.

"Wagner," replied a hoarse voice.

"Are you by the table? There is a lamp there. Light it," said Dreeme.

The match spurted like a tiny firework and great shadows sprang up on all sides. A dancing ring of Jinns. Wagner's red beard hung like a sultry smoke above the chimney. The man lowered his head and peered at Dreeme across the table.

"What is it, Wagner?" inquired the doctor. "Is Westcott's leg bad?"

The shaggy head shook slowly.

"That's all right," he replied. "I wash it now. I'm real good at it."

His eyes narrowed under his bushy brows and his yellow teeth glowed through the mass of hair.

"She said you was to meet her by ten in the back room of the burned mill," he said slowly in his rusty sepulchral voice. "She told me to tell you."

A faint throb of anticipation tugged at the doctor's mind.

"Deborah?" he asked. Wagner said:

"Missus Westcott."

Dreeme's mind stopped dead. Automatically he said:

"Tell her I won't come."

"She said she guessed you would all right," replied the hoarse voice.

To think now. Leaning over the well. The white nape of her neck. Heavy boots dragged across the floor.

"What does she want?" he asked softly. There was no response. Boots dragging. A puffing. Dreeme floundered in a sea of amazement. He repeated his question loudly.

"What does she want, I say?"

This silence! Collecting his wits, he peered about the dimly lighted study. Empty, of course. He had gone out. Gone right by him. Dreeme walked over to the table and sat down in the easy chair by it. A tiny white moth dipped and volplaned about the smoky chimney. Now what was this? He would have to think about it. He leaned back in his chair and pulled at his cold pipe.

The faint ticking of the clock was like the tiny regular beating of a miniature tomtom. The minutes danced to it, shaking their small feet in an unending circle. They tripped by him, hands joined, and infinitesimal tapping heels maintaining a regular time that measured off the softly-flowing hours. He watched the vain moth dashing its white wings desperately against the smoky chimney. Sooner or later it would get scorched and flutter to the table, a charred and crumbling pinch of powder. Life was a curious thing. Breathed into a bit of dust it became a moth. Or a man. Something was happening to him now. His two years of dreary silence were breaking down and he was beginning to grow morbid about things in general. He was getting nervous, acutely aware of invisible tentacles that seemed to reach out of this darkness that encircled him on all sides and touch him softly. Humphrey Lathrop had said that it was nerves. But perhaps it was more than that. Perhaps it was a sixth sense slowly coming to birth inside him, a sense nourished by his loneliness that was reaching out into new dimensions. He was pursuing phantoms, hunting through the sun-shot fields about Marlborough for invisible essences that drifted deliberately and had a particular semblance of their own. He was going to solve an intense and formidable riddle. He was going to track down the secret of an atmosphere, the aura of a community. It sounded absurd enough but it was only the absurd things that mattered greatly after all if a man desired to be more than an eating, sleeping, laboring animal. To be a man, and all that *that* meant, was to walk arm in arm with phantoms, to discourse with shadowy substances, to resolve high mystical riddles. Ah! The moth shrivelled against the hot glass and dropped to the table. So that was that! He turned it over tenderly with a paper-knife and then pushed it to the floor.

Now then! He looked at the ticking clock from which the joined minutes were tripping their fantastic and regular dance. It was nine-thirty. Then it would be in half an hour. His thoughts, held tightly by the leash of his will, were set free and they sprang forward like a pack of ravenous hunting dogs. Up the Leeminster Road they sped and his spectral self followed them as an eager hunter follows his baying hounds. For an instant the face of Deborah flashed in the dark air and then it disappeared, left far behind by this rout of yelping coursers. He had said that he would not go. But she knew that he would, that his curiosity would carry him as far as the mill at least. What she wanted he did not know but he could suspect it. She was assuredly a lonely caged-in creature. She stood at windows and watched the night-sky and wondered about the life that went boiling so turbulently by on the great highroads to the west and the east of her locked doors. She sat in a room lined with books beside a cloven-headed man and a secret sat there with them and she had nobody to share that secret with her, no one, that is, except the man himself who *was* the secret. Perhaps she wanted to tell him things, to pour out the subterranean stream of her consciousness. He could imagine her muffled voice speaking in the darkness of the mill. It was not strange that she had sent for him, after all. It would have been stranger if she had maintained her silence. Dreeme rose slowly from his chair and blew the light out. Well . . .

II

She was seated in an embrasure formed where a portion of the brick wall had fallen away and dropped into the yellow-scummed water of the mill-pond. He could see the dark silhouette of her head as it turned sideways against the smoky light of the moon, and for a moment he paused in the doorway watching her, noting the regularity of her boldly-cut features and the cold sensuousness of her rounded lips. It was almost symbolic to find her so, no more than a silhouette, a face seen in a single aspect, a profile clean-cut and set against unsteady light that flowed with the rippling of milky waters. She was like this. She was the outline of a mystery, a part of that riddle that somehow he must solve if he was to have any peace of mind. It was dark and gloomy in the mill. Its fire-blackened walls retained the horror of an old debacle. Two men had been incinerated here. She said:

"I was sure you would come."

She had not turned her head. She still sat sideways against the moon. But her hand moved. It was pale and indistinct as it shifted into the dim light. He advanced toward her slowly, his footsteps sounding hollowly on the cracked cement floor.

"What is it?" he asked. "What do you want?"

Her head turned and although her face was a blackness he could feel her eyes studying him, fondling his features with a glance that was both tired and expectant.

"I was tired," she answered in a muffled voice.

That seemed to explain something and he continued his advance until he was beside her. She drew back slightly into her corner of the embrasure and he sat down on the cold crumbling bricks. He said:

"You mean . . . of loneliness?"

Her shoulders quivered a trifle. She did not need to answer that. Her movement dislodged a fragment of brick and it dropped with a sharp plop into the mill-pond. Dreeme started nervously at the sound.

"Why were you spying on me through the stone wall to-day?" she asked suddenly, and then went on, not waiting for an answer. "I knew you would come. You mustn't loiter about the house, though. It isn't safe. He would be sure to find it out."

Dreeme felt like a drowning man, and he made a valiant effort to save himself.

"I had business Leeminster way," he replied in an uncertain tone. "I just happened that way. I wasn't spying. I . . ."

"You needn't lie," she returned coolly. She put her hand on his knee. She said:

"You are the first young man I have talked to alone for years."

The electric touch of her fingers filled Dreeme with a nervous excitement. He fumbled vaguely for words, but his mind was like a great empty sack. Explore as he might there was nothing there.

"He keeps me shut up," she went on. "I have to . . . but no matter."

Dreeme still sought blindly for words. Her voice and her vaguely-outlined face were dead weights on his intelligence. He could not rise above them or push them aside.

"I like you," she said. "Does that sound silly? Let it. I liked you the minute I saw you."

"I think . . . I mean . . ." began Dreeme.

"You were like a boy with the weary lines of a man's face impossibly stamped on you," she remarked slowly. Her eyes studied him a moment. She asked softly:

"Are you afraid?"

His silence, complete and emphatic, was the mute answer to her question. In the milky light he could see that she was almost smiling.

"Don't be afraid," she said as though she were speaking to a child.

"I'm not afraid," replied Dreeme with an effort. "What is there to be afraid of? I don't understand. That's all."

Her face was level with his, and she looked at him for a moment steadily, her dark eyes under their heavy lids full of a vague surmise.

"How long have you been here?" she asked presently.

"Two years," answered Dreeme much as though he were a school-child being examined.

"So long?" she murmured. "You see how ignorant I am. Men pass outside my window and I never see them."

Dreeme, in spite of his confusion, doubted that.

"What do you know about me?" she proceeded. There was a faint breathlessness in the question.

"Practically nothing," he said.

She sighed, and it seemed to Dreeme that she sighed in relief.

"We are not children, are we?" she asked irrelevantly.

Dreeme shook his head.

"It has been so long since I conversed with anyone that I have almost lost the use of words," she said half to herself. "Yet words were once my favorite playthings. I would shape them into all sorts of patterns."

She removed her hand from his knee for an instant and then put it back. It seemed to Dreeme as though there had been a brief flaw in the electric current that was pouring into him and which so unsteadied him.

"Be silent, then, and let me talk," she went on. "I need to say things. I am tired of talking to myself and inanimate objects, tired of reading, tired of working, tired of listening to things that I do not much care about any more."

She paused for a moment but Dreeme said nothing.

"You see," she said. "I needed someone." Her hand closed about his wrist softly. "I needed you. I had not been in the room more than a minute before I realized that you were that sensitive type about . . . Do you remember looking at me? Weren't you trying to say something to me, trying to say it without words?"

Her speech had suddenly become a husky caress. She leaned forward. She murmured in an almost inaudible voice:

"Say it now."

Dreeme fumbled for words. Had he desired to convey any message to her? He could not find it in the welter of his mind.

"I was wondering," he stuttered. "I mean, it seemed strange to find that room full of books, that curious man, and . . . you."

He was suddenly aware that he did not desire this relationship between them to establish itself too quickly and too firmly upon a basis of mystical understanding. It was too silly. Two strangers did not reveal themselves so nakedly to one another. He clutched eagerly at the tattered cloak of his New England reticence. She did not appear to understand that he was attempting to convey a polite snub, a discreet hint, as it were, to resume the formal disguises of casual acquaintances, but her hand slipped from his wrist. Dreeme almost breathed with relief.

"It is good to be away from that house and to be able to talk as I wish," she proceeded. "It is an evil house. It is dominated by an evil man."

Dreeme said nothing. He sat gazing at the mill-pond in a phlegmatic manner. Her dark eyes narrowed a trifle as she watched him.

"I, too, am evil," she added.

Her tone was matter-of-fact, as though she were stating a thing already understood. At the same time, there was an implied challenge in it. Dreeme felt that he should say something.

"I don't think you are evil," he protested. There was but little conviction in his voice.

"All that is relative, though," she went on in a voice almost indistinct. "Do you like to ponder over things, to intellectualize them? So do I. Evil is relative. Perhaps he is not evil according to his own lights. Sitting alone in the house I have evolved my own scheme of things."

"What is it?" he asked suddenly. "What is it in that house? Why is he different from other men? What is it in Marlborough that . . . what . . ."

He waved his hand expressively, showing for the first time a curious liveliness.

A slow startled look suffused her face. She gazed at him steadily for a moment, and then the corners of her mouth quivered. Behind the cold mask of her face she seemed to smile.

"I will not tell you," she answered. "At least, not now."

There was an implicit promise in her voice. But no sooner had she conveyed this slight intimation of future explanations than she seemed to regret it.

"There is nothing," she said. "It is the loneliness. It is the ingrowing. It is the days passing along and every day the same."

"Have you lived here all your life?" he asked.

She paused a moment. She said:

"All my life. I have never left this valley. I have never found the door that leads out into the world."

She was a liar. Dreeme knew that at last. Her voice had again become a husky caress. It strove to reach out and embrace the dubious young doctor. He was conscious of a vague note of insincerity in it. Far back in his mind a sly intuition manifested itself, and it suggested that this woman was very near to acting, that she was cautiously feeling her way into his emotions. She wanted to find out if he could be swayed by passion, pity or intellect. He must be careful, terribly careful. He must avoid the almost overpowering magnetism that emanated from her white slumberous body.

"Life should proceed," she said, her words sounding like slow calculating steps through the difficult labyrinth of her thoughts. "It should go on and touch different places and different people, accepting and rejecting, considering all. It should meet the passions and accept them all and live through them and with them. But my life is not like that. I am cut off, set apart from things, bounded by walls and the will of one man. My thoughts boil in me to no purpose. My mind revolves and it achieves no friction, no flashing of sparks. It is just an insane wheel whirling endlessly in a vacuum. That is what it really is. I cannot go on like that and remain sane."

Dreeme did not know what to say. He knew that he was beginning to be frightened.

"I do not live in that house," she went on. "I exist in it. I stare out of the window in summer and see parched fields stretching to eternity. In the winter it is all an expanse of untrodden snow. Sometimes voices come to me from the road. That is all. That is all, I tell you."

Her voice rose, deep and husky. Louder than she had spoken before she declared:

"I was born to great acceptances."

Dreeme was becoming more and more frightened. He did not want to hear these things, these somber intimacies of a household that was no part of his affair and yet he could not stop listening. Her words were a warm web that caught up all his thoughts. He could not stand up and say, "I'm sorry, but this is not my business." It would be cowardice. He opened his mouth to say something, perhaps that very thing, but she continued to speak as though to hold his wavering will in the balance.

"I don't have to describe my life to you," she said. "You know. You know because you know Marlborough, and the strength that exists in the walls of the houses of Marlborough. But there are things that you do not know. You do not know that my husband is . . . but why should you know? He is like God, but I cannot tell you what I mean by that."

She stopped, apparently expecting some exclamation, but Dreeme sat in silent bewilderment and said nothing.

"He directs destinies," she went on. "He lets nothing stand between him and the objectives he has planned for himself. Not even me. Least of all, me. He has great power over the minds and futures of people when he chooses to exercise it. It is impossible to be independent with him. Once inside the walls of his house there is no individuality left to the visitor,—or rather the intruder, for no one enters his house except intruders. He spreads like a great force over everything. Freedom becomes a secret possession then, something to be cherished darkly at one's bosom. It is only in an escape from that house that one may assert one's unique unity. It is by slipping away that I keep myself sane. I have slipped away now. He is busy at his books, and the new girl moving about will, perhaps, seem to be me."

"What books?" asked Dreeme abruptly. If he could find out what Westcott read he could find out what he thought. That was Westcott's own idea. Even as he asked the question he realized that he was crudely diverting Martha Westcott from her self-revelation, and he flushed at his unconscious rudeness. She did not seem to notice his divagation. She said:

"I don't know. He buys old books, sends to Europe constantly for items he finds in the catalogues that come to him, but I never look into them. My mind is my book. I think that he is formulating a new religion from them."

He was aware of her untruthfulness again, of something held back and reformulated in the mind, of a desire to impress him and yet not to tell him anything substantial.

"A new religion?" he repeated with a shade of curiosity.

She dismissed it vaguely. She said:

"He is fashioning a new god in his own image."

It sounded silly to Dreeme. He wanted to smile. A cloven-headed man on an avoided farm in a forgotten valley creating a new god. He felt like blurting out, "Oh, come now. That is a bit too thick." Instead he declared:

"We all fashion God in our own image. It is our unfortunate weakness."

She was getting impatient with this topic. She did not want to talk about anything but herself.

"But not his kind of a God," she replied, a vague note of irritation in her tone. "Perhaps, after all, he is fashioning himself into the image of an old god. Would that be unusual? I really can't tell you. I don't know. I am only a part of the furniture in that house. I, too, have my philosophy of living."

She paused for a question.

"Yes?" said Dreeme politely.

She stirred uneasily, and her knee, warm beneath her skirt, struck against his leg. In moving her head bent forward and the fragrance of her hair swept his face. Suddenly he was enveloped in the hot disturbing atmosphere of flesh. He wanted to rise to his feet now, to terminate this ineffectual interview, to explain to her that though she might upset his mental equilibrium by the magnetism of her body, the subtle insinuations of her mysterious eyes, and the leashed ardor so like a caged tigress that moved behind her pale flesh, he was yet aware of her cunning licentiousness that would use him for her own malicious ends. He could view her with a cold intensity from a distance now, could speculate as to her designs; yet, at the same time, he was aware that in her immediate presence she dominated him by a power that was not entirely beauty. It was this that made him uneasy and unsure of himself.

"Yes," she said, low, husky, half-passionately. "I have my philosophy of living. It is to drink to the dregs the opportunities vouchsafed us by Time, to take advantage of that cruel gaoler, Destiny, and fool him at every turn. We are born free and we should live free. Our blood whispers messages to us and we should answer those low calls that ring in our ears if we are to vindicate ourselves to ourselves. Have you ever rested your head against a woman's breast and heard the blood racing furiously through all its arteries? What are we put into the world for? We are the fruit of suppressed joy, are we not? It is the liberation of self for which we are ordained. There is only one way of being actually free, and that is to surmount the thousand and one petty laws and dogmas that hedge us about. We speak constantly of obligations, but what do we mean by them? Do we mean the suppression of our free instincts and the obliteration of our integrity before the selfish demands of another's welfare and peace of mind? Is not that a slavish instinct? What is our debt to humanity but the reverse of humanity's debt to us. There is a freedom based upon the destruction of all laws, political, religious and moral, a freedom where we may tread the earth as gods in a great tranquil equality, and it is to that freedom that I turn my face. If I am free in myself, if my thoughts and secret passions move as they please, why not this flesh which I carry travel in freedom also?"

He heard the soft sound of her breast struck sharply by her hand.

"I do not say 'no' to anything," she went on. "I merely say 'does it satisfy me and fill me for the moment?' If it does it is good. If it does it is an end in itself. Let men and women think what they please and move about with free wills. I abolish slavery."

It all sounded like a set speech to Dreeme, something she had written out and memorized, something that she had evolved to sap the spiritual integrity of whosoever she might meet in this mood of attack. Well, he would show her that he was adamant.

"You are an anarchist," he said. He strove to say it lightly, to fashion it into a mere flippant rejoinder. To his chagrin he heard his own voice trembling.

"I am a woman," she replied. "All women are anarchists at heart. The only laws they respect are the laws of their desires. I am an anarchist of the soul, of the mind, of the flesh. Nothing but the limitations of my body shall stand in my way. And through the limitations of my body I will find my own deliverance."

She stopped at that as though expecting a sudden flood of answers on his part and her eyes were fastened upon his face. He said nothing but waited.

"I am lonely," she murmured in a low, almost inaudible voice.

Dreeme, turning his face directly toward her, looked into her eyes. She was speaking through them, steadily, mercilessly. For a moment they stared at one another, and then Dreeme, his face flushing and his body shaking, stood up. In the moonlight so diffused and cloudy her eyes dilated like those of a tigress.

"Have I told you nothing?" she cried. "Have I said nothing to you?"

Her voice was loud and raucous, a terrible sound that caused Dreeme's body to sway. It was as though she were lashing him with a whip.

"You have told me many things," he answered in a trembling voice, "and most of them I did not want to hear."

She stood up before him and put her hands upon his shoulders, the nails of her fingers pressing into his flesh.

"You coward!" she said. "You miserable coward!"

He took her hands from his shoulders, but still retained them in his own. Her hands were cold and the palms were moist.

"I am not a coward," he answered in an uncertain voice.

She breathed deeply, a long shuddering inhalation, and then put her mouth close to his ear, her long body resting lightly against him.

"Listen!" she said in a husky whisper. "Are you as lonely as I . . ."

Suddenly she stopped and twisted about toward the door of the mill, a door that yawned on the road and framed in its square a clouded milky haze.

"Do you hear it?" she asked in a low monotone.

He had already concentrated his faculties and was listening intently.

"Yes, I do," he answered. A cold fever settled on him as he replied, and he knew that he was perspiring icily at every pore.

Over the narrow wooden bridge that spanned the Saccarac River sounded slow footsteps. He could hear them distinctly in the nerve-racking silence of the night, a measured advance that increased in sound as the invisible traveler neared the mill. One of the bridge-boards creaked beneath the weight of this unknown, and then there was a brief silence. The unseen wanderer had apparently paused, and Dreeme could imagine him leaning on the wood rail of the bridge and gazing into the black water that flowed so sluggishly beneath the cloudy sky. There were no stars reflected in that water. There was not even the reflection of the face of the noctambulist who was leaning over and gazing into nothingness. Even as the thought flashed through Dreeme's mind he heard the tread resumed, this time to the accompanying crunch of gravel. Whoever it was had crossed the bridge and was following the path that skirted the ruined shell of the mill. Suddenly, with surprising strength, Martha Westcott thrust Dreeme away from the broken embrasure where they had sat in the murky glow of the half-drowned moon and against the charred side-wall of the mill. From that dark corner they could stare obliquely at the door. They stood there crushed against the wall, the acrid smell of burned timbers in their nostrils, while the crunching footsteps deliberately progressed toward them. The invisible wanderer was passing the angle of the mill now, following the blackened wall, just about to cross the milky square of the doorway. At this moment the sound ceased, stopping with a startling abruptness as though the hidden prowler had paused with one foot in the air. Dreeme could hear the woman beside him catch her breath in a tiny strangled sob. Both of them, flattened against the blackened beams, their shoulders touching, watched the dimly-glowing frame of the entrance with dilated eyes. In the silence that surged back about them like a dark wave, Dreeme could hear Martha Westcott's heart beating. It was like a drum. It seemed to increase in volume until the whole interior was throbbing with the sound. Then slowly, ever so slowly, a dark shadow obscured the doorway, although there were no accompanying footsteps. The shadow hovered for an instant as though it were poised in the air, and then, to Dreeme's horror, a low monotonous humming filled the wrecked room. The shadow, enlarged by the deceiving rays of the cloudy moon, appeared to sway, to diminish, to swell in rhythm with this unceasing drone. Dreeme, his nerves at the breaking point, started impulsively forward, but the tight clutch of Martha Westcott's hand on his wrist caught him back. At this moment he recognized a melody in the low humming. "Rock of Ages." Somebody was standing in the doorway of the mill and monotonously humming, "Rock of Ages." Immediately Dreeme's imagination shaped before him a shallow-faced figure in a frayed frock coat. A lean figure with dead eyes.

He had barely time to identify the man in the doorway before the humming ceased, and the shadow withdrew as noiselessly as it had appeared. There was the instant's pause and Dreeme suddenly recollected that there was a patch of soft earth before the mill door. Of course. The loiterer was crossing that, returning to the gravel-path again. Even as his mind began to function rationally once more he heard the crunching footsteps, this time decreasing in sound as the wanderer progressed along the road to Marlborough. They were slow, casual, a retarded crunch-crunch, a deliberate and unexcited dwindling. Presently there was silence. Dreeme, relaxed and almost smiling at the fever of fear into which he had been thrust by the nocturnal rambler, turned to Martha Westcott. He expected to find her relieved, but instead of this he could faintly decipher a concentrated expression of mingled fear and anger on her face.

"Well," he said, "our unexpected caller has departed."

"You knew him?" she asked.

They were both walking toward the door, tacitly admitting that the rendezvous was at an end.

"The worthy Burroughs?" said Dreeme lightly. "Of course. He was taking his usual evening promenade."

She said nothing until they reached the milky square of obscured moonlight. Then she asked:

"Will you meet me here tomorrow night?"

"No," said Dreeme.

She frowned at that.

"I have certain things I want to tell you," she went on. "I need your advice about a number of matters."

"Why don't you come to my office?" he inquired.

"You know very well why," she replied.

He said nothing but stood restlessly outside the door, anxious to leave her and unwilling to be too abrupt.

"Burroughs didn't see us anyway," he said inconsequentially. "It was too dark in that corner."

She opened her eyes wide at that and regarded him with a mocking expression.

"It isn't wise to meet in this clandestine way," he insisted. "Somebody might see us, and you know how people gossip. I don't like gossip when there isn't any reason for it. It's . . . it's too nerve-racking."

He teetered on one foot and turned toward Marlborough. She was leaning easily against the door. She said:

"I will tell you a great many things tomorrow night."

Dreeme made an impatient gesture, and started to walk away.

"He did see us," remarked Martha Westcott, not so much to the young doctor, as to the night about them. "Of course he saw us."

Dreeme did not turn about, but kept on his way down the road. The air was cool and frolicksome, and it ruffled the hair on his forehead. It was fresh and pleasant. It was not like the acrid smell of burned wood. Two men had been incinerated in the mill. That was a long time ago, and still the charred timbers stood there waiting for somebody to rebuild them. He wondered how late it was. There was not a single light in any of the houses. If he turned back now he would see Martha Westcott leaning against the door of the mill, her heavy-lidded eyes and archaic mouth turned toward him. He would not turn back though. The road twisted a trifle, and he knew that the mill was hidden, that if he looked back he would see nothing but the sprawling angle of a stone wall. An invisible weight seemed to fall from him. He had not realized he was so tired.

Chapter Five

I

The girl beat with her hands against the door, whimpering softly as the steady concussions shook the white-washed planks. The morning sunlight caught her by the shoulders in warm hands and seemed to shake her. She did not pause to listen for any approaching footsteps, but continued to hammer at the wood as though in a half-trance, and but semi-conscious of what she was doing. White clouds ballooned upward in the bright blue sky and watched her from a distance. They were snowy-plumaged hawks observing the peregrinations of a lice-like humanity upon a rolling ball of earth and sea. The girl was a far-away mote to their far-seeing eyes, a speck of dust without form or meaning. She moaned to herself and shook the door. Dreeme heard her thin voice so broken by suppressed and breathless sobs as he hurried down stairs, turned the key in the rusty grating lock, and flung the door open. She stumbled into the hall, her tear-streaked face lifted like the face of a wounded animal, and lurched against him with a sudden paralysis of knees, clinging tightly to his arm. Dreeme pushed the door shut and half-carried her along the hall to the little study.

"Why Deborah!" he cried. "What is it? Sit down. Shall I get you a glass of water?"

She refused to sit down, but continued to cling to him still whimpering. Her face was streaked with tears and dust, and her mouth shook convulsively. The pupils of her eyes were dilated, and she did not seem to see him.

"What is it?" he repeated. "What is it? You must tell me, you know. What has happened?"

She gazed about the little study in a vague manner, and for a moment appeared to strive for the mastery of her feelings. Her mouth opened and coherent speech seemed about to issue. Then she broke down completely and, relinquishing his arm, dropped to a chair beside the table upon which she buried her face. Dreeme, hearing her unrestrained sobs and noting the convulsive quiver of her pathetically small shoulders, realized that this was better than the stifled whimpering with which she had entered the room. She was giving full vent to her outraged nerves now, letting them run away with her until, tired and exhausted, they would once more be subject to her reason. The young doctor sat down calmly and waited.

Outside the morning moved on leisurely sun-shot feet through the cool lane. Sparkles of light caught at the flawed panes of the windows. In the sky the clouds hovered like white hawks. Birds chirped loudly in the ancient trees, and a creaking wagon drawn by a heavy-hoofed farm-horse protested its way toward the general store. Dreeme listened as the creaking axle-tree and softly-jingling harness grew fainter and finally died out. He heard the far caw of a crow as it sped in feathery darkness toward some field unguarded by an ungainly scare-crow. It was all peaceful and unvexed, a crystal tide of morning, a time for calmness and not tears. He waited patiently. He inspected the atrocious wall-paper that closed him in from the sun, and cleared his throat with dry humor. The wall-paper designer must have been a practical joker. Finding nothing better to do he drew his watch out and looked at it. The heavy, old-fashioned, silver-cased heirloom blandly announced that it was quarter past seven. He forced it back into his vest pocket, and stroked one freshly-shaven cheek meditatively. He had not slept so well. He . . . had been troubled by dreams. He thought of . . . no, he wouldn't think of her now. Mrs. Slater would be along with his breakfast soon. He raised his eyes to the ceiling and waited. Flyspecks. Blackened rings of lamp smoke. It was cracked in the corner. That was where the mice nibbled and made little crackling noises during the night. Did they live on wood or plaster?

The girl lifted her head suddenly and pushed back her disheveled hair. Her eyes were like wet violets, a soaked blue so deep as to be astonishing. Dreeme smiled at her gently and said nothing. She looked at him in a surprised manner.

"I feel better," she announced in a very small voice.

"I'm glad you do," he replied. "Shall I get you a glass of water now?"

"Please," she nodded.

When he came back with it she had wiped her tear-stained face with a small handkerchief, smoothed her hair, and brushed part of the dust from her gray dress. She drank the water in slow sips, gazing at him over the top of the tumbler. Dreeme leaned back in his chair and observed her. Curiously enough, although he had seen her but once before she was like an old acquaintance now. It was as though he were sitting in the room with what, in his New England, would be dubbed "family." A tacit feeling of confidence established itself between them. Her intensely blue eyes, her misty bronze hair, her small mouth and nose, even her thin arms and slender wiry hands, were part and parcel of an old knowledge. It was pleasant to be like this while the mysterious white hawks in the sky hovered so far above them.

"I'm not like this generally," she informed him as she put the tumbler down. There was a wise and confidential intimation in her voice.

"I know you're not," he answered. "You've been terribly frightened."

His statement was almost a question, and the pupils of her eyes dilated again as she nodded assent.

"I'll tell you all about it directly," she said.

She was small . . . small. That was his main impression. But intelligent. Wise. He waited with a seeming patience praying fervently that Mrs. Slater would not appear until he had found out the source of Deborah's trouble. He could guess part of it, but he did not want to let his mind stray too far along the vague pathways of unsubstantiated surmise. The girl closed her eyes and obviously strove to adjust herself in a reasonable manner to the subject which was in her mind. It was patent that she did not know how or where to begin, and that she was fearful of not being able to communicate the essence of her story to Dreeme. She wanted to speak reasonably now. To assure herself, perhaps, of her own rationality. He would help. Like a doctor.

"Begin at the beginning," suggested Dreeme. She opened her eyes. She said:

"I don't know how to tell you and make it seem like anything. It's . . . it's more feeling than anything else."

He nodded sagely, and, after a moment's hesitation, she began.

"You see I have to do something for my living. Father was killed at the court-house in Leeminster, and he was all that I had. We lived there . . . Leeminster, I mean . . . and father was a constructor. He built houses. There weren't many to be built, of course. He was working on the ell of the new court-house and the men mixed cement on the roof of the front porch. One of the bags was pushed off in some way, and it fell on father. He died in half an hour. That was a month ago. Then I had to close up our house . . . such a little one, sell things, and help finish up father's business. I had a very good lawyer, Mr. Stopes. Perhaps you knew him?"

Dreeme shook his head.

"Lawyers," he said, "are out of my line. They never get sick."

"He was a very good lawyer," she insisted. "After the estate was set-tled there was just enough to pay his fee. Then Aunt Slater sent for me. It was only yesterday that I came over. I walked all the way. I thought I should stay here and help Aunt, but it seemed that Mr. Burroughs had heard about me or seen me in Leeminster . . . he preaches there sometimes . . . and he told Aunt that Mrs. Westcott needed somebody to help around the house. I didn't want to help because I am not a servant, and I told Aunt so, but she said that she couldn't afford to keep me. I thought that was funny, because, after all, she *had* sent for me. I'm telling you this because I want to show you that I was feeling bad in my mind anyway, and perhaps exaggerated some of the things that happened later."

Dreeme nodded. Mrs. Slater was like that. She was a New England aunt.

"I didn't have to come," proceeded Deborah. "I might have stayed in Leeminster and taught school. Father was very careful about putting me through my studies. Well, I went over late yesterday afternoon to the Westcott farm with Mr. Burroughs. We walked because he said he thought I would like to see the country. I didn't like the country, and I didn't like Mr. Burroughs. He is like the country, dull and ghostly and green and sad. I think I first became afraid and nervous on that walk, for Mr. Burroughs, after we started, never said a word to me. We just plodded along, and he would look at me sideways with his funny eyes. I tried to say something once or twice, but he only nodded. I felt as though I was walking into a nightmare. The Westcott farm seemed terribly dreary to me, and I was frightened as soon as that horrible little boy appeared at the fence-gate."

"Miles," said Dreeme.

"Is his name Miles?" asked Deborah. "I didn't know. He had a great growling dog on a rope, and he let it walk after me up the path. It snarled all the way. He started to say something, but Mr. Burroughs just waved his hand and the boy went off through the bushes. We went into the kitchen and Mrs. Westcott was there. Mr. Burroughs introduced me, and I went right to work helping Mrs. Westcott. There were piles of dishes to wash. After that Mrs. Westcott showed me where I was to sleep and where I was to put my things."

She paused for a moment and shut her eyes, seeming to revisualize inwardly the appearance of Mrs. Westcott.

"She's quite beautiful, I think," Deborah proceeded. "But it is what I would call . . . something frozen-like, you know."

Dreeme shifted slightly in his chair.

"If you could imagine cold fire, fire that was just like ice, I think that would be Mrs. Westcott," went on the girl. "She didn't have much to say to me. She moved around the kitchen like some . . . like some queen, like somebody who didn't want to be there and didn't mean to be there very long. Presently she went away with Mr. Burroughs, and I finished up the work in the kitchen and went into the living room. There wasn't anything to do there, and I kept on into another room that was full of books. It was just like a library, shelves all around, and such tattered books. There wasn't one that was new. The only thing that I could think of to do was to dust the books. So I found a bit of cloth and started in on them. It would take a life-time to dust those books. I had removed an armful from one of the shelves and was about to dust the shelf itself when I saw a lot of little dolls in a row against the back of the shelf. They were terribly amusing, and I took two of them out to look at them more closely. One was a tiny man and he had needles stuck in his eyes. The other had a needle thrust into the knee. I pulled it out. It was while I was holding the dolls in my hand that I felt somebody standing in back of me. At first I was afraid to turn around. I was sure that my knees would give way. I put the dolls back, and stood there looking at the shelves. Then something began to turn me, and I faced about, and there stood that awful man in the doorway, with his head thrust forward, and his still eyes watching me with a sort of smile way back in them."

Deborah paused and thrust a small tongue over her dry underlip.

"I first began to be really frightened then," she added. "You see, I have nothing to go upon but sensations and intuitions."

Dreeme sat motionless in his chair, his entire intelligence concentrated upon her story. She said:

"It came over me like waves, and I began to feel like somebody in deep churning waters. There was no reason for it, just something inside of me telling me to be afraid. He stood in the doorway and looked at me, and I stood there unable to move or say a word. I could see the ridges on his head. 'Who told you to come in here?' he asked. 'Go back to the kitchen,' he added. 'When I want you to dust the books I'll tell you so.' His voice was low and snarling. I don't know how I got to the door, but I did, and he must have passed me, for just as I was stepping out of the room he shouted, 'You damned little fool!' He was standing by the shelves with one of the dolls in his hand."

Dreeme frowned. Something about wax dolls with pins thrust into them. He had read it somewhere. He could not recall it now. He put the subject away for the time being, and resumed his calm rôle of auditor.

"Nothing more happened till suppertime," Deborah was saying. "I stayed in the kitchen and helped with the cooking. Then we all sat down at table. There was Mrs. Westcott, and the boy, and Wagner, the hired man, and myself. Mrs. Westcott wanted to say something to Wagner. I could see it on her mouth and in her eyes. And Wagner wanted to hear what she had to say, for he sat like an attentive bull-dog waiting for a caress. But before she could say anything *he* came out of the library, lurching along in an awkward fashion, for he is lame in one leg, and sat down. None of us spoke then. The dishes were passed in silence. Mrs. Westcott sat with her eyes lowered to her plate, although every now and then she would glance under her long lashes at Wagner, who sat on the edge of his chair with a puzzled expression on his face. He was just like a bull-dog that is trying unsuccessfully to comprehend what its master desires it to do. Mr. Westcott saw them every time, and he would smile in the most malevolent manner. That supper was terrible. I thought that it would never end or that I should suddenly scream and run out of the room. Do you know that taut feeling when your nerves seem strained to the breaking point? I was like that. The boy . . . did you say his name was Miles? . . . ate like a greedy little animal. Wagner was puzzled and surly. Mrs. Westcott was terribly excited, although on the surface she was as still as snow. I could sense the fever in her. Mr. Westcott was the only calm person, and his calmness was like the breathlessness that is in the air before an electric storm breaks. You know what I mean. When you can hardly breathe. And I was thinking how terrible it was to be there, and how miserable and frightened I was. How could I stand it? How could I stay there? The silence, it . . . it seemed to crawl around the room, to move like a great lazy snake, to slide under the table and up the backs of the chairs, and across the face of the clock. The air was heavy. Like before a storm, you know. Like . . ."

She stopped abruptly, plainly at a loss for words to convey the strange nuances of that meal. Dreeme sat uneasily in his chair, dimly conscious that he was involved in this imbroglio of ominous silences. He began to feel like a man sitting at the edge of the crater of a slumbering volcano. Sooner or later it would erupt, and he would be destroyed by unimaginable fiery lavas. He could picture to himself the silence of that supper without the aid of Deborah. Around a table sat a group of wax figures with living eyes. The eyes spoke, but the mouths were speechless. These eyes whispered, laughed, threatened, fought invisible duels. They were glittering assassins moving stealthily toward their defenseless victims. Deborah was a victim. He was a victim. Anyone who blundered into that death-like circle of wax figures was a victim. Deborah's voice cut across his brooding. She had given up the attempt to picture the Westcott supper with any degree of vividness. She said:

"After supper, we rose from the table without a word. Wagner hurried away. He went like a ghost. I heard the door close softly behind him. Mr. Westcott heard it, too, for it seemed to be a signal for him to go into his room of books. He said to Mrs. Westcott, 'Leave me alone now. I'll see you to-morrow.' She said, 'Don't make a fool of yourself.' He smiled at that and said, 'That's your prerogative.' Then he went into the library and closed the door behind him. I helped wash dishes. Pretty soon Mr. Burroughs came. He slid into the house humming to himself. He loitered about the kitchen for a while and talked to Mrs. Westcott about what sort of a year it was, and how he was going to preach Leeminster way on Sunday. Mrs. Westcott just laughed in her husky way. 'Preach!' she said.

'You're an insane humorist, George.' He smiled, too, and looked at me in that sly still way. 'Watch out for my little Paschal Lamb,' he said, nodding at me. Then he went to the door of the library and knocked, and pretty soon he went in, leaving the door ajar. I could hear him talking with Mr. Westcott. I continued to work about the kitchen, but the door that led into the sitting room was open, and so, too, was the door to the library, ajar, I mean. I could hear men's voices, but it was hard to distinguish the words. I didn't notice when Mrs. Westcott went away, but when I looked for her to ask her about something, she was gone. Once I heard Mr. Westcott's voice raised. He cried out, 'I tell you she'll do, George. At the place called Dagon . . .' Then I heard footsteps coming toward the door. 'The master . . .' began Mr. Burroughs, and the door was closed with a slam. I couldn't distinguish any more words. When I went into the sitting room I could just hear Mr. Burroughs' voice. It was monotonous, as though he was preaching, and it sounded like some foreign language. Maybe Latin."

She stopped and looked at the silent attentive figure of Dreeme.

"It doesn't sound like anything, does it?" she asked.

"Go on," said Dreeme briefly. Queer word, Dagon.

"I'm getting to what really frightened me now," she said. "All that went before was a mere leading up, a series of nothings that put me in a nervous state of mind. I wanted you to know, though. I went to bed rather early because I was tired. It was a long time before I got to sleep. You know how a strange bed feels, and when one is nervous. But I did get to sleep finally, and I guess I slept pretty heavily. I don't know how long I slept, but I am sure that I was awakened by three horrible screams. I started up . . ."

"You heard somebody screaming?" asked Dreeme. She shook her head. She said:

"No, I didn't hear anything. But I am sure that I was wakened by three screams. I don't know . . . I . . . I sensed the echo of them, I guess. I started up wide awake and half-mad with fright. I knew instantly without looking that the door to my room was open. There was a little moonlight straggling in at the window and when I looked toward the door I could see him standing there. I could see his face very plainly, and the ridges on his skull. He . . ."

Dreeme uttered a stifled exclamation.

"You mean . . ." he began.

"Yes, yes," she said, the shadow of fear starting up in her eyes again. "Mr. Westcott was standing in my doorway and looking at me. He was leaning forward a little, his head lowered on his breast, and staring at me from under his eyebrows. The moonlight rippled across his uneven head and his flat nose. His eyes were large and dark and still, with that awful stillness that seems to say so many things. He stood there and stared, and everything seemed to die inside me. The blood paused in my veins, and a queer sort of dizziness came over me. I was conscious of nothing but his eyes, and of an enormous will in his eyes that seemed to but half-reveal itself. I seemed to swoon, to float upward, while his eyes grew into huge circles that swallowed me and the room. Far off, as though from another world, I heard a low voice saying, 'At Dagon. At Dagon. For the master.' He did not say that, for his lips never moved, and even if he had spoken I could not have heard him, for my ears were like dead things. It was through his eyes that everything came to me. And it was looking into his eyes, being drowned in his eyes, that I saw . . ."

For a moment she lost the faculty of speech and lifted a small white frightened face to Dreeme. Her lips fumbled for words, and the young doctor could see them moving dumbly.

"Wait," he said. "Don't tell me any more."

In the back of his mind a faint light was beginning to dawn. It was far away as yet, as far away as those snowy hawks that hovered over the valley. He would have to mount as high as those clouds if he was to see everything spread out like a simple map before him.

"I must," she said with an effort. "I must try to let you know. It was all in his eyes. An unutterable evil. A concentration of everything that is horrible and bestial in this world, or, for all I know, out of it. His eyes were telling me of all the sins and perversions and horrors that have existed since before the beginning of time, of reptile urges and . . . I can't explain it, you see. I do not know how to handle the words. But I saw . . . the horror of time . . . and . . ."

She could not go on. But she did not sob again. She sat with trance-like eyes and said nothing.

Dreeme was staring at her intently, and, from a half-shocked mind, striving to piece together her stumbling narrative of mingled fears and menaces. Curiously enough he did not doubt the authenticity of her mental fever. This was no mere hysteria, no nightmare. It was as though the hidden facet of an admitted evil had been slowly turned toward him. The far-away light continued to shine in the deepest recesses of his mind. He felt all that she felt as he heard her story, and understood vividly enough the aspect and profundity of that terror which moved her, and which she conveyed so haltingly. She had sensed something that could not be adequately expressed in words, just as he had sensed something in the community that was beyond the power of speech.

Deborah began to speak again. She said:

"He turned and went out noiselessly, and the door made no sound as it closed behind him. I could hear the clock ticking somewhere. It was the first time I had heard one in that house, and somehow it made the night and the world real again. I could not sleep again. It was too much to expect. I lay there staring at the door for hours, and sure that there was somebody on the other side of it, somebody standing there with his head thrust forward and still eyes that grew as large as moons. It began to grow light, that skimmed-milk-like color that the early cloudy morning has, and I kept saying to myself, 'I must go away from here. I mustn't be found here in the morning.' It was only by a terrific effort of will that I forced myself to get up and dress. I can't tell you how blinded with panic I was when I pushed the door open. There was no one there. There wasn't a sound in the house as I crept down stairs and out of the kitchen door. I reached the road and looked back at the house. It squatted there like a dead thing with blind eyes. It couldn't see me. I began to run then. I ran all the way here. I thought I could hear things running after me, but when I looked back the road was empty. I even thought I heard someone laughing in the air. I came to you first because . . ."

The door swung open and the small plump figure of Mrs. Slater appeared behind a breakfast tray. Her eyes opened with amazement when she saw the drooping figure of Deborah, but she said nothing until she methodically placed the tray on the table and removed the napkin from the food. Then she turned to the girl, a thin disapproval curling down her mouth.

"Land's sakes," she said in a querulous tone. "You're in town early."

Deborah gazed from her aunt to Dreeme, a mingled defiance and supplication in her blue eyes.

"I've run away," she said. "I'm not going back. I won't stay there."

Mrs. Slater arranged the breakfast plates in a deliberate fashion. Her eyes fluttered as she moved about the table. She said:

"You can't run away. Girls don't run away in Marlborough."

There was no interest in her voice, nothing but a faintly-aggrieved protest.

"She has run away," remarked Dreeme shortly. "Can't you see her in front of you?"

Mrs. Slater ignored him. In a voice entirely lacking in curiosity she inquired:

"What was the matter, Deborah?"

"I . . . I was frightened," replied the girl. "I don't like that awful place and those awful people."

She stopped abruptly at that. Dreeme understood that she realized the impossibility of explaining anything to Mrs. Slater. He undertook to fill the gap.

"Deborah is a highly nervous girl," he said. "It is necessary that she have surroundings that are favorable. A lonely farm and a brutal farmer who peers into one's bedroom at night, and who is up to the devil knows what, are not the surroundings for her. Speaking as a doctor . . ."

"Your coffee's cooling," said Mrs. Slater. She shifted the sugar-bowl uneasily. Dreeme poured a cup of coffee and handed it to Deborah.

"There's plenty of breakfast in the house of your relations," announced Mrs. Slater, the wan ghost of indignation in her voice.

"But not plenty of room," added Dreeme. He sat down angrily to his breakfast, and proceeded to eat. Mrs. Slater stood looking at her niece.

"You know I would do for you," she said, "but Walden has about all he can handle with the children. The land's mighty poor."

She ignored Dreeme completely. The young doctor visualized a picture of a stoop-shouldered man struggling all day with thin soil that noisy little mouths might be fed. He cultivated a stone and strove to make bread of it. Well, it was no circus. Still . . .

"You can't place Deborah where she is frightened and unhappy," he said.

"Mrs. Westcott is the only neighbor around here who wants somebody," remarked Mrs. Slater. There was a hopeless and dispirited note in her voice.

Neither Dreeme nor Deborah replied. Mrs. Slater stood by the table stolidly, her eyes fluttering.

"There's nothing to be frightened of at the Westcott farm," she added. "Nothing at all."

Dreeme passed a slice of toast to Deborah. Curious. All his life. He knew she sat that way. Mrs. Slater moved closer to the table.

"I don't see why you should be unhappy there," she said. "I don't see, at all."

"Well, we'll talk it over later," interposed Dreeme. "Let Deborah recover her equanimity."

"It's hard on me," said Mrs. Slater. She stooped to lift an empty plate, and tiny lines rippled across her plump face. It was sagging a bit now. The earth seemed pulling it downward. She was aggrieved at life in general and Deborah in particular. Dreeme she plainly regarded as an interloper, an officious stranger, who thrust himself into affairs that did not concern him. For an instant he was angry. It was hard on her! He opened his mouth to expostulate, even to deliver a long speech on her unkindly attitude, when a measured thumping sounded in the hall leading to the study. It was a rhythmical alternating sound, now loud and then soft, the sound of a man, perhaps, with a wooden leg. A man with a wooden leg or . . . Before the door swung open Dreeme knew who it was. With calm eyes, therefore, he raised his face to Jeffrey Westcott who stood in the doorway. He said:

"Good morning. You are into town early."

Westcott nodded slightly. His eyes were fastened on Deborah.

"You're abroad early also," he remarked to her. His voice was low and casual. The girl did not answer him but turned appealingly to Dreeme. Westcott smiled vaguely, the mere flash of an ironic humor that was undisturbed and sure of itself.

"How are you, Mrs. Slater?" he asked.

Mrs. Slater fluttered her eyes and coughed an intimation that she was not so well. Dreeme perceived that she did not like Westcott, but was making an effort to conceal her instinctive antagonism. There was fear in this effort. The farmer's eyes roved about the room, casually inspected the books in the little case, and then reverted to Deborah.

"I've the horse here," he said to her. "I'll take you back now."

"She's not going back with you, Mr. Westcott," interposed Dreeme dryly. "She's not going back at all."

Mrs. Slater opened her mouth with a cluck.

"Not at all," repeated Dreeme, giving him a defiant look.

Westcott continued to regard the girl.

"Weren't you coming back with me, Deborah?" he asked in a low silky voice.

A strange thing happened. Deborah rose to her feet slowly and took a single step toward the farmer. His dark eyes were fastened piercingly upon her now. Dreeme jumped from his chair and turned the girl around. Instantly she burst into tears.

"Don't let me go," she pleaded.

"I know now," said Dreeme. He faced Westcott with a smile. He added:

"Try that on me. See if it will work on a man."

Westcott lowered his cloven head.

"Really, doctor," he said in a mild voice, "I don't understand you."

He, too, was smiling slightly.

"You neglected to send your bill," he went on.

Fumbling in his pocket he drew forth a brand-new five dollar bill, and, limping forward, laid it on the table.

"There," he said. "We are quits. Let us hope that we may remain quits."

He opened his eyes and gazed full into Dreeme's face. There was absolutely no expression in his look. It was like the meaningless stare of a blind man. Paying no more attention to Deborah he turned to Mrs. Slater.

"Is Walden in the fields?" he asked.

She nodded, and he swung on his heel.

"Good morning, doctor. Good morning, Mrs. Slater," he said. He ignored Deborah. An instant later they heard his lame thumping through the hall, and then the closing of the front door. Dreeme absently picked up the bill. On it was scrawled: "Even a fool may learn wisdom."

II

The Reverend George Burroughs stretched his long yellow hand out and grasped a slice of bread. He made it a point to take the fattest cut. Dreeme, watching from beneath lowered lids, noted that the preacher's hand was shaped like a claw. The fingers curled back like the crazy-shaped bits of driftwood he had seen washed up on the tip of Cape Cod years ago, when, as a boy, he had made a vacation trip to those rolling dunes of white sand. Indeed, the Reverend George Burroughs himself was very like something that had been washed up on the beach. Some sort of skinny sea-monster, an old merman who was half sea-horse. It was time to keep an eye on the preacher. Dreeme looked up at Burroughs and discovered that the man of God apparently was thinking the same thought, for his expressionless eyes were fastened upon the young doctor over the bread that he was cramming into his capacious mouth. Burroughs masticated loudly and continued to stare at Dreeme. The pupils of his eyes were like two black shoe buttons. He had never done that before. He had always averted his eyes or dropped them to the heaped plate above which he constantly hovered so eagerly. Dreeme was less startled than amused. If he had entered into the old hypocrite's line of vision at last so much the worse for the old hypocrite. He would give him something to look at. Something to think about. The old night-wanderer! The old fool who poked his horse-like face into burned mills to see what he might see! The withered employment agency for the Westcott farm! Dreeme remarked calmly:

"You enjoy evening strolls, preacher."

Burroughs, his mouth clogged with bread, nodded slowly.

Dreeme awaited an answer, and as none was forthcoming apparently, he transferred his attention to the rest of the table. He had sat so many times at this board and had seen nothing and understood everything. Now he saw everything and understood nothing. This noon, for instance, it was simple enough to perceive that a general unrest pervaded the secretive diners. It was even communicated to the children, who gazed frightenedly from face to face, seeking for the reassurance of an unslipped mask, for a visage that did not suggest the complexities of perturbation. Mrs. Slater, her cheeks heightened in color—tiny scarlet flags mutely calling for aid—and her eyes fluttering, was plainly disaffected and at odds with circumstances. Walden Slater was so upset that he ate meagerly. His long camel-like upper-lip closed half-heartedly over the mouthfuls that he balanced precariously on the flat blade of his knife. The preacher was puzzled, a bit startled, perhaps, to find Dreeme thrust into his scheme of things for he must have heard all about the young doctor's championship of Deborah. Deborah! She, at least, was real. Though Dreeme did not know these other people he knew *her*. She smiled briefly across the table at him, and it was as though she had flung him a flower. A small blue flower with a starry heart tossed across a table of strangers. A flower as blue as her eyes were blue, as starry as the pupils of her eyes. He smiled back at her broadly. The smile was intercepted by everybody at the table. He enjoyed their reactions to it. Mrs. Slater nipped at it as a parrot nips at a cracker. The children thrust little faces of ice between it and Deborah. Walden Slater retreated from it in a bewildered manner, and then, to Dreeme's pleasant surprise, wrung the doleful ghost of an accompanying smile from his long lip and tossed it gingerly to Deborah. The Reverend George Burroughs observed it impassively and blew a little cloud of darkness over it. The busy knives and forks played a greedy melody.

"In the cool of the evening it is good to walk," announced the preacher. He spoke as though he were delivering the text for a sermon.

"And much may be seen by night that is invisible by day," returned Dreeme facetiously. He felt in a high good humor, light-minded, puffed up with a malicious playfulness. He was quite fearless of the community and its inhabitants. "I will not be here long," he thought to himself. He, after all, was but a sojourner. He did not belong in Marlborough and he was glad of it.

"The true heart of man is often bared to the darkness," agreed Burroughs in a sententious voice. For an instant Dreeme thought the preacher was laughing at him, and he gazed at the yellow face before him suspiciously. There was no hint of a smile upon that long countenance. It was a sober blank, quite clear of any subtle writing. Indeed, it was a little too guileless. "Perhaps," Dreeme thought, "I am not as self-sufficient as I think I am." His eyes returned to Deborah. She was looking at him brightly. Well, he would have to be self-sufficient for her sake. Still, these people were accepting his interpositions too quiescently. He knew that they could not be as weak-willed as that. Humphrey Lathrop had intimated too much. He, himself, had observed too much. Did not Burroughs know that he had met Martha Westcott in the burned mill? Had not Burroughs told all this to Westcott himself? Or had the darkness concealed them from the inquisitive eyes of the preacher? Martha Westcott had said "no" to that and he had believed her. And why had Westcott received his interference in the matter of Deborah's return to the farm so blandly? What was he planning behind his smiling face and hypnotic eyes? That was it, of course. Westcott was fooling with hypnotism. He had hypnotized Deborah that night and even when he had come for her this very morning he had, for an instant, subjected her will to his. Dreeme scraped his plate clean with outward unconcern but inwardly he was perplexed. "As a matter of fact," he thought to himself, "I am all at sea." He was not self-sufficient at all. He was aware of a great many questions, but he could offer but a meager handful of answers. These people were leagued against him, and they intended to do what they pleased with him when the psychological moment came. And that would be when he interfered too strenuously in their designs, when through fool-luck he clogged their purposes. That would be when? The scraping of knives and creaking of chairs aided and abetted his inquiring mind. He pushed his plate back and scowled. Then his features lightened. Of course! A thrill of triumph ran up his spine, and the far-away light in the depths of his mind glowed brighter. It would be when he found the place called Dagon. It would be when he stood on that spot and faced these farmers in the very heart of their mystery. Even as the unfamiliar name flashed across his consciousness the preacher's yellow hand closed upon his wrist. He lifted startled eyes to the calm equine face.

"I asked," said the Reverend George Burroughs in his solemn voice, "if you enjoyed strolling in the evening."

Still at it, eh?

"By myself, yes," replied Dreeme. The yellow hand disappeared beneath the table.

"It is good to be by one's self," remarked the preacher. "He who goes by himself need fear no man."

The stilted voice of Burroughs rose like the neigh of a horse.

"That is not exactly the saying, is it?" inquired Dreeme politely.

The preacher wiped his mouth with the back of his hand and said nothing.

They had finished eating now. The defeated platter lay in greasy subjection. The knives and forks reposed upon the stained field of battle like discarded weapons. The buzzing flies hummed above the débris monotonously. With a clattering of steel-tipped shoes the children squirmed from their chairs and fled through the door. Mrs. Slater and Deborah rose and staggered toward the kitchen under loads of plates and cups and gravyboats. They were Trojan women carrying the shields of their warriors. The three men still sat in their places as though there was something to be said between them. Walden Slater opened and shut his mouth. He looked helplessly from Burroughs to Dreeme. His sweaty shoulders seemed to climb up about his tanned leathery face. A remnant of bread swung like a miniature acrobat from his chin.

"It'll be a poor crop," he mumbled.

"Poor crop," echoed Burroughs.

"Why will it be a poor crop?" asked Dreeme.

Walden Slater opened his mouth and eyes very wide at that. After a moment he answered weakly:

"Because it will be a poor crop."

Several minutes of silence ensued.

"The Lord will provide," remarked Burroughs finally. Walden Slater did not brighten perceptibly at these glad tidings. He had put his trust in the Lord before, and he knew exactly how much it was rewarded when there was too much sun and not enough rain. He corrugated his brow in the unusual travail of thought.

"I guess . . ." he commenced.

"If rain . . ." started Burroughs.

"How much . . ." questioned Dreeme.

All three men had started at once, and at the surprising medley of voices they ceased abruptly. Each one waited for the other to speak. No one dared to begin. Mrs. Slater and Deborah had removed all the dishes. The red and white table-cloth was folded up and put away. The hot afternoon sun splashed through the windows and flooded the dining room floor. Burroughs cautiously withdrew his chair from the golden pool. Walden Slater spoke with unusual rapidity for him.

"About Deb," he said, "I guess if she wants to stay, she can. I told Jeff Westcott that. I said . . ."

He stopped as abruptly as he commenced.

Dreeme wanted to jump up and fling his arms about the weary farmer. This was what had been on Walden Slater's mind. This was what he had desired to communicate to Dreeme. Having delivered himself of his pronunciamento he rose painfully to his feet and turned toward the door. The Reverend George Burroughs picked his teeth meditatively with a wooden toothpick he had drawn from his black vest pocket. Then he blew his nose with a rare fish-horn effect.

Dreeme fumbled for his pipe contentedly. Well, Walden Slater was a friend. He was an ally. He was stretching a grotesque gnarled hand across the imbroglio of nights and days to Dreeme. The young doctor watched the farmer's bowed shoulders disappear through the door. He was going back to his meager sun-parched acres where he would labor all the harder that he might feed one more mouth. Dreeme lighted his pipe, pushed his chair back, and walked slowly across the room. Before he reached the warm flood of sunlight he was halted.

"Doctor Dreeme."

The Reverend George Burroughs stood beside the table with a half-raised yellow claw. His stringy black hair stood out above his frayed coat collar.

"If you enjoy the pleasing scent of the evening air," he declared in his neighing voice, "perhaps we may stroll together some time. I am a silent companion, I fear, but equally a lover of nature. If you desire I shall be pleased to give you some information about the flora and fauna of this neighborhood."

"Thank you," responded Dreeme. "I generally stroll alone when I do stroll, which is not often. Sometime, however . . ." He waved an inconclusive hand.

Outside he wondered. "Now, what the devil does he mean?" He turned at the gate-way to meet a corpulent red-faced man who came running heavily down the road. The fellow was waving his arms in excitement. "Doctor," he called as he came nearer, "Doctor." Dreeme waited for the excited individual. When he came abreast of the doctor he stopped and puffed furiously while he mopped his ruddy face with a ruddier handkerchief. "Cardiac trouble," thought Dreeme. Aloud he said:

"You shouldn't run in the sun."

The individual flourished his active hand.

"They've found a body by the Saccarac River, almost under the bridge," he bellowed. "I'm Barnson. I don't know nothing about it. My farm's just above the bridge. My son, Simon, found the body. You remember, you treated him for blood-poisoning in the foot last Fall."

Dreeme was uncertain as to whether he had treated the body or Simon for blood-poisoning in the foot, but he turned with Barnson and started to walk hurriedly with him up the Leeminster Road.

"Whose body?" he asked.

"Didn't wait . . . to find out," puffed Barnson. "My boy, Simon, found it. You remember . . . the boy you treated."

He sat down heavily by the roadside.

"Dang it, I'm winded," he declared. "You run ahead."

"The body won't run away," said Dreeme.

Nevertheless he mounted the incline at a trot, his exertions and the sun covering his face with a freely running river of perspiration. The dry red sand puffed about his feet and sifted into his shoes. As he turned the arc of the road by the burned mill he saw a knot of men standing by the river below the bridge. They were leaning forward, their shoulders almost touching. He scrambled down the bank, the wiry weeds catching at his clothes and thrusting up his coat-sleeves as he half-slid and half-stumbled toward the low baked bank of the river. The men drew apart at the sound of his scrambling feet, and a freckled-faced youth with a bobbing Adam's apple, whom he recognized as Simon Barnson, turned to him as he approached the group.

"It's Wagner, Westcott's man," he called in a shrill voice.

Dreeme waved the men aside and approached the limp bundle of clothes that huddled before him. Wagner lay on his side, his heavy-booted feet sunk in the muddy ooze of the Saccarac River. One arm was twisted across his face. The two or three farmers who stood in a knot conversing in low tones, observed Dreeme curiously as he went methodically about his task of investigating the condition of the corpse. It was only by a violent effort that the young doctor moved Wagner's bulky upflung arm sufficiently to study the dead man's face. He started back with an exclamation of horror at the sight. Wagner's eyes had been torn out and a wooden peg had been driven into each socket. Streamers of blood had flowed from these wounds and coagulated along the tanned cheeks and in the red and bushy beard. The purple lips were drawn back over the yellow teeth in a last ghastly smile of anguish. In the back of the hired man's head, a trifle above the lined red neck, was an open wound, a gaping orifice of blood and splintered bone, that might have been made with some fairly sharp instrument, an axe or a heavy chisel.

"He's dead all right," said Dreeme, rising to his feet. "How long since he was found?"

The farmers stood in stolid silence until Simon Barnson constituted himself spokesman.

"I found him 'bout half an hour ago," he said. "Then I run home and told Pa. Then I run to Bidwell's." He indicated a tall farmer standing near. Bidwell backed hastily away.

"Don't you be talking too much, Simon," called a voice from the top of the bank. "You'll be talking yourself into jail first thing you know."

Dreeme glanced up and saw the elder Barnson sitting on the ground and mopping his fiery face. His lips curled, and he turned back to the silent farmers. He said:

"It's murder, you know. I should say the man's been dead about three hours. We'll have to find out who's been across this bridge during the last three hours."

The farmers shuffled together.

"I reckon there's authorities'll find that out," said one of them coldly. The others nodded in agreement.

Dreeme felt helpless and out of place. He addressed himself to Simon Barnson.

"Has the coroner been sent for?"

Bidwell, the tall farmer, spoke up at that. He said:

"Yessir. I sent my man with the mare out to Leeminster right away as soon's Simon told me. He'll pick up Westcott on the way back."

"Oh, will he?" said Dreeme. He stood beside the body gazing down at it. Wagner stared up at him with a fixed grin upon his ensanguined face. He lay like an old sack half-filled with boneless flesh. He was worm's meat now. All his toiling in the hot sun and the fierce rains had come to this. His heavy feet had crunched through the last field. His hands, so calloused and split with labor, would guide farm implements no more. Dreeme looked down at the clenched hand that he had forced from the disfigured face and he saw clutched in the black, broken-nailed, stumpy fingers a bit of paper. It was curious that he had missed it before. He knelt down and tried to force the stiff fingers open. The farmers watched him from a little distance curiously, their necks craned, their eyes narrowed to slits in the sunlight. It took all his strength to open these dead fingers but with one last desperate effort he heard them break with a crackling sound and the slip of paper fluttered to the oozy bank. He snatched it up before it drifted into the river. Standing up he held the paper before him and looked at it. There was nothing upon it except the tiny drawing of a goat's head. Dreeme stared at it in perplexity.

"I reckon you'd better save that for the coroner, Mister Doctor," remarked Bidwell.

He heard them break with a crackling sound and the slip of paper fluttered to the oozy bank.

"I intend to," replied Dreeme shortly.

None of them trusted him. He was a stranger and they wanted their own kind around, men who talked and thought as they did, who understood without words the springs of hidden actions. Well, to hell with them! Let them all go to hell! He heard the creak of the coroner's buggy and the clop-clop of the horse on the bridge-boards above him and lifting his eyes he saw the thin-mouthed Leeminster official. One of their own kind at last! Beside him was Jeffrey Westcott, hatless, his cloven skull gleaming blue in the sunlight. The farmer turned his head downward and stared coolly at the body of his hired man. Then he transferred his attention to Dreeme. There was no expression in his face.

"Down here, coroner, down here," called Simon Barnson.

"Hold your horses, son!" replied that official. "I'll be right there."

He lumbered heavily from his buggy and slid down the bank in a sitting posture, adjusting his steel-rimmed spectacles as he came.

Chapter Six

I

Dreeme sat gloomily in front of Humphrey Lathrop and waited for the old doctor to deliver any advice that he might have to give.

"There you are," he had concluded, an exasperated perplexity lining his face. "I'm out! It's a closed community so far as I am concerned. A murder is committed, a murder as obvious as the nose on your face, and I can do nothing about it. I've tried. I've run about town in the boiling sun all afternoon. I've even been to Leeminster. What's the result? Nothing!"

Humphrey Lathrop pursed his great lips and looked wise. "He's the frog," thought Dreeme. He was thinking of the old story of the frog who puffed herself up until she burst. The little frog had seen a cow. He had described it to his mother. It was big, enormous. "Was it as large as this?" she had inquired, puffing herself up to formidable proportions. "Larger," the little frog had said. The big frog scowled (imagine a frog scowling!) and had puffed herself still bigger. Her abdomen had distended to an horrendous bulge. "As large as this?" she had asked proudly. "Larger," responded the little frog. The mother was beside herself. She had puffed valiantly again and her green skin had stretched and swelled wonderfully. She was a rotund circle of emerald. "As large as this?" she had shrieked. "Oh, larger," the little frog answered gloomily. He had probably become a bit bored by this time and had wanted to go off and sit on a lily pad and snap at flies. With a last desperate effort the great frog indrew a huge breath. There was a pop and then no frog. The little frog had looked up in the sky and then down at the ground but he had failed to discover his mother. She had burst into fragments, disappeared entirely. Humphrey Lathrop puffed himself up in this way. Some day he would burst and disappear. And then Dreeme felt quite ashamed of his malicious analogy. Humphrey Lathrop was a kind helpful old man. His importance was only the privilege of age. He was not consciously puffing himself to impossible proportions. He was merely trying to ease Dreeme's mind, to act the wise counsellor. The young doctor observed him and nearly smiled. Then his levity abruptly died away as his reason thrust him back among his grievances.

"There you are," he had said. "What's the result? Nothing!"

"It's always the result," said Humphrey Lathrop gloomily.

Dreeme reiterated himself.

"After I saw the body I questioned the coroner. I wanted to study the wooden pegs. I gave him the scrap of paper with the goat's head on it. I wanted to talk about time, about possible murderous weapons, about a dozen and one things. He put me off with silly generalities. I went to Bidwell, who seemed to have the confidence of those infernally silent farmers, and pleaded for an investigation without loss of time. He evaded me. I talked to the damned selectmen or whatever they are, Winship and Collender. There was nothing doing. Nothing but antagonism in sleepy little suspicious eyes. The constable was busy getting in some parched hay. He knew nothing about it and didn't want to know anything about it. He was a hopeless fool. Finally I went to Leeminster. The officials there referred me back to Marlborough. I tell you, Humphrey, it is impossible to start a serious investigation of this murder. By God, I'll write to Boston. I'll telegraph Washington."

He paused breathless. Lathrop broke into a low chuckle.

"You can't do anything," he said.

They sat in silence after that and Dreeme smoked moodily. The twilight drooped its dark wing over the valley. The white hawks that had hovered in the sky were gone now. Shadows crept up the tree-lined street and squirmed into the corners of the houses. There was a shadow over the Saccarac River. A shadow over the trampled bank where Wagner's body had crushed the reeds. It would be night soon. The sable mantle would drop and the lights would be extinguished.

"It's impossible," said Lathrop. The great chair creaked as he shifted his huge body. "Go away, Daniel. Don't worry yourself. Marlborough will look out for itself as it has always looked out for itself. You can do nothing about it."

The air seemed to sigh about them.

"An investigation is not too much to expect," said Dreeme doggedly.

Lathrop shook his mountainous shoulders. His three chins quivered with the gesture.

"Don't expect anything here," he said after a moment. The shadow of night was in his eyes.

II

Dreeme walked down the road to his house. The night was extraordinarily clear, the heavens being covered with a huge wheel of glittering stars. Lifting his head the young doctor could see the Great Dipper, the Little

Bear, the steadfast North Star. The Milky Way was a shoal of misty light pricked to diamond points by infinities of sparkling gems. Between the hosts of stars and the road were the crowded tops of the ancient trees interposing their thick foliage. The huge branches idly shaking their multitudes of leaves made moving patterns upon the road, crazy designs and impossible arabesques. Dreeme stepped through these checkered patterns unseeingly. Two shadows walked on either side of him. One was a shadow of ruddy gloom, the secret lustre of a beryl; the other, a shadow of dim light, the shy reflection of crystal. He walked between them and the moon moved like a lantern in the hand of some sky-traveler above him. The shadows crept closer to him and he instinctively spread his arms to keep them from him. There was no sound in the quiet evening and yet they were speaking to him. The ruddy shadow said:

"I do not say 'no' to anything."

Dreeme walked faster. The shadow of dim light said:

"I had a very good lawyer, Mr. Stopes."

"I do not hear you," said Dreeme. His pace increased until he was trudging along at a furious rate.

III

In his study Dreeme turned the pages of the book impatiently. Finally he closed it and placed it upon the table. He would think. He wondered if he ever stopped thinking, if, indeed, his cerebral efforts were ever more than an ineffectual attempt. The clock struck nine and he noted it automatically. Another day had fled by. A day of excitement and terror and perplexity. He sat desolately and watched the yellow flame of the lamp as it sputtered despondently. The chimney was soot-stained. Mrs. Slater should clean it. There was small reason to think when he could find no answers to his thoughts. Perhaps Humphrey Lathrop was right, after all. If he had troubled his mind about nothing his mind would not be troubling him so fiercely as it undoubtedly was now. Perhaps the time had come for him to pack his books, his trunk, and his bags, and take his way eastward out of the valley, leaving the dour natives to live their lives in their own way and to continue to clutch the mystery that permeated the community to their secretive bosoms. Why should he stay here where he was a barely-tolerated stranger and prescribe cures for unthankful patients who viewed even his ministrations with suspicion? It was no career for a young man. The rewards could be counted neither in money nor in friendships. He was a fool, an infernal fool.

And thinking these thoughts he reached a hand to pick up his book but paused, the hand poised in mid-air. She had asked him to come to the burned mill again that night. During the troublous surprises of the day he had forgotten all about it. It was inconceivable to imagine that she would appear after the unusual happenings of the day, happenings that had touched her so closely. Was she not sitting in her room, understanding, perhaps, why Wagner had been killed? Dreeme shuddered at the approach of the thought which he had kept so resolutely out of his mind. To go to the burned mill now would be a very fool's errand. He would find nothing there but blackened bricks and charred beams and the disturbed dust where he had sat in the broken embrasure with her and watched her obvious efforts to entangle him. He had even told her that he would not come, told her so brusquely and with no pity for her demands. What had she said to him? "I will tell you a great many things tomorrow night." What had she meant by that? What was she driving at, anyway? His hand dropped to his lap and he sat gazing vacantly at the yellow lamp-flame.

The first time he had seen her. She had fascinated him. He supposed that was the word for it. Anyway, he had felt her presence, had sensed the magnetic appeal of her power, the outrageous suggestion of her will. Nature had endowed her with certain unusual attributes and chief among them was this curious power of disturbing the rational equilibrium of the men about her. She was sly and skillful in her amoral way, determined to have what she wanted regardless of the consequences. There might be some things to be said on her side, particularly by the special pleader who, dominated by her undoubted beauty, perished in the spell of her personality. But Dreeme knew that she could not dominate him in this way although at the first she had disturbed him greatly. Even now he knew that he would be visibly excited in her presence. The man in him would tremble before the woman in her. She could not touch his brain, though, for that was an insuperable bulwark between them. It was his stout shield of defence and beat upon it as she might with the sharp sword of her loveliness she could not hack her way through. She was like the beautiful and heartless wife of the Afrit in the Arabian Nights, the one who possessed the vast number of rings, each one a souvenir of a time when she had betrayed her sleeping lord. Well, *he* would not be a victim. No ring of his should join that glittering and invisible chain that he suspected Martha Westcott wore about her white throat. He was safeguarded from her by a welling desire that rose in his heart, by a desire that he knew would keep him in Marlborough until the time came when he might go away not alone. A shadow of dim light, the shy reflection of crystal, stood near him now and his eyes brightened as his thoughts shifted.

He had helped *her* anyway. He had stood between her and the callous-ness of her reticent relations, between her and the despairing selfishness of her helpless aunt. She had wanted to bury her on a lonely farm, to engulf her in the very mystery that tormented all his faculties. He wondered if she was sleeping now in the house next door, lying with one thin pathetic white arm stretched across the bright patches of the crazyquilt and dream-ing, perhaps, of him. Dreeme smiled at the yellow lamp-flame. He was growing sentimental. Her confident helplessness, her blue-eyed surrender to circumstances, her ultimate faith in the goodness of humanity, her un-questioning dependence on him, all these things touched him acutely. He felt his eyes grow moist at the thought of her. She, at least, was real. He had said that to himself before and he would say it again and again for it gave him a strange strength. She counted and made the whole thing worth while. He could depend on her as she depended on him. He would con-stitute himself her champion, the fighter who would stand between her and . . . Dagon. The name sprang spontaneously into his mind. "Dagon," he said aloud, listening to the sound of the word in the little study. "Dagon." It meant something. It was a place.

His mind turned back. "I will tell you a great many things tomorrow night." Did she mean anything, after all, by that statement? Or was it merely a snare, a bait to inveigle him back to a rendezvous that he found in itself distasteful? Would she, for instance, tell him about Dagon, describe it to him, indicate where it was, explain what it meant? If pushed to a last extremity of desire she might. He flushed at the thought of so befooling her. Still . . . He was fighting with whatever weapons he could grasp. If only . . . The clock noisily announced nine-thirty. Of course, she would not be there. She would never dare to come after what had happened the night before. Go . . . stay . . . go . . . stay. The clock was ticking it now. Still un-decided he rose up and reached for his hat. It would do no harm to take a walk anyway, to stroll in the cool of the evening as the Reverend George Burroughs would say. Dagon . . . Dagon. He closed the door softly behind him and stood in the moonlight.

IV

The burned mill stood in the bright moonlight, its charred door yawning on the road. It looked like the sun-dried skull of a buffalo resting forlornly on the dry sand of a parched plain. Yet about it were the trees shot through with a milky light and beyond it was the silver blade of the

Saccarac River. Dreeme walked slowly through the door wondering if she would be waiting there for him. Inside he paused with a brief start of surprise and anger as his eyes located the figure in the broken embrasure. The moonlight flowed in crystal over a cloven head bowed forward in a listening attitude. This shaven cranium seemed phosphorescent in the rich glow.

"Good evening, doctor," said Jeffrey Westcott. There was the hint of a grim levity in his voice. He stood up, his powerful arms swinging ape-like at his sides, waiting for the young doctor to approach closer. Dreeme eyed him speculatively and without fear. Of course. He might have known if he had thought clearly enough about it.

"I'm afraid that this is an abrupt surprise for you," remarked the farmer. His tone was studiously polite, the tone of a man about to have business dealings with a stranger. The snarl that had permeated it the first night when Dreeme had removed the bullet from his plump calf was missing. The young doctor approached him slowly and sat down in the embrasure. Well, if he was in for a scene . . . Westcott turned, the moonlight rippling across his flat face. His eyes and teeth glittered in the flood of light.

"It is a surprise," said Dreeme calmly. "I expected to meet your wife here."

He might as well have it over with at once.

"She is detained," answered Westcott softly.

"You must not misunderstand me," proceeded Dreeme, a trifle stiffly. "Your wife and I . . ."

Westcott spread a broad hand deprecatingly.

"I know my wife," he said in a very low voice.

There was silence then while Dreeme shifted his eyes from the farmer to the scummed waters of the mill-pond. They were like an old opaque mirror in the moon. Did he know his wife, though? Did anybody know his wife? Astarte Syriaca. The wife of the Afrit. What was she?

"No, no, doctor," resumed Westcott as though he were reading Dreeme's thoughts. "My wife's little vagaries do not disturb me. She discommodes me at infrequent times but I have a remedy for it."

Dreeme glanced at Westcott's long powerful arms.

"I suppose you beat her," he remarked shortly.

The farmer flung back his head and laughed, a low rumbling laugh, a hollow burst of merriment that rattled among the blackened beams.

"Nothing so simple as that," he said, after he had recovered himself. "Nothing so simple as that. You're a trifle primitive, doctor."

There was a faint hint of hysteria behind the calmness of Westcott. Dreeme could sense it, a far-away excitement that was kept under control only by an effort of the mind. The farmer was laboring under an unrest that he desired to conceal. The young doctor sat coolly gazing into the scummed mirror of the mill-pond. There were no faces there, not even the reflection of the silver drum-head of the moon, nothing but a glow, a blank meaningless glow. The farmer sucked in a long breath suddenly.

"When are you going away, Doctor Dreeme?" he inquired. There was a finality in the question that made it as much an order as a query.

"I don't expect to go away," said Dreeme.

So that was it? He was to be forced out of town, was he?

"Do you find much that holds you here?" Westcott's tone was studiously innocent, devoid of any sly innuendo. Yet the implied order was there.

"I find much that interests me here," answered the young doctor. He wanted to add, "Even you," but thought better of it. Let the farmer show his teeth in his own way. Suddenly he felt Westcott's broad hand on his shoulder.

"Doctor Dreeme," the farmer said. "You had better go away from here. The farmers don't want you any more. They are suspicious and ill at ease with you. You are fashioned from a different kind of flesh than they are. Your mind works differently. There are doctors who can come from the outside, from that world of cities where everybody is more or less the same in social relationships, and settle here and be of some use but you are not one of them. Old Doctor Lathrop was like that. You are too . . . too speculative, too eager to find out things, too unwilling to permit the valley to go its own way and employ its own methods. The itch of curiosity is too strong inside you. These men who scrape at the soil do not want active intelligences about them. They distrust strangers. Go away. Forget that you were ever here and forget the people who are here. The world has forgotten them and they desire no less than to stay forgotten. This is good advice that I am giving you for I know what I am talking about. I may not mingle much with these people but I know their minds. After all, I am one of them. I tell you to go away . . . before you are sent away in a manner humiliating to you."

The heavy hand dropped from Dreeme's shoulders. The dark eyes studied him curiously.

"Thanks for the advice," said the young doctor. "I'll stay."

"Why are you so obtuse?" asked Westcott sadly. Behind the intonations fluttered the tiny scarlet bird of hysteria.

Dreeme became a trifle angry.

"I'm not obtuse," he snapped. "That's why you want me to go away. You're afraid of what I'll find out. Of what I'll discover about your wax dolls and your goats' heads and your hypnotic charlatanry and your murdered hired man and . . . and your place called Dagon!"

Westcott's face became distorted in the moonlight. The scarlet bird flew upward with a feverish beating of wings.

"You fool! You fool!" he cried, in a strained raucous voice. "That's it! You must be made to leave this valley even if you are carried out of it!"

Dreeme laughed shortly.

The blazing eyes of Westcott moved closer to his face.

"Do you think we care one tinker's damn about you?" he shouted. "Do you flatter yourself that we are afraid of you? You simple idiot! We are doing our best to get rid of you without hurting you! You mean nothing to us. You are stumbling about in the darkness and don't know where you are. You are pitting your puny mind and strength against a power that is as old as the Egyptians, a power that established itself in this valley nearly two hundred and fifty years ago. We who have listened to the voice of the Master need fear nothing but deliverance from the Master."

"Have I gotten on your nerves as badly as that?" cried Dreeme maliciously.

Westcott's voice had changed and a crazy ecstasy was in it. The scarlet bird filled the burned mill with a hysteric swishing of wings.

"He walks on the hills at night. He whistles to the Sacred Goat and snaps his fingers at the moon and stars. In the dark palms of his hands is all the power of the earth. He stands at the place called Dagon and his feet are rooted like mountains."

Dreeme rose to his feet. Westcott was swaying like a drunken man and a thin white froth bubbled on his lips.

"Aie-e-e-e, Asmodeus!" he screamed. "Sweep this man out of my father's holy place!"

Dreeme thought he was about to fall upon the ground and he stretched out a hand toward him. Westcott shuddered all through his heavy body. Then, as suddenly as it had come, his delirium passed away. The madness died out of his eyes and voice and he sank down in the embrasure. The scarlet bird had flown away on the wind.

Westcott lifted his hand to his eyes and sat for a moment in silence. Then he turned to Dreeme.

"I am taken with seizures," he said rapidly. "I am an extremely nervous man. You must not take my outbreak too seriously. You are a doctor. You know."

Dreeme sat down opposite him in the embrasure. The far away light in the depths of his mind was glowing so brightly that it dazzled his reason. Shapes passed before it and they were familiar but he could not quite identify them. He glanced sharply at Westcott. The farmer, quite himself, was smiling slyly, secretively.

"Nervous delirium," he said confidentially, tapping his cloven head. "I lose control of myself."

Dreeme eyed him searchingly.

"I am not so sure," he said. "Are you all right now?"

Westcott nodded. The young doctor noted that the farmer's hands were quivering, however.

"As you admit I am a doctor," he said, "perhaps you will give me a doctor's privilege of questioning you. Do you ever take drugs?"

"I do not take drugs," replied Westcott, "and I do not give you a doctor's privilege of questioning me. When I need a doctor I send for one. I do not need one now."

The bright moon placed a silver sword between them. Westcott rose to his feet.

"I have given you my advice," he said. "You will do as you please about it."

He turned toward the door.

"Wait," cried Dreeme. Westcott turned on his heel and regarded him smilingly.

"Will you answer three questions?" the young doctor asked. Westcott said:

"Ask them and I will answer or not as I see fit."

"Why did you hypnotize Deborah?"

"I didn't hypnotize Deborah."

"Who killed Wagner?"

"I don't know who killed Wagner."

"Where is the place called Dagon?"

"I never heard of the place called Dagon."

"Three lies in as many seconds," said Dreeme bitterly.

"Only two of them were lies," remarked Westcott. He actually chuckled. His hands had stopped trembling and he stood easily, nonchalantly, watching Dreeme sardonically with his large dark eyes.

"No, doctor," he said. "You are beating at a stone wall. When I first saw you I detested you. Later I revised my reaction to you. In fact, I feel a sympathetic pity for you. You are so . . . so obtuse. Sooner or later you will cut your own throat."

"You say you belong here," broke out Dreeme, ignoring the farmer's remarks. "I don't believe it. You don't talk like a farmer. You have nothing in common with Slater or Bidwell or Barnson. You live alone out in that secluded house. Are you so ashamed of yourself that you exist so secretly?

What are you up to in that room lined with books? Are you fashioning yourself into the image of an old god?"

The last question had popped into his head suddenly. He was quite fearless, indeed, he experienced the peculiar sensation that there was a conversational *rapport* between him and the farmer if he could only find the key to it. There was no doubt in his mind now that Westcott was mad, that he was ridden by some monstrous theory, that he pursued some irrational objective. He suspected that if he could discover the proper opening Westcott would pour out as much of it as he dared. He began to believe that the farmer was a theoretical fool masked as a lion. His last question had arrested Westcott who had already turned to go.

"What's that?" asked the farmer. "What's that?"

He turned slowly. He said:

"What do you know about old gods?"

"Perhaps I know more than you think," insinuated Dreeme craftily.

Westcott eyed him suspiciously and with some concern.

"I wonder . . ." he mused to himself and then broke off. He surveyed Dreeme coolly.

"You picked that question up somewhere?" he said. "You never thought of it yourself."

A light dawned on him and he smiled.

"Ah, dear Martha," he murmured. "Dear talkative Martha."

He came back and sat down in the embrasure. The moonlight flung great silver arms about him.

"You bring to life an inborn loquaciousness," he said. "I had forgotten the need of conversation. Doctor Dreeme, I am not an ignorant man. I have studied in three countries and I bear a degree from one of the most famous German universities. I have traveled in Arabia and in Persia and in India. I have lived among the secret priests of unknown religions. Behind all their conflicting dogmas I discovered one objective. Years ago the peculiar circumstances of my birth pushed me into a specific line of investigation. The seeds of that particular knowledge for which I sought were buried in this valley and I settled here with the determination to foster them and cause them to grow. You say that I have nothing in common with the farmers of Marlborough but that only reveals your ignorance. I have this in common with them,—they, too, know of the seed. They, too, keep the ground fertile that it may grow in its appointed time. Their lives and the lives of their forefathers are but a preparation for the time when that seed will sprout. I am the self-constituted gardener. I am the man who directs."

He paused and gazed across the moonlit room. His eyes were filmed, trance-like, and he seemed to be looking inward at the secret growths of his mind.

"To fashion myself in the image of an old god," he murmured. "That is a crass way of putting it. There are no old gods. There are only new gods, gods builded out of our invincible wills and forced by the strength of intelligence into the domains of high powers. The greatest of all gods is man's will. If a man possesses enough knowledge he can do anything, shape the destinies of those about him, influence the comings and goings upon the surface of the earth, cause wars and the breakup of nations, and even, when the seed is sprouted and the tree has flowered, defeat the purpose of death."

Westcott seemed entirely unconscious of Dreeme. He was talking to himself now.

"'And the will therein lieth which dieth not,'" he quoted. "The instincts of man are constantly drawn toward what, for want of a better word, we call evil, as a filing of iron is drawn toward a magnet. Evil is therefore the fountainhead of life. All the gods, Buddha, Allah, Christ, are the enemies of the will for they pretend to dominate it. The only god is that demon of the mind who places himself in bold antagonism to the high tyrants of the heavens. Satan is the only god and he is the god that we daily create out of our will. All that we are springs out of evil. We have misunderstood evil so long, masked it in outrageous masks and clothed it in obscene garments, that we forget that it is a pure essence, that it is evil—as we understand evil—only when we compare it with our artificially created good. The animals know no evil because they know no good. They know nothing but a great impulse pulling them one way always,—the way of self-emancipation. It should be so with us. There is neither evil nor good but a sole purpose and that purpose is the domination of the will over matter, the power of regulating time by the exertion of the will. Within us the sixth sense lies dormant. We taste, touch, smell, hear and see but these are animal functions. The sixth sense is to will. When that is discovered we shall be the lords of creation. How can we develop and strengthen this weak will that staggers like an infant child in the dark corridors of our brains? The old magicians did not know. I have read all their books and my house is filled with them. Can the will be sharpened by symbols, by monstrous symbols that tear our time accustomed minds from the old impulses and subserviencies? May we by building an artificial structure of liturgies and ceremonies and sacrifices, by constant allegories that call the imaginative faculties of the will into exertion, discipline and exercise that weakness that is our shame today? In other words, may we by a complete reversal of all those religious mummeries that subjected our will and made it puny before the imaginary gods, destroy the prison walls we have builded about ourselves? We made the gods by worshiping them, by fearing them. Can we unmake them by reviling them, by walking boldly before those pillars of hollow smoke? There was once a group of people who believed that the will might become paramount if they followed the dictates of their mystic senses regardless of so-called good. They called the will by a symbolic name and they met in secret forest clearings. They made a pledge with evil and they barely understood why they did it. They . . ."

Westcott stopped suddenly and looked at Dreeme. The trance-like light died out of his dark eyes.

"I will not tell you any more," he said. "Why should I talk to you of these things. You do not understand."

"There are some things I understand," answered Dreeme. "You associate Satan with the free will. You imagine you can strengthen your own will to superhuman dimensions by denying the impulses of good. You . . ."

"I deny no impulses," said Westcott roughly. "I follow the solitary impulse."

He rose to his feet.

"Good-night, doctor," he said, "Take my advice and go away."

"Go away!" cried Dreeme. "Why should I go away??"

"Because," replied Westcott, "even a fool may learn wisdom."

He strode heavily to the door, his injured leg swaying his body from side to side as he walked. He did not even turn back as he passed out into the full moonlight. A moment later Dreeme heard his uneven stride as he passed over the little bridge. Dreeme sat alone in the burned mill and looked at the scummed water of the quiet pond. One thing was certain. Westcott was a mad man. He was a megalomaniac eaten up by a ridiculous theory that gave him an excuse for any excesses he desired. Anything might fit into his theory of strengthening the will. Even murder. Constant brooding upon his purpose had awakened an hysteric ecstasy in him and there were times when this ecstasy broke into an uncontrollable display. Dreeme tried to remember what he had read about these lunacies in the past. Somewhere, he was sure, he had learned that an abnormal intellectual power went hand in hand with an infant-like abandonment to symbols. For instance, one of these fanatics might display the most brilliant intellectuality in building up an elaborate and mystically logical structure and this structure might be built upon the most absurd and impossible foundation. Or, again, the mad man might reveal the most refined cunning to a certain point and then observe a cloud in the sky, a leaf on the ground, the note of a bird in the darkness and be swung abruptly from his purpose. Such men were dangerous. Any slight incident might provoke their madness.

Dreeme had an instantaneous picture of Westcott sitting alone among his books and searching through the yellowed leaves for the secret of the mastery of the will, building up impossible theories out of insane hints, drawing into the crazy net of his mind all the obsolete mysticisms of the dark ages, of the Egyptians, of the Indian fakirs, of the Satanists. He was partly sane and partly mad. One half of his brain functioned with surprising agility; the other was a dark morass of supernatural superstitions and primitive impulses. It was plain that he was employing the community for his dark purposes and it was equally plain that the community, because of some secret injection of blood, favored these impulses. These farmers were ridden by an ancient fear which Jeffrey Westcott kept alive. They did not see him often but they knew that he was there and while he was there, sitting in his lonely house and avoided by those about him, he would continue to dominate the valley. He employed some legend for his own ends and the farmers were in some way the inheritors of that legend.

Dreeme rose to his feet and proceeded out of the burned mill and down the road toward Marlborough. He had never seen the moon so white, so lustrous. It was as though the valley were bathed in a crystal liquid, as though the air were full of sparkling essences that flowed through the tree-tops and along the fronts of the farm-houses. He drew in long draughts of the clear cool air as he went his way, a little surprised at it for the day had been so hot and the sun had been so like a fountain of pale fire spraying the dry streets. As he walked along he wondered why he had ever feared Westcott. It was easy enough to handle a man like that. One had but to keep an eye on him. That was all. And yet . . . Dreeme was not so sure. Westcott's actions were unpredictable. The actions of any lunatic were unpredictable. He might be smiling and suave one minute and a ferocious beast the next. What had he desired with Deborah, for instance? In what way could she serve to strengthen that will that was apparently his only god? It was too much to believe that he desired her only as an aid to his wife in the farm-house. In some way Deborah entered into his crazy scheme. Well, he would keep his eyes open and his wits sharpened. He would stand between Westcott and Deborah to the end of time. The end of time. That was a long period but it was not long enough for him to watch over Deborah.

His mind reverted to the interview with Westcott. It was funny. Why had the farmer shown so little rage at the idea of Martha Westcott's meeting with him? Was Martha playing her game with the connivance of her husband? Dreeme was inclined to think that this was not so, that Westcott, sure of his power over his wife, let her run to the end of the rope which he held and then pulled her back when he thought she had gone far enough. Perhaps he practiced his will upon her, forcing her to do the things which he did not want her to do only for the pleasure of stopping her when he felt like it. Dreeme turned in at his gate still brooding and was about to open his door when he heard the creak-creak of Walden Slater's rocker. He would go around the house and see if he could engage the taciturn farmer in conversation.

Walden Slater sat slumped in his chair, a corncob pipe stuck at a crazy angle in his wide mouth. He was looking at the moon.

"It's bright tonight," remarked Dreeme, sinking down on the stair to the little back piazza.

Walden Slater grunted, removed his pipe, and rubbed his long upper-lip with a huge hand.

"Aren't you up late?" asked Dreeme.

"Uh-huh," said the farmer.

"It must be about eleven o'clock," continued Dreeme.

"Ten-thirty," said the farmer. "I just heard the kitchen clock."

"What's wrong?" questioned the young doctor.

Walden Slater rocked slowly. Creak-creak. Creak-creak.

"I dunno's there's anything wrong," he said mildly.

"Have they done anything about Wagner?" asked Dreeme.

Walden Slater squirmed about in his chair and put his pipe down on the floor.

"Took him to Leeminster," he said ungraciously.

Dreeme laughed aloud. He said:

"You old curmudgeon!"

Walden Slater grinned with some difficulty and then remarked:

"I'm thinking."

Dreeme rose to his feet, still smiling.

"This is a nice social neighborhood," he said to the moon.

Walden Slater thrust his pipe back in his mouth and resumed his inspection of the great white globe that floated in the heavens above him. Dreeme turned the corner of the house slowly.

He didn't feel sleepy. The night was too fine, too exhilarating. It was like a heady wine, some mystic vintage that ran through his body and sharpened every impulse, every wit. It was on a night like this that the imagination might spring hawk-like into the air and bring down fair and impossible prey. Dreeme wondered how far the mind might travel through the starry immensities above him, through the glittering star-fields un-plowed by Time, before it reached . . . something. Humphrey Lathrop did not believe in the supernatural. He clung to the theory of the supernormal, of mysteries that might be explained as the intelligence of man lifted itself higher and higher and even of mysteries that might never be explained but which were yet felt in the intuitive senses as supernormal and not super-natural. Poor old Humphrey! The dear old frog swelling larger and larger! He sat in his cottage retired from Time and Lucinda squabbled about his frequent potations of apple-jack. He was happy, though. As happy as any-body could be who had long ago put ambition behind him and had not very much before him to expect.

Dreeme paused before his own door and half-put out a hand to turn the knob. The door was ajar. That was funny. He was sure he had closed it carefully when he started out for the burned mill. He stood looking at the door vacantly, his mind wheeling about elsewhere, wheeling through the enormous starry arc that revolved in the sky above him, wheeling through the cool and quiet expanse of the sleeping valley. Why should he go in and sleep when there was no sleep in his eyes? He was not tired. He would continue to walk until he was wearier than he was now. He turned from the door and retraced his steps along the path to the road. As he turned into the sandy stretch he heard the creak-creak of Walden Slater's rocker. The farmer was thinking, doggedly following some faint light that glim-mered before him. Poor Walden! Dreeme smiled to himself as he stood in the sandy road and listened to the faint protest of the rocking chair. He was beginning to pity everybody. Was this a testimony of his own exhilara-tion, a sign of his unsought superiority? He began to whistle softly some old tune that crept back into his consciousness. He didn't know what it was but it seemed to fit the night.

The sound of the Slater front door softly opening caused him to turn his head. Who would dare to walk through that blank closed parlor stiff with its horse-hair stuffed chairs and its lumpy sofa and its colored por-traits of dead and vanished Slaters? He stood by the fence, his face turned toward the door and waited. A slender form came down the steps and along the path toward him. She walked slowly, almost with diffidence, and she did not speak until she was standing close beside him. He noticed that her dress was white, her party dress undoubtedly. The moon poured its silver light over her and she stood like a white ghost in a white world, her blue eyes sparkling and her small mouth curled in a faint smile. Reaching out his hand he drew her toward him.

"I've been waiting by the window all evening," she said.

Chapter Seven

I

Not that way," said Dreeme hastily as Deborah instinctively turned up the Leeminster Road toward the Saccarac River.

Everybody seemed to head in that direction as though there were a magnet at the end of the road attracting them irresistibly. He would change the scheme of things by facing another way, by facing an opposite direction than that in which lay the Westcott farm, the burned mill, the trampled bank of the river, and the creaking bridge that had groaned with the weight of the coroner's buggy. She wheeled on her small feet and followed him obediently and they passed the dark front of his little house and the tarnished brass plate upon which was inscribed "Dr. Daniel Dreeme." A moment later they were walking side by side through the main street of Marlborough, a main street that speedily opened into a tiny square faced by the small church, the post office and general store, and Mrs. Larkin's boarding house where nobody ever boarded. The blank fronts of the scattered buildings gloomed at them incuriously. Though this was the heart of the community Dreeme could not hear a single beat. The heart had stopped pulsing for the night and even in the daylight it functioned but sluggishly. No lights glimmered from the windows of the houses for all the inhabitants had long ago crept into their beds and stretched out beneath their home-made quilts to wait uneagerly for another early rising. Yet the moon flooded the square and made it as bright as day and in that crystal bath they walked slowly, feeling the cold light run along their faces and ripple over their arms.

"Did you expect to see me tonight?" asked Deborah. Her voice was a thin silver wire plucked by a soft finger.

"No," said Dreeme. "But I wanted to see you. I didn't know it, though, until you came down the path like a little ghost."

"I'm not a ghost," she said. "I wanted to see you all evening. I sat by the window and waited."

"Why?" he asked.

She was silent at that and only shook her head.

"Have you anything to tell me?" he inquired.

She shook her head again.

Moved by a sudden impulse he put his finger under her chin and raised her face. Her violet-blue eyes gazed at him calmly but something in them, some far-away message, set his pulses pounding furiously. He dropped his hand and looked away. Unconsciously they hastened their pace, passing through the square and the narrow side street that led toward the lower end of the town. The houses thinned out, falling away like specters from them, and an instant later they were trudging along a country road.

"If you follow this road far enough," he said with an effort at lightness, "you'll reach the real world."

"I shall travel on it soon," she answered. There was a break in her voice.

"What is the real world like?" she asked after a moment.

"It is full of people," he said. "It is full of cities. It is like a noisy jungle. It is easy to hide there."

She did not answer him. For a long time they walked in silence, their shoulders touching lightly as their bodies swayed over the uneven road. His hand rubbed against hers as they moved along the sandy stretch and for no reason whatsoever he resisted the temptation to take her small fingers in his own. There didn't seem to be anything worth saying although he was conscious that she was waiting confidently for something to be said. He knew what it was and she knew, also, that both of them were saying it without words, without the use of futile speech. Their brushing shoulders said it to one another and their touching hands made it unmistakably plain.

"We'd better turn back," he remarked finally. They were far along the road now and no houses loomed their dark bulks against the white sea of the flowing moon.

They turned and retraced their steps, walking swiftly through the loose sand and pebbles of the road. She continued to look straight ahead and occasionally he would glance sideways at the cool oval of her face. It seemed but an instant before they were back among the squatting houses, closed in by the silent walls and shut away from the full light of the moon. In the shadow of the frame-building that served for post office and general store she stopped and turned to him and said:

"I put my best dress on."

A moment later he realized that both his arms were about her and that he was saying:

"I love you! I love you! I love you!"

He kept repeating it and she did not interrupt him but leaned against him listening contentedly. When he stopped she looked up at him and said:

"Shall I tell you that I love you?" He said:

"I'm babbling like a fool. I've been wanting to tell you this all day and I didn't know it till just now."

"I led you on," she said soberly. Then she laughed with a quick feverish gaiety.

"I didn't need to be led on," he declared. "It was the getting started that was difficult. I'm a slow idiot. I wasn't sure. I'm not sure even now."

"That you love me?" she gasped.

"That *you* love *me,*" he returned.

"Oh, *that!*" she said.

She put both her slim arms around his neck and embraced him tightly. For an instant he seemed to be wearing a necklace of fire.

"It was because I loved you that I ran to you this morning," she announced. "I wanted you to protect me."

"Good Lord! Was it only this morning?" he exclaimed.

"It was only yesterday that we met," she said. There was wonder in her voice, too.

He bent down to her and kissed her for the first time. Her lips were like damp rose-petals and they clung to his greedily.

"If it was only yesterday," he said, "how long our Paradise will be."

She disengaged herself from him and they walked slowly up the street toward the Slater house, hand in hand.

"Some day," he said gravely, "I'm going to ask you what your last name is."

A small ripple of laughter broke from her.

"It's Morton," she announced. "My name is Deborah Morton."

"My first name is Daniel," he declared. "At present I am in the lion's den. I haven't been bitten, though."

"Daniel and Deborah," she repeated softly to herself.

At the gate to the Slater house they paused and he looked down at her, noting her fresh white dress and the fragility of her small figure.

"You are nothing but a child," he said. "What is this?"

He touched the square brooch on her breast. She unpinned it and handed it to him.

"Do you want it?" she asked. "I've had it always. It was given to me by my mother. My father gave it to her and his father gave it to him. It has been in the Morton family for years, for ages."

He held it up to the moonlight and inspected it and as he saw what it was an exclamation of amazement broke from him.

"What is it?" she asked. "Have you seen it before?"

"No," he said, handing it back to her. "Keep it. It must be some sort of an heirloom."

She pinned it back on her breast and lifted up her face that he might kiss her. "Good-night," he murmured, and an instant later her ghost-like form hurried up the path to the front door. Dreeme turned toward his own house, wondering why Deborah should have a brooch upon which was the finely cut cameo of a goat's head, the exact replica of the drawing he had wrenched from the dead hand of Wagner.

II

Dreeme heard the solemn-toned clock in the Slater house striking as he pushed his own unlatched door open and stepped into the narrow hall. One hollow sound. A single and ineffectual blow at the star-lit night. It must be eleven-thirty, he thought, for Walden Slater had mumbled something about ten-thirty when he had paused at the back piazza an hour before. Time for all good men to go to bed. Time for all good men to come to the aid of their party. After he pulled the door shut behind him and shot the bolt and turned around he realized that the lamp was glowing in his little study. For an instant he stood in stupid perplexity, wondering how he could have been so excited as to leave the light aflare and the door ajar when he had hastened forth two hours ago to the burned mill. Was he actually as absent-minded as that? "I didn't leave them so," he said to himself, shaping the words silently with his lips, and then walked slowly along the hall to the study. Through the angle of the partially opened door he could see a patch of black dress against which a long white hand hung languidly, the fingers idly curled. He stopped and observed it, not with surprise—indeed, subconsciously he had expected it—but with a vague distaste that wrinkled his forehead and tightened his lips. She was sitting in a listening attitude waiting for him to turn the corner of the door. He was tempted to turn and walk out hastily, letting her have the house to herself until the loneliness and weariness of waiting forced her to return to her own home. He was tired and didn't want to talk. He had ridden a wave of excitement all day, a towering tidal wave that had swept him high and far, and now he was exhausted, let down, filled with the glow of a faint triumph, to be sure, but pleasantly hollow inside. He was like a swimmer who had outreached his strength but achieved some goal in the endeavor. He desired nothing more than to climb into his bed, stretched out beneath the great square patches of the coverlet, and sleep dreamlessly, to renew his benumbed faculties for the day that was to follow. What on earth could she have to say to him now? Had his attitude not settled everything last night when he had left her at the mill without turning back? She had called him a miserable coward. Well, let her think so. Perhaps that was the safest way for him. All he desired now was to get out of the valley with Deborah. Let them continue as they willed with their own theories. They were all mad and perhaps it would be a good thing if they killed each other off in the process of their lunacies. His curiosity about them was sleepy now. The unrest that had pervaded him at the thought of the mystery hovering over Marlborough was slothful. It was more important to go out into that real world with Deborah and begin to live. Here, he was in a valley of shadows. He stood, therefore, in the shelter of the door peering through at the lighted room in sleepy impatience and lethargic anger. She sat there listening. She knew he was lurking just out of her sight. He could see her hand crumple up in irritation.

"Will you come in?" she said in, a low husky impatient voice.

He crossed the lintel reluctantly and stood facing her. Her eyes glistened in the saffron glow of the lamp as she observed him coldly. It was only by the heightened rise and fall of her full breasts outlined beneath the dark fabric of her dress that he could see how enraged she was. Vaguely he wondered how long she had been sitting there and waiting for him.

"Since ten o'clock," she said as though in answer to his thought. "I heard you walk about the house an hour ago. I heard you stroll away with that . . . that servant girl. I heard you come back with that . . . that servant girl."

He decided that Deborah did not need any defence so he complacently ignored her contemptuous speech.

"Are you as lacking in ambition as you are in courage?" she inquired maliciously in her peculiar husky voice.

Dreeme nodded. He didn't care what she thought as long as she left speedily. She could not rouse him to anger by anything she said. With an excitable gesture she stood up and paced swiftly about the room, her long shadow flickering across the atrociously-papered wall. Dreeme watched her objectively. She was magnificent. There was no doubt of that. Like a tigress. A great slumberous tigress in whose arteries ran a secret and smoldering flame. Full breasted, long in the thighs, wide cheek-bones and great eyes, hair like a blue-black smoke curling over her white forehead, archaic mouth. He had pictured her in so many ways. Medusa. Astarte Syriaca.

Wife of the Afrit. Tigress. A creature of the imagination compounded out of dark and passionate urges. Yet his veins ran slow snow at the thought of her. She could not touch his emotions again as she had that first time in the lamp-lit library when he had felt her presence like a dim magic in the room. He could look at her coldly and say, "Please go. I do not want you here. I do not trust you. You belong in this unreal world and I am not a part of it. There is the shadow of blood on your mouth." He even opened. his mouth to say these things and then thought better of it and closed his lips tightly. She stopped in front of him, her face a few inches from his, and studied him fiercely. The bitter-sweet aroma of her hair rose about his nostrils. He thought fixedly of the frail ghost-like figure of Deborah and observed her coolly.

"You have a new mask," she said shortly. "Where is my weak doctor now?"

"He never existed except in your imagination," he replied.

In spite of her anger she smiled.

"Do you think so?" she said.

She continued to study his face. Her large understanding eyes were disconcerting and he looked away from her finally.

"Did you go to the mill?" she inquired.

"Don't you know?" he returned.

"So did I," she added. "But he was there waiting. I know he was waiting for you. I told you that Burroughs saw us. I came here, then, and waited."

Dreeme moved over to the table and she followed him, seating herself by the side of it.

"Did he tell you to come here?" he asked. "How could you have passed me on the road?"

"He did not see me. He does not know I am here," she said. There was a flash of anger in her eyes. After a second she added:

"I cut through . . . in back of the Slater house. There is a path there. You must know it."

He nodded absently. He didn't care, after all.

"What do you want, anyway?" he demanded. "I'm tired. I want to sleep."

She looked at him appraisingly.

"I want you to take me away from here," she answered coolly.

He smiled at that and shook his head.

"Wait!" she said, lifting her hand. "I will be faithful to you. I will give you more than any woman has given any man. I will give you strength . . .

which you lack, and intelligence . . . which you lack, and confidence . . .
which you lack, and . . . Do you want love? I have an eternity of it stored
up inside me."

She spread her arms and her ripe bosom rose with the gesture.

"I don't want any of these things," he said in a low voice.

"That little girl has befuddled you," she said in an angry voice. "You are
like a somnambulist, a man walking in his sleep and afraid to wake up. You
are dreaming like a schoolboy of a little empty face. I tell you I will take you
up on the mountain-tops of the world and show you all the riches of Time.
You can pick what you will and with me beside you it shall be yours. I will
pour strength into you and make you one of the proudest of men."

The lamp sputtered fitfully between them and Dreeme sat looking at
her sleepily. She was like a Sibyl now, muttering some incantation. All that
she did was in the vein of play-acting. Even her rolling sentences seemed
out of some old drama. Then, Dreeme thought of Westcott's brief delirium
and wondered how many of them Martha Westcott had heard to talk in this
vein. Both of them were acting in life. Both of them were archaic masks.

"I don't want the riches of Time," he said wearily. "I'm satisfied as I am."

He sat up suddenly.

"No!" he cried. "All I ask is to be let alone."

"You don't understand," she said in a patient voice as though she was
speaking to a child. "You are frightened and you don't understand. You are
frightened out of your wits at the idea of living life fully. You want to
spend it in little ways beside a little fire with a little face in front of you.
That is not life. That is merely a subterfuge for living. Life extends beyond
the lighted square of the fireplace. The path leads upward to the high rocky
places, to the granite cliffs, to the place where the free winds blow. There
is a continual excitement there and no peace. The brain is sharpened in
that rarefied atmosphere and the will is hardened. It is there that living is
its own reward."

Still he shook his head.

"I know!" she exclaimed fervently. Then she paused and seemed to cast
about in her mind for some conclusive argument that might move him from
his sleepy lethargy. "Shall I tell you about myself?" she asked at last. "Last
night I tried to tell you what I thought, the sort of philosophy that I had built
up out of the dreariness of my days. Shall I tell you who I am now?"

He did not answer but sat gazing at her weariedly. She took his silence
for assent.

"My people came from Salem," she began, "but that was a long time
ago. It was back in the days of Cotton Mather. I was named for my first

ancestor,—Martha Carrier. When I was a young girl I used to lie in bed and dream about that woman whose name I bear. Once I actually saw her. I do not think it was a dream. She really came into the room and stood beside my bed and there was a pale light all about her. She was a tall dark woman with a secret mouth and she walked like a queen. She leaned over the bed and said something to me but I forget the words if, indeed, I ever heard them. When she bent above me I saw a red stripe about her white neck and knew that she had been hanged. I was frightened at the sight and hid my face in the pillow but not before I heard a mingled sound of voices muttering and shouting and caught a glimpse of shadowy shapes swinging against the moon. I didn't know, then, what it was all about but I know now. I was to learn all these things in the years that followed while I grew up alone in the valley here. My father died on the day that I was born, Peleg Carrier his name was, and so, of course, I never saw him. My mother died when I was three years old. She was a shadow, something that I cannot catch in my memory, strive as hard as I may. When my father died Jeffrey Westcott appeared in the valley and took charge of everything. He had been a friend to my father in those days when he had been a student in Germany. I was brought up by Jeffrey Westcott. We lived out on the Leeminster Road in an old house very near where the farm is now."

Her eyes softened and she appeared to be turning back in memory to that house. Dreeme, whose faculties had quickened as her husky voice proceeded with her tale, had automatically drawn his pipe out and was filling it. She said:

"I carry that house about inside me. It was an old rambling structure. It must have been centuries old. My forefathers had lived in it since the first one came into the valley and raised it. It was a house that was full of the Past, full of the essence of times gone. When I wandered through the many rooms and the floors creaked beneath my feet and the shadows leaped out of the yawning closets and the huge stone fireplace. I seemed to be constantly accompanied by shapes in steeple-crowned hats and muffling cloaks. These shapes were always trying to say something to me, to whisper some secret, to tell me, perhaps, of a treasure that was hidden somewhere in the musty recesses of the building. There were so many things in that house, so many reminders of the past, that it was a haunted house. Jeffrey Westcott and myself lived there for thirteen years and it was rarely that we saw anyone. There were not so many people in the valley then and Jeffrey did all the house-work until I was old enough to take it over. Until I was thirteen or fourteen years old I was free, free to roam about as I pleased, and I became a wild creature. I loved to wander in the woods and along the bank of the Saccarac River and down the muddy roads. I was never lonely for I seemed to find living spirits in the river, the trees, the few houses. I could sit and converse with these invisible beings. Each season brought me something, a deposit of mystical knowledge. In the winter everything was mantled in white and the trees, covered with a crystal coating of ice, stood like crazy shapes blown out of glass. The wind roared down the valley and the branches rattled and clashed like pendants. The shivering deer trooped along the river bank and there were bears in those days. The thought came to me that the heart of nature was a frozen thing and that the natural state of the earth was cruelty, that only light and heat and fructification meant anything at all. Then the spring would come and the ice on the river would crack, split into whirling sheets, and vanish, and the earth became black again and tiny shoots of pale green would thrust out on the stark branches. There were early flowers and the pale sun would give out a thin warmth. Here, I thought, is the vague beginning of passion, the indomitable urge to live pushing against the ice of Time, the defiant gesture of the earth against itself. After that the full-flushed madness of the summer would descend on the valley and the wide fields would bear their yield and the heat would buzz in the air. August was a feverish madman running through lush grass and waving his fiery torch. This season became to me the end and purpose of being, the complete passion of the sensual earth, the triumphant vindication of self. The earth became a ruddy murderer standing above the pale shadow of itself and sucking its warm passion from its own secret heart. Out of the dead body came forth the living body. And then came autumn wearing a colored blanket striped with red and yellow and brown, walking through the flowers like a proud Indian chief in full head-dress of tufted feathers. In his eyes was a gray sadness and there was a mist about his mouth. The smoke from his pipe of peace curled over the valley. He was a tired man stirred by the last embers of passion. This was to me the period of weariness after the full flame of passion had died down. It was in this way that I became a mirror to the seasons, reflecting them in my moods, walking with them all the way. I dramatized myself. I became the earth alternately dead, fecund, full-flowering, and weary. You see how imaginative I was, how different from other children."

When she paused Dreeme lit his pipe and the sharp flare of his match danced about the room. Martha Westcott's cheeks were glowing with the ardor of her memories. She seemed to take on a girlish aspect as she spoke of her girlhood and her face reflected the seasons as she enumerated them. When she spoke of the winter her cheeks were as white as snow and when she described the summer they were flooded with rich blood that glowed through her pale skin. She was like some rare sensitive instrument reacting to the moods that flowed through her. Dreeme's antagonism to her began to dissipate and a creeping interest manifested itself in his attitude, as, puffing upon his pipe, he leaned forward and listened to her recital. If she noticed this weakening on his part she gave no sign of it but continued to dwell among her memories whole-heartedly, snatching out of the past whatever came within the net of her words.

"Once," she said, abruptly diverting the thread of her memories, "I was wandering about in the old house, poking into odd corners, opening forgotten chests, creeping under the stairs, investigating the numberless tiny closets that occupied so many curious places in the walls. It was a summer day and I can recall the buzzing flies that hovered about me and the sound of Jeffrey Westcott's footsteps down-stairs as he moved about the kitchen. I was running my hand along an up-stairs fireplace, thrusting my fingers between the bricks when one of them moved. With an effort I pulled it out and discovered a hollow into which I could force my whole arm. I fumbled about and my fingers closed on something that felt soft. Drawing it out I discovered that I clutched an old book in a soft black leather cover, apparently a notebook for it was filled with a strange writing in archaic characters and symbols and a map. I was sitting on the floor investigating it when Jeffrey Westcott came upstairs. I could hear him walking behind me and pausing and looking over my shoulder. Suddenly he cried out, 'Old Uriah's black book!' and snatched it from me. He retired to his room with it and passed the rest of the evening there. It was on that day that Jeffrey went mad. Old Uriah was my grandfather, Uriah Carrier. He . . .'"

"I know," said Dreeme, removing his pipe from his mouth. He remembered Humphrey Lathrop's description of the old sea-captain. A hunter of whales in the Pacific who had terrorized and robbed the natives of Tahiti. A blackbirder off the African Gold Coast. A man with the devil in his tobacco pouch.

"What was in Old Uriah's black book?" he asked. She shook her head.

"I did not find out till years later," she replied. "I know but I will not tell you. It is not part of my story."

She dismissed it with a wave of her hand.

"Jeffrey Westcott changed from that day," she said. "His relations to me changed. He was no longer the kindly guardian but a silent malicious man eaten up with a mad dream, with an idea, with a monstrous theory. We met and ate in silence and he would have nothing to say to me. A year or two after that the old house burned down. It was struck by lightning one day while Jeffrey was in the fields working and I was wandering by the river. I saw the smoke and flames rising in the dark stormy air and then the storm burst. But it was too late. There was nothing but a black gutted ruin after the rain cleared and the last ember expired. For a while I thought my past had gone up in fire and smoke and then I began to realize that houses may burn and people may die but the past is indestructible. We carry it about inside of us and nothing can smash it to pieces. Jeffrey was not too demoralized by the fire. He said, 'It was time. It is a symbol. It means there is nothing for me to find here until I have studied there.' He decided to go away. I remember the long ride to Boston, the wait for the boat, and the longer trip to Hambourg. It was in Hambourg that Jeffrey married me. He said that it made things easier, that it smoothed the difficulties of traveling. It was in Germany that I grew to maturity, grew to a lonely maturity while Jeffrey dragged me from town to town and city to city, wherever there was an old library or an old withered man full of insane notions. He had been in Germany before, had studied there as he had studied in other parts of Europe and Asia. He left me much by myself and I read a great deal, all sorts of quaint old books, philosophy, poetry, history, and the natural sciences. At first I loved Germany. The little towns with their quaint houses delighted me and the homeliness of German life soothed me. As time went on, however, all this became an old story and a vast weariness descended on me. I knew that I did not love Jeffrey Westcott and he knew that he did not love me. I grew in upon myself, became silent and morbid, passed my days revolving the various thoughts that came to me out of old books. A reticence fell over me. I could not talk to people. I was eaten up by a desire to be myself and I knew that I could not be myself as long as Jeffrey Westcott dominated me. His will grew stronger and stronger as the days passed and I could feel it concentering on me as the attention of a doctor fixes itself upon a rabbit he is about to dissect. I found that I could not fight against his will, that something iron in his nature forced me to go the way that he wanted me to go. As his will developed he grew more and more morose, absenting himself from the society of people. Soon I was entirely cut apart from any common intercourse. It was then that he returned here, bringing me with him—a reluctant ghost. He bought the farm on the Leeminster Road and we have been there ever since."

Dreeme's pipe had gone out and he made no attempt to relight it. He felt a strange pity welling up inside of him for Martha Westcott and yet a faint voice within the dark convolutions of his brain told him not to pity too much. His mind, at the same time, was setting scattered facts together and he began to realize the situation in the valley. He felt now that there was only one thing left to discover—the place called Dagon. After that, everything would be made clear.

"My life here," she said, "has been a waiting. The seasons have passed by and I have wandered like a ghost about that lonely house waiting for somebody to come, waiting for a rescuer. All these years Jeffrey Westcott has sat immersed in his books or conducting his strange experiments and his will has made me a part of those experiments. I will not tell you what they are because I desire to forget them. They must not be a part of my life in the future."

She paused again and glanced at him curiously.

"Yes," she said then, "I will tell you one thing so that you may understand how he has dominated my mind. I will tell you this because it concerns you indirectly, because it was the thing that brought you into my life. One day he came out of his library and said to me, 'I can make you shoot me in the leg.' He sat across from me at the table and kept repeating it to himself. 'I can make you shoot me in the leg.' I set my will against his and laughed. 'There will be no pain,' he said, half to himself. 'I shall will that there be no pain.' He sat across the table from me. He kept saying that. I thought I should go mad. I rose up from the table to clear away the dishes and then I found myself in front of him with the rifle in my hand and smoke curling from the muzzle. 'I will not,' I said. 'I will not shoot you in the leg but some day I will shoot you through the brain.' He laughed at that and said, 'You have shot me in the leg and there is no pain. Send for the doctor. Send Miles for the doctor.' I looked down and there was blood running along his leg. It was running into his shoe. Then you came."

Dreeme believed every word she said. He put the cold pipe on the table and pushed back his chair. Far away he heard a clock strike midnight. Mrs. Slater's window must be open, he thought. Perhaps Deborah was lying awake listening to that chime that marked the end of a day. He felt restive and stood up from his chair. Martha Westcott felt his unrest and spoke rapidly.

"Then you came. We looked at one another and I knew that I might be saved from this living grave by you. You were the first young man I had seen to talk to since I left Germany. You were not like these bent-backed farmers who scrape at the soil and bow beneath the old horror that Jeffrey Westcott conjures up before them. You are different, a man from the outer world. You knew that I was different, too, for you trembled all over when I walked to the door with you that night. I thought of you all the time. I thought so fiercely that my thoughts brought you back to me the next day and you hid behind the stone wall and watched me draw water from the well. Something began to laugh inside me then. That was why I sent Wagner to you. That is why you met me at the burned mill. That is why I am here now."

The yellow lamp-flare was burning dimly but Dreeme felt as though the little study was filled with a strange incandescence, a milky glow that lighted up both of their faces. He who had been so sure of himself was frightened again for he felt his pulses quickening in their beat and that trembling that had assailed him before in her presence was upon him like a palsy. He should not have listened to her. He should not have permitted her to creep into his mind, to envelop him with the warm mantle of her personality. He walked jerkily around the table toward her and she stood up as he came. Her eyes became luminous pools as he neared her and she half-raised her hands.

"I won't have it," he said in a grating voice. "I won't have you say these things to me."

She dropped her hands but remained standing in front of him, very near, her eyes studying his face.

"Are you entirely a stranger to passion?" she asked him. "Is there no pulse of life in you?"

He tried to talk rationally, to shake his anger from him. He said:

"I've heard what you have to say about yourself and I'm sorry. You have been the victim of a hard life and I pity you. But I do not feel toward you in the way that you seem to imagine. I am not in love with you and I shall never be in love with you. You surprised me, took me off my guard, so to speak, when I first saw you that night. I had not expected to see anyone like you. I was curious. You seemed to represent something, some part of the secret in this valley, and I thought about you a great deal. But that is all. If my emotions were stirred . . . they were the . . . the . . ."

He fumbled for adequate words for his thought was slipping from him. In the first place, he had never actually analyzed his emotions toward her, never satisfied himself as to the reason why she could at times make him tremble. It was certainly not because she was beautiful, although he realized as she stood there in front of him that she was very beautiful. No, it was not that. It might be ascribed to a certain magnetism that flowed about her and drew him insensibly toward her. Yet was not that a part of her beauty? Lost in conjecture he stood before her and observed her with tired eyes beneath a frowning brow. She had listened to him quietly, watching him closely all the time, and when he faltered and became silent, she placed her hand on his arm.

"You are reasoning," she said. "You are trying to destroy me by reasoning, but you find that you cannot do it. I am in your mind and I shall stay there."

"I shall root you out of my mind quickly enough," he said brutally.

"Is it that little girl?" she said. "Do you think that I am afraid of that little girl?"

He shook his head impatiently.

"I will not discuss her with you," he declared. "You have nothing to do with her . . . or me, either."

"Good-bye," she said then, and put both her arms about his neck. He felt the heat of her long body against him, and instinctively held her to him.

"Good-bye," he muttered against her blue-black hair.

His arms tightened about her as he felt her body pulsing against his, and he shut his eyes tightly. Waves of sunlit heat seemed to roar about him. She was no more than a creature of flesh and blood, after all, a warm breathing woman frantic with primitive urges, and unsuccessfully disguising them in a web of pretentious phrases. The thought of her lonely life crept into his beguiled consciousness, and a feeling of tenderness, of pity, swept through his blood. If he could help her, he would. But there was no way to it. She must go on and fight her own battle against life, against the close prison of the valley, and against the madness of Jeffrey Westcott. He was not a part of that arduous struggle. He was but an onlooker, a nonparticipant, a traveler who would shortly go away. And yet . . . her body contained a kindling heat . . . the scent of her hair was about his face . . . he could hear the shuddering ecstasy of her breath.

Suddenly she drew away from him and stood in the center of the room, breathing rapidly. He could see her dilated nostrils and her archaic lips slightly parted. Her dark hair had fallen about her shoulders. Her hand was raised to her shoulder. For an instant she poised like a living statue, and then with a quick gesture, she tore the black dress from her shoulders, and the snow-white flesh rippled to gold in the lamp-light.

"Daniel Dreeme," she gasped in a husky tone. "Daniel . . . you . . . you . . ."

He stood rooted to the spot, staring at her right shoulder, at the golden-white flesh that shone in the lamp-light and at the blue figure, no larger than the palm of his hand, that disfigured the glossy skin. It seemed to leap to his eyes at the instant conclusion of her abandoned gesture. He could not take his gaze from it, for it seemed to burn luminously by itself, a tracing of blue fire that writhed before his strained eyes. It fluctuated, drew near, retired from him, grew larger, and then diminished in size. He wanted to cry out, "What, in the name of Christ, is that!" but he could not force a single word through his lips. She had sensed the direction of his eyes the instant she had torn the dress from her shoulder, and a horrified hopelessness had swept across her face. She could see that the brief bond which had held them together was instantaneously snapped, that the charm was shattered. He was thinking no longer of her, no longer stirred to tenderness by her, or to passion by the whiteness of her body. Slowly she drew together the torn fragments of her dress and covered herself. Without a single word she walked slowly toward the door. She stood there with her back to him for a full minute and waited, but he said nothing. He still stood by the table, his eyes on the spot from which she had walked. His mind was an amazed welter of thoughts through which constantly moved the cold dead hand of Wagner, and the frail ghost-like figure of Deborah. He could piece nothing together, make sense of nothing, find no rational explanation of anything. The lamp began to sputter, shooting its thin protesting flame upward in the chimney as the oil burned out of the wick. In a minute it would go out and leave them in darkness. Every time the flame shot upward the shadows lengthened in the room and every time it went down the corners filled with curling pools of blackness. Dreeme walked slowly toward the lamp. It needed oil. It should be put out. His mind strove to function automatically as he stretched his hand out toward the lamp. He heard Martha Westcott move in the doorway, and he turned toward her. She was disappearing into the hall, walking slowly. Suddenly his voice came back to him.

"The goat's head," he said. "Where did you get the goat's head?"

He could hear her feet walking down the hall, and he stood listening as the front door softly opened and then closed again. Leaning over he blew the light out and stood, in the darkness, frowning.

Chapter Eight

I

When Dreeme awoke late in the morning he heard the heavy roar of rain on the roof, and, hurrying through his morning ablutions, he proceeded down stairs to his breakfast, finding the covered dishes on the table in the little study. Mrs. Slater had been there and had not waited, and he was thankful for this. He did not care to see her standing beside him, her eyes fluttering with excitement, and a repressed rancor in her pursed mouth. She resented his interference on Deborah's behalf, and a strong distaste for her had grown in the young doctor's mind. A regular New England aunt. A narrow-minded, overly-righteous, cold-hearted descendant of icy-natured forebears. The devil take her! Dreeme raced through his breakfast, not minding that the eggs were cold and coagulated on the heavy china plate, that the coffee was insipid and luke-warm. He would probably never get good service again from Mrs. Slater. Well, he would not need her services long. He would not be here in this small two-storied, two-room building that whined in the strong winds and drew in all the unpleasant heat of the summer. He would be in some large city, Boston or New York, and Deborah would be with him. There were lots of places where a young doctor could find a refuge. Finishing his meal he rose from the table and strode through the hall to the door and thrust it open. A wind-blown gust of rain dashed in his face, and he drew back from it. The weather had changed all right. Last night the largest moon he had ever seen had poured its silver light over Marlborough, but some time in the night it had disappeared, devoured by angry storm-clouds, and now the community lay prone beneath a furious down-pour. The farmers would not complain at this. Here was fecundation enough. Reaching for his rubber-slicker Dreeme adjusted it about his shoulders and stepped out into the storm. The heavy drops snapped against his face and drummed on his hat. The trees across the road were mere misty shadows. It was dark, too. Dreeme noticed that the lamps were lighted in the Slater house.

A New England rain-storm was a desolate phenomenon. It turned the entire vista gray and sodden green. Great puddles widened in the road, and the unceasing whir of falling water made a monotonous sound in the ears. Dreeme supposed that he should have put on boots, but he did not feel inclined to turn back into the house. He desired too much to go on and to finish up the business that was in his mind. He was going to face Humphrey Lathrop, and stay with the huge old doctor until he had made everything clear to him. He would tell Lathrop everything that had happened. Lathrop would help him, for, after all, Lathrop was a wise man. Even if he did look like a swelling frog at times. Dreeme sloshed through the puddles and mud on his way to the old doctor's cottage, his mind a chaotic mixture of problems and unasked questions. He had all the facts now, but he could not put them together until he possessed the key. With the key he could unlock the last secret door, and when he did this everything would fall into order, and his curiosity about Marlborough would be satisfied. He crossed the square and saw nobody but the tall spare figure of Bidwell standing in the shelter of the porch of the post office and general store. Bidwell did not return his greeting, but stood immovable watching the young doctor who proceeded on his way, head down against the driving rain and wind. Dreeme smiled sarcastically to himself. He was certainly a popular man in Marlborough. The rain dripped in an unceasing stream from the front brim of his hat and got into his eyes. It flowed into the back of his neck. It was in his shoes now. Every time he stepped he made a sucking sound. But it was cool and not altogether unpleasant. It quenched the restless fire of his body, and soothed his torn nerves. He felt as though he could walk for miles with this heavy down-pour beating upon him and that he would be all the better for it. The front of Humphrey Lathrop's cottage, small and gray in the rain, loomed before him, and he opened the rickety gate and walked up the path. He would find out everything now, and he would not leave Humphrey until he did.

II

Dreeme pushed the untasted tumbler of apple-jack away with an expression of disgust, and stood up and pointed a questioning finger at the old doctor. He demanded:

"Where is the place called Dagon?"

There was a finality in his voice that rang through the room. Humphrey Lathrop's jaw dropped and his three chins quivered like jelly. He pushed back his reinforced chair from the table with a mighty effort and an enormous scraping sound. For an instant Dreeme feared that the old man's eyes would pop out of his head. There was amazement in them, consternation, something very like terror. For the first time since Dreeme had known him the old doctor was completely taken off his guard, surprised, and routed.

"Where did . . . where did . . ."

Lathrop fumbled for speech unsuccessfully, his tongue sticking to the roof of his mouth. He glanced cautiously about the room as though he expected invisible foes to spring up on all sides. Dreeme, amazed at Lathrop's reaction, stood with outstretched hand and pointing finger, awaiting his answer with an obvious determination that no beating about the bush might distract. The rain dripped from the bottom of his trousers, and made a dark pool about him on the round rag carpet. The clock ticked desolately as he waited. Lathrop spoke slowly and with evident reluctance. He said:

"Where the bones were buried."

He appeared to have given up all hope of dissuading Dreeme from the subject.

"Bones? What bones? What does that mean?" cried Dreeme.

Lathrop's voice was monotonous.

"The bones of the Salem witches."

A great light seemed to flood Dreeme's mind, that light that had once been so far away, but it was too dazzling for him as yet. A voice deep inside him was talking feverishly, saying things, explaining, indicating. He could not catch the sound of the words. The voice was talking too fast. The words ran together. They were a febrile blur of sound.

"You must explain everything, Humphrey," he said in a calm voice as he sat down. "I'm in this thing too deep now. Somebody I know . . . is affected."

The old doctor nodded, and then, reaching for his tumbler of applejack, drank the entire potion down in a single draught. He choked and wheezed for a moment.

"You hit me amidships then," he remarked soberly. "Where did you hear of the place called Dagon?"

"Never mind," returned Dreeme. "Don't stave me off with questions. Tell me things."

"I'm going to," answered Lathrop mildly. "I'm going to tell you things. You're going to have it all now, and much good may it do you."

His eyes roved about the room. Then they reverted to Dreeme.

"Suppose you tell me everything first," he said in a wheedling voice. "I want to know what you've found out. There is no use duplicating the few facts and suspicions that I possess."

Dreeme eyed him impatiently.

"All right," he said shortly, and plunged immediately into his tale. In a rapid condensed form he told Lathrop of the first visit he had paid to Westcott's house, of the two conversations with Martha Westcott, of the death of Wagner, of the strange fright of Deborah, and of the goat's head. He strove to reinterpret the theory of will which Jeffrey Westcott had put forward in the burned mill. He explained his suspicions of the Reverend George Burroughs. Lathrop listened attentively, his head on one side, and his great lips pursed so that they thrust out like the snout of a pig. Occasionally he would nod. Once or twice his eyes opened very wide. In one instance he emitted a triumphant cluck as though some suspicion he had carried in his mind for years were verified.

"Will you fetch me down that big black book?" he said softly when Dreeme concluded his tale, indicating the little shelf that was nailed high on the wall behind him. Dreeme strode over and drew forth a bulky volume that was covered with dust, blew it off, and brought it to the table where he placed it. He deliberately read the title on the back of the tome as he laid it down. The name "Cotton Mather" was printed there in faded gilt letters. Lathrop smiled, a smile with no humor in it, and drew the book toward him. Then he adjusted his spectacles and leaned back very much like a judge about to give a decision.

"I tried to keep you away from this," he said, "for good and sufficient reasons, and chief among them was the peace of your own mind and the degree of your success in Marlborough. Well, you have lost the peace of your mind, and there is no longer any reason to suppose that you will ever have any success in Marlborough. There is no reason, therefore, why you should not know as much as I know. I will tell you, Daniel, that what you have told me has made some dark places clear to me, and verified certain suspicions which I have wisely kept to myself. Therefore, in making plain to you what I know I shall adjust some of your own information into the scheme of things."

After this preamble he cleared his throat loudly, searched through the huge volume before him until he found a certain place, closed the book upon a pudgy finger that retained the page, and glanced soberly at Dreeme.

"It's witchcraft we have to deal with," he said mildly. "It's a cursed madness that has ruled this valley since 1692."

Dreeme nodded without surprise. He suspected this, indeed, he knew it.

"Yes, sir, witchcraft," repeated the old doctor. "You probably don't believe in it. No more do I. But the outward forms of it exist just as surely as the outward forms of the Christian religion exist. It has its established hierarchy, although I believe today that it is the weapon of madmen, charlatans, and fanatics."

He sighed loudly.

"This is a mad world, Daniel," he said. "We are all more or less insane. Well, I'm getting nowhere. As I age I grow more discursive."

Dreeme moved restlessly and the old doctor lifted a hand.

"Let me tell you this in my own way," he said. "You'll have it all before I am done."

Lathrop cleared his throat and fastened his eyes upon Dreeme.

"In 1692," he said, "the little town of Salem went insane. You've read your history and you know all about the witch scares and the hangings on Gallows Hill. You know how the children cried out that they were possessed, and gave testimony against various men and women in the community, and how the judges and preachers strove to battle with this strange outbreak of insanity. I don't have to give you a résumé of that history. It is enough to remind you of it. It is the common conclusion of most scholars that all this was a form of religious mania, and that the people who were hanged were not professed witches but victims of hallucinations and enmity. I don't believe it. I believe those people belonged to a secret and blasphemous order that met all over the world, that they were divided into covens or parishes, that they each had their leader in the shape of a Black Man who represented the Devil, that they worshipped Satan, and that they attempted to practice magic. I believe that they were unhinged to such a degree that they could imagine themselves flying through the air, that they were addicted to hallucinations and delusions and visions, that, like the whirling dervishes, they could fling themselves into hysteric trances and dwell in the domain of their sick imaginations. They believed those things, Daniel. They had faith in Satan. And they attained a malevolent strength through their faith. They could superimpose their will on innocent people and make those people sick by the power of suggestion. There is nothing supernatural in that, after all. It is supernormal, perhaps, but you know my views on these things. The trappings and the ceremonies and the results might seem supernatural, but that was because the people in those days did not know about such things as thought-transference, auto-suggestion, and the impulsion of the will. In a measure, these people were liberating themselves from time, moving beyond the limitations of their days, subsisting in an arcane of their own manufacture through the full strength of those fanatical beliefs, which, after all, is saying no more than that they liberated their wills and believed in the strength of their wills. Well, in 1692 all this was brought to a halt by the hangings and the persecutions of the witch-judges. The Salem coven was demolished and scattered. Do not think, however, that all the witches were strung up on Gallows Hill. Others fled into the woods and sought far places where they might conduct their orgies and ceremonies in their own way. The larger group, and now, Daniel, I am telling you something I read in a book of which you have heard, hovered in the wilderness about Salem for some weeks, living on roots and berries and what the Indians might give them, for the Indians, too, believed in witchcraft. By night they ventured to the desolate graves of their hanged companions and dug up those bodies and bore them away with them into the thick forest. They pushed westward, avoiding the little settlements in the clearing, passing north of Springfield, crossing the Connecticut River, and eventually they came to a valley and discovered it to be a lost cul-de-sac in the hills, and there they settled down. With them they had the black book of the order, a book filled with ceremonies and liturgies, and in which a scribe set down the account of their wanderings. Can you guess where they settled, Daniel?"

Dreeme nodded.

"Here," he said. "They settled in this valley. These farmers are their descendants. The black book they carried with them was the black book of old Uriah Carrier."

Lathrop wagged his head up and down.

"That's right," he said. "As a boy I looked into that book and was frightened out of my wits. Yes, Daniel, they settled here, still carrying on their frightful ceremonies, still calling upon the devil by night and meeting in the secret forest-clearings to dance in the light of the moon. One place they kept sacred. It was a hidden place, known only to the adepts. It was there that they buried the bones of the hanged witches, those poor bodies that they had carried for two hundred miles through the thick wilderness. There, too, they raised the Devil Stone upon which the Black Man stood during the great ceremonies. They called the place Dagon and strewed it with ashes. I can picture that place lighted by torches at midnight. I can picture the rapt faces of the witches and the compelling eyes of the Black Man as he stood above them and called on Satan, on Beelzebub, on Asmodeus, the fiends that he imagined served his purpose. I can hear the laughter of the women and see their glistening eyes as the madness took them. By day they were taciturn people, carrying on the quiet masquerade of pioneers, building up homes in the clearing, pushing the forest farther and farther back; but when the moon rose the madness that was in their blood swept them out of themselves and they became other creatures employing pagan symbols and ancient phallic ceremonials. They existed in a domain out of place and time, then, a land of hallucinations and dreams and primitive urges. It was a land where they celebrated the Black Mass and the Witches' Sabaoth, and gave full rein to the frenzies of the blood and brain. I've never seen the place called Dagon, Daniel, and I never hope to see it, but I suspect where it is. I suspect that the Devil Stone is still there, and if one dug deep enough one would come to crumbled bones, if, indeed, bones last that long."

The old doctor drew a long breath and paused. He reached for the apple-jack bottle and poured himself a drink.

"I'm developing into an old drunkard," he remarked. "Imagine it. At my age!"

He drank half the tumbler of amber liquor and set it down on the table. The roar of the rain filled the room and Dreeme, gazing toward the window, could perceive nothing but a silver opaqueness that ran and glittered. He waited for Lathrop to go on, knowing that the old doctor could tell his story best in his own way.

"Now then," said Lathrop, wiping his mouth with a fat hand. "Where was I? Where, for that matter, are any of us? That's philosophy, Daniel."

He summoned up a smile, but it was lost in the earnest attention of the young doctor. He said slowly:

"I didn't actually lie to you, Daniel, but I did conveniently forget to tell you some things the other day. I thought there was no need of spreading a story that had better not have existed at all in the beginning. Well!"

He sighed wheezily. Then he resumed his story.

"It was not alone the descendants of the Salem witches who wandered into this valley and established homes," he said. "You've heard of Thomas Morton of Merry Mount, haven't you?"

Dreeme nodded. Of course, he had. Why, Deborah . . .

"Morton," said the old doctor, "was a rascal who headed a colony of loose fellows. They sold liquor to the Indians, disregarded the Puritanical laws of living, laughed at religion, and injected a licentious scarlet into the gray cloth of the old New England. You can imagine that carousing colony near enough to Boston to cause the good Puritans a prodigious loss of sleep. It was something that they hated and feared because it stirred in them the covered embers of their own suppressed excesses, I suppose. Uncommitted sins that are buried in the blood and brain are fearful things, Daniel. I imagine that most of the Puritans sublimated their fleshly longings into a religious ardor but this would make them fear the downright honesty of openly committed sin more than ever. Anyway, when news reached Boston that the Morton colonists had reared a huge May pole and were dancing about it with their skins full of good liquor and debauching all the likely squaws they could lay hands on, they decided that something drastic should be done. So a body of armed men (crusaders of the Lord, Daniel) marched to Merry Mount, cut the May Pole down, strewed the place with ashes, cursed it and called it Dagon (you see how the name crops up?), and scattered the befuddled revelers. What was more natural than that some of these topers and lechers should push westward into the wilderness, having, so to speak, their bellies full of Puritanical oppression? To the west they came, then, following an old trail that led north of Springfield and across the Connecticut River, and eventually they found themselves in this valley. Leeminster was the town settled by them. So there you have the two towns, Daniel. I don't know which was settled first. It doesn't make any difference. They were near enough for daily intercourse, and I suppose there was some intermarriage. Whether the witch-fever spread to Leeminster or not is a mystery. I am on dubious ground now, for most of the opinions I have arrived at are the result of deduction and there is no documentary proof to bolster me up. That is why I am chary at giving vent to them. Some of the things that you have told me seem to substantiate a few of the suspicions I have had. My voice, Daniel, is getting awfully hoarse."

He paused and finished his tumbler of apple-jack.

"You are going to be reeling in a minute," said Dreeme impatiently.

Lathrop wheezed and chuckled.

"No, sir," he said. "When you see me reel you'll see a sight."

He chuckled again. Dreeme observed an apoplectic glow on his fat cheeks, however, and it made him uneasy. He was afraid that the old doctor's head would loll to one side, and that the continuation of the story would be a series of sterterous snores. He had seen it happen before for Lathrop plied the apple-jack not wisely but too well.

"Where was I?" inquired Lathrop mildly. He rolled his blue eyes at the ceiling in thought.

"Oh!" he said in faint surprise as he unexpectedly lighted on the thread of his conversation. "Oh, yes!

"Marlborough and Leeminster proceeded on their solitary way while the land developed," he declared. "Towns sprang up on all sides of them, but they were protected by their valley and the fact that no large artery of travel cut through them. They were in a cul-de-sac. They accepted the modernities of living suspiciously and in a gingerly manner. Being farmers, the natives subsisted by themselves and without too much aid from the outside world. As time passed on I imagine the witch practices ceased, although the memories of them were handed down from father to son, and mother to daughter. They were not so much ashamed of these practices, at first, as they were reticently jealous. The very fact of them made them different from other men and women. When I came here I found no signs of secret practices. I did find a dour reticence, perhaps a more antagonistic one than you have run up against. But I paid no attention to it, and I minded my own business. I did not ask questions. I did not watch people. I admit that I thought a lot. I read a great deal of history, and tried to orientate these people. It was from old Captain Uriah Carrier himself that I got my clew, for, thinking me no more than a mere boy and being a boastful old scoundrel, he told me that he was the last Black Man, and he even, in a burst of drunken recklessness one night, showed me the book that had been in his family for generations. It was easy enough for me to put two and two together after that. Being wise though I put them together by myself and kept my convictions to myself. I . . . ."

Lathrop developed a choking fit and sputtered for a few minutes while Dreeme waited impatiently. The old doctor made a half-gesture toward the apple-jack bottle, thought better of it, and withdrew his hand reluctantly.

"You see Marlborough today," he said wearily, leaning back in his chair, "and you see a community that has hugged a secret to its bosom for centuries. These men and women are alive to the past, to the terrible heritage which they possess, and they desire to eradicate it from common knowledge, to bury it, as it were, in the dust-heap of gone things. That is their first impulse. They do not want strangers to know that they have descended from condemned witches. Now there's Jeffrey Westcott."

He paused and blinked his blue eyes.

"Who is he?" he proceeded. "I don't know. You don't know. But we can guess what his purpose is. You've told me all about his maunderings about the mightiness of the will, the theory he hinted at to you in the burned mill that night. Now this is what I see, Daniel. Westcott fell in with Peleg Carrier in Germany, learned from him about the witch-cult that had existed here, and came to find out more about it. He had a theory of his own, a theory in an inchoate state, and he fancied that witch practices might be subdued to the ends of that theory. When he was settled here he found that he could start nothing, for these people had ceased to practice the so-called Black Arts. What he needed was a key, a weapon to drive the farmers before him. He found that weapon in Captain Uriah Carrier's black book. All he had to do was to startle the morose inhabitants of Marlborough and its outlying district with the testimony from this book, for the will toward witchcraft was already a part of their blood's inheritance. I believe, Daniel, that he reinstituted witch meetings, formed a coven here, and made himself the ruling Black Man. That's why he's avoided; that's why his farm is shunned territory. He commands the dark side of the nature of Marlborough. These people lead two lives, and one of them is the surface life that we see going on about us. The other is the secret life that centers about the

place called Dagon. Westcott drives them through their fears and their secret weaknesses, weaknesses that they might fight against and successfully
conquer if he were not here. When he goes the whole scaffolding of mummeries will break down, these people will become normal inhabitants, and
all this stuff will seem like some wild dream. That's what I think, Daniel."

Dreeme nodded an assent.

"That's it," he agreed. "Now what can we do about it?"

Lathrop scowled heavily.

"I," he emphasized, "can do nothing about it."

"Something must be done about it," urged Dreeme.

"Then you do it, Daniel," said the old doctor. "And God be with you."

He shook his head dolefully.

"I'm not a witch-hunter," he explained mildly. "Neither am I Don
Quixote or Bayard or Sherlock Holmes or . . . or . . ."

He continued to roll his head from side to side slowly.

"No, Daniel," he protested, "I'm the man who sits in a chair all day."

He reverted to the phenomena that Dreeme had adumbrated during
his story.

"The various things you've told me," he said, "clear up, as I've pointed
out before, some of my suspicions. Let us take up the wax figures first,
those little puppets that Deborah Morton found behind Westcott's books.
That's an old witchcraft trick. A doll is made and baptized with the name
of some living person against whom the witch desires revenge or evil.
Then needles are thrust into those places where the person is to be injured
and charms are recited over the little figure. Westcott, I believe, imagined
this mummery would sharpen and direct the invisible strength of his will.
You say one of the dolls had a needle thrust into its leg. Well, Westcott got
shot in the leg, didn't he? I imagine that was his first charm, a charm
against himself. And it worked. Never ask me how it worked, but it did.
The other doll had needles through its eyes. Well, how about the wooden
pegs driven into Wagner's eye-sockets?"

Dreeme shuddered as he recalled the disfigured face grinning up at
him from the bank of the Saccarac River.

"I don't believe Westcott killed Wagner," added Lathrop. "No, sir. I
believe he wanted the hired man dead because he found out that the poor
fellow was acting as a go-between for Martha Westcott and yourself. Now
into whose brain did Westcott force the thought of and will for this murder? Find that out, Daniel, if you can."

"I intend to," said the young doctor, his mouth a thin line of determination.

"But don't forget," remarked Lathrop, "that there may be a little doll somewhere christened Daniel Dreeme with a needle through its heart."

"I'll take my chance," said Dreeme.

"We come to the goat's head," proceeded Lathrop. "That puzzles me. I know its origin but not its purpose."

Dreeme was visibly excited at this topic.

"Here we sit like two Sherlock Holmes," chuckled the old narrator, "and we're really two Doctor Watsons. Amateurs, Daniel, amateurs."

Suddenly he sobered up.

"The goat's head," he explained, "was the seal of Thomas Morton of Merry Mount. It is still extant upon legal documents which he left behind him. I'll venture to assert, Daniel, that your Deborah, who wears that seal, apparently, about her neck, is a descendant of the Morton clan. Old Thomas left enough illegitimate progeny, God knows, and there is no reason why some of these women may not have taken the rascal's name. Why the goat's head should have been clutched in Wagner's hand or why it is branded on Martha Westcott's shoulder is beyond my reasoning faculties. Those are things that you will have to find out."

Slowly he opened the bulky black volume before him.

"Daniel," he said, "listen to this. I am reading from Cotton Mather."

He bowed over the page and read slowly:

". . . this Rampant Hag, Martha Carrier, was the person, of whom the Confessions of the Witches, and of her own Children among the rest, agreed, That the Devil had promised her, she should be Queen of Hell."

He looked up solemnly.

"That, I take it," he remarked, "is the fountainhead of the Carrier family. You notice she had children. She was the Queen of Hell, Daniel, the Queen of Hell. That's a brave title for a Puritan lady."

He turned back to the book and searched through a few pages. Finding what he sought for, he cleared his throat and looked up.

"Now then," he said, and began to read again.

"'Richard Carrier affirmed to the jury that he saw Mr. George Burroughs at the witch meeting at the village and saw him administer the sacrament.' And here's another interesting bit. 'He,' . . . that's Burroughs, Daniel. . . . 'He was Accused by Eight of the Confessing Witches, as being an Head Actor at some of their Hellish Rendezvouses, and one who had the promise of being a King in Satan's kingdom, now going to be erected . . .'"

Lathrop closed the book with a snap and a puff of dust started up from it.

"And there," he said, "is the stock from which your sallow preacher-friend, the Reverend George Burroughs, descends. I point these things out to you, Daniel, so that you may understand how clear the stock has come down from the Salem witch-days. There's another place in this book, if I recollect aright, where the witches accused George Burroughs of bringing puppets with him and sticking thorns into those puppets. Burroughs, I suppose, was the Black Man, or one of the Black Men, who ruled the New England coven. There we are, Daniel. Now you know all that I know and I imagine you can see why I wanted to keep it from you. I thought the ancient fever would die out and that there would be no need of all this speculation. It seems not."

He wheezed heavily and shook his head.

"What must I do, Humphrey?" asked Dreeme.

Lathrop opened his eyes very wide and pointed a pudgy finger at the young doctor.

"Do?" he said. "Why, be a wise man. Take your little Deborah Morton with you and get out of the valley and settle elsewhere and live your life without worrying about these things. This situation cannot last. Westcott is undoubtedly mad, and he will blow himself up in some devilish experiment, or some farmer will do for him. Why should you stay here rooting into things that, after all, are no concern of yours? If these fools want to play at being witches, let them. Much good may it do them! Your life is all before you, and it moves on another arc than the existence in this gray town of Marlborough."

He sighed and glanced at the silver-streaked window where the runnels of rain slid unceasingly.

"I'm anchored here," he said sadly. "I'm an old hulk rotting in a forgotten dry-dock. Time has forgotten me. All I can do is sit in this chair and watch absolutely nothing go by and cogitate upon it. It's a bright prospect, Daniel, a bright prospect."

"I shall go away," remarked Dreeme slowly. "Just when, I don't know, but soon . . . soon."

He, too, watched the rain beating against the window-panes and listened to the confused roar of the storm as it beat over Marlborough. It was pleasant to sit in a dry warm nook and observe the elements raging vainly outside. The valley was full of the gray smoke of the down-pour; and the greedy soil, that had parched beneath the hot sun, was drinking the cool water, bringing its measure of relief to the tiny thrusting roots that fumbled about in the darkness for nourishment. It had not rained since the night he had first gone to the Westcott farm, since he had stood in the dark doorway with Martha Westcott listening for the sound of wings in the air; and that had been but a brief storm, a swift and vanishing interruption of the parched season that had hovered over the valley. That had been but a few days ago, and yet how far away it seemed. Wonderingly he watched the rain beat against the window and listened to the whirring music that filled the cloudy air.

III

Walden Slater had drawn his rickety rocker back against the wall and he sat just outside the curtain of water that dripped from the eaves of the back piazza. He looked through the swinging silver hangings of rain soberly, his empty corncob pipe drooping disconsolately from his wide mouth. It was evident that he was deep in the concentration of difficult thought for his brows wrinkled and his head bowed still lower as he twiddled a small bit of wood in his hand and gazed blankly at the whirring rain. Dreeme stood in the back door and watched him. Behind the young doctor in the kitchen Deborah moved about, her small clear voice raised as she attempted unsuccessfully to converse with the reticent Mrs. Slater who paraded back and forth with dishes and answered her in grudging monosyllables. There was an excited quaver in Deborah's voice that moved Dreeme, the note of a stifled excitement. They all had something on their minds. They were all concealing something from one another. The very atmosphere induced an ingrowing that was unhealthy and unnatural. Dreeme coughed loudly and shifted his position. Walden Slater did not stir. He still sat crouched in the rocker rolling the bit of wood between his stumpy fingers.

"I should think the rain would cheer you up," remarked Dreeme.

Walden Slater turned his head slowly, inspected the young doctor with a blank eye, and then resumed his study of the rain.

"Won't it be good for the crops?"

"Umph," said Walden Slater. He twiddled his bit of wood and looked at the sky.

"I'm going to marry Deborah," announced Dreeme.

Walden Slater turned deliberately around and stared at the young doctor. He looked first at his shoes, then his trousers, then his coat, and finally into the doctor's face. His eyes were opaque mirrors. He cleared his throat. He said:

"Be you?"

His tone was mild and there was no surprise in his voice.

"I reckoned so," he added after a moment.

"Any objections?" asked Dreeme.

Walden Slater watched the rain carefully.

"Do you ever whittle?" he inquired.

Dreeme laughed aloud.

"No," he said. "I don't even carry a knife."

His mind flashed back to dour farmers seated morosely before the post office and general store whittling away at small pieces of wood, industriously carving nothing to pass away the endless time.

"No objections at all," remarked Walden Slater mildly.

Both of them heard the humming of the Reverend George Burroughs as he came through the kitchen from the dining room, and Dreeme drew back with some distaste as the tall sallow figure pushed through the door to the back piazza.

"The Lord gives plenteously," intoned the preacher as his black expressionless eyes roved from the faces of the two men to the gusts of rain that swept across the green foliage beyond the house.

"Lend me your knife," requested Walden Slater, twiddling the bit of wood in his hand.

The Reverend George Burroughs extracted an old clasp-knife from his pocket and passed it over to the farmer. Walden Slater began to methodically whittle the bit of wood he held to a fine point. The tiny shavings fluttered to the floor.

"A fine rain makes a fine crop," announced the preacher.

"A fine crop makes a fine profit," added Dreeme, saying the first thing that popped into his mind.

"A fine knife makes a fine point," declared Walden Slater. "This knife is dull."

He handed it back without any thanks, and the preacher stowed it away in his pocket. Dreeme drifted back through the kitchen preparatory to returning to his study. The conversation was altogether too dull.

IV

Dreeme was jerked out of a sound steep by a strong hand grasping his shoulder. He started up with an uncontrollable cry of amazement.

"Get into your clothes," said a voice. "It's time."

He recognized Walden Slater's voice. Without any questions he leaped out of bed and hurried into his trousers and shirt. A heavy rain pounded on the roof as he completed his brief toilet, and shook his head violently to recover his partially benumbed senses. Walden Slater moved before him as they hurried for the stair-case and ran down it to the entrance hall. Before dashing out through the door into the rain Dreeme flung his still soggy rain-coat about him. A moment later they stood in the road where the heavens seemed to open and let down an unimaginable flood upon them. Walden Slater snatched up a storm-proof lantern from the ground by the gate, and as he stooped his heavy coat gaped open and Dreeme caught a glimpse of the butt of the Smith and Wesson revolver thrust into his belt.

"What is it, Walden?" gasped the young doctor. "For God's sake, find your tongue."

"I can find my tongue when I want it," replied the farmer. "You come with me."

They splashed through the puddles up the gradual rise of the Leeminster Road, bowing their heads to the fierce blows of the frantic gusts of rain that sought to thrust them back. Dreeme was running in his bare feet.

"Walden!" he gasped. "Walden!"

"Deborah's gone. Disappeared completely," cried Walden Slater with unwonted vigor. "So's Burroughs. Does that tell you anything? Dreeme, I've thought this whole thing out. You come with me."

He ran all the faster, and Dreeme followed him while a mounting rage seethed within him.

"I know what I know," the farmer called back over his shoulder.

Dreeme seemed to be borne along by the furies within him. He accelerated his pace and soon was abreast of the farmer. For a time they ran doggedly, the breath whistling in their lungs. Under their feet drummed the boards of the bridge that spanned the Saccarac River. A moment later they were on even ground. Deborah gone! How or why she had gone Dreeme did not know, but Walden Slater knew, and that was enough. It would be time enough later to ask questions. Yet Dreeme, leaning his head closer to the farmer, did ask something.

"Where are we going?" His voice rose in a shout. "To the Westcott farm?"

"Dagon, damn it, Dagon!" shouted back the farmer. "We're going to the place called Dagon!"

They ran all the faster through the relentless rain.

Chapter Nine

I

As Dreeme, racing close at the heels of Walden Slater, circled the West-cott farm-house, he glanced up curiously at the windows. There was no light. The building gloomed in its cluster of trees just as it had that first night when he had stumbled after the boy Miles along the uneven path and entered through the back door. It was like a house of the dead, a dwelling-place from which the rose-colored actualities of living had long ago vanished. Around it, the tall dark trees kept their somber watch, standing like ghostly sentinels. The spark of Walden Slater's lantern sent strange beasts of shadows scurrying into the underbrush that lined the hummocky path. At the back door the farmer set down his light and hammered upon the wood with the butt of his revolver. The sound seemed to echo inside the house. It was like the echo that comes from a musty tomb when the iron grille that guards its dead from the living world is shaken. If there was anything in back of the wood against which Walden Slater was hammering so vigorously, that shape or being or spectre was standing mute.

"Of course not," muttered the farmer. With a fierce kick of his heavy boot he crashed the door open and it smashed against the wall on broken hinges. The intruder entered slowly, holding the lantern before him in one hand and grasping his cocked revolver in the other. Dreeme followed at his heels. The small beam of light darted about the room reflecting the stuffed chairs, the wax flowers under glass, the photographic enlargements on the wall. Dreeme's mind automatically swept back to that time when he had followed Martha Westcott through this room trembling from the magnetism of her strange personality. Walden Slater circled the sitting room slowly, lifting his lantern to view the pictures and examining the tables and the chairs. He seemed to be looking for something, some hint that might indicate the direction that he desired. "Uriah," he muttered, pausing before one picture, a particularly large and atrocious piece of workmanship that hung above the wax flowers. Dreeme caught a glimpse of a glittering eye highly touched by the painter's art.

"What are we searching for?" he inquired. "Shouldn't we get on?"

Walden Slater said nothing but strode toward the door that led to the library. He kicked it open unceremoniously and entered and Dreeme followed close at his heels. It was just as the young doctor remembered it. "Light the lamp," said the farmer. Dreeme fumbled at the chimney and wick, and an instant later the pale yellow glow illuminated the room. The crowded book-stacks leaned forward, and the ancient volumes seemed to watch the intruders speechlessly. The young doctor walked impatiently about the table where he had once seen Jeffrey Westcott seated. He felt that they were wasting time, that Deborah was confined somewhere in some secret place from which she should be rescued as speedily as possible. He wanted to say this to the farmer, to get him started on the way to the place called Dagon, and yet he refrained from speech, for Walden Slater was obviously looking for something. He, too, circled the room, inspecting the backs of the books with a swift and keen eye. Dreeme paused near one case and read a few faded titles. "Certainty of Worlds of Spirits" by Richard Baxter. "De la Démonomanie des Sorciers" par Jean Bodin. "Sadducismus Triumphatus" by Joseph Glanvil. "Daemonolatria" by Nicholas Remigius. "Discourse of the Subtill Practises of Devilles" by George Giffard. He turned abruptly to the farmer.

"What are we looking for?" he asked.

"The goat's head," replied the farmer. He had ruffled through the papers on Westcott's table.

"Do you know what that means?" exclaimed Dreeme.

Walden Slater nodded.

"Be patient," he said. "It's the signal for the Esbat."

He continued to rummage about the room.

Suddenly he snorted in triumph, and started for the door. Dreeme followed close at his heels. The farmer, still holding his lantern, turned a corner and they began to climb a narrow flight of stairs. Behind them in the deserted library the oil-lamp perched precariously on the corner of the table and quivered at each gust of rainy air that swept through the window.

They wandered through two bedrooms, the feeble flare of the lantern illuminating neatly-made beds, and came to a closed door that apparently opened into a room on the rear of the house. Walden Slater, employing his usual tactics, kicked it open and they entered into a small chamber that was entirely unfurnished except for a raised stone slab on three perpendicular pillars of granite in the corner. The farmer made his way immediately toward this strange bit of furniture and held his lantern over it, inspecting the corrugated surface of the stone. Dreeme, standing beside him, saw dark stains on the slab and a small keen-bladed knife that appeared more like a lancet than anything else. The knife glittered in the ray of the lantern and the young doctor was overwhelmed by a sudden fear. He stared wide-eyed at the farmer, and Walden Slater's long upper lip quivered in the dim light. Dreeme struggled between an absorbed excitement in their discoveries and his intense concern for Deborah's safety. She was somewhere not far from them, her mind a riot of fear, waiting frantically for him. He was sure of that. But what had happened to her in the meantime, during those hours (and he was not sure how many they had been, for the taciturn farmer had vouchsafed no specific information on this point) she had passed since Burroughs enticed or kidnapped her from the Slater house, he could not even guess. If any harm had come to her (and his heart nearly ceased beating at the thought) he would not leave the valley until he had killed Jeffrey Westcott and George Burroughs. A cold determination seemed to freeze the emotions in him as he came to this decision. His thin lips tightened and his eyes became like blue steel.

"I shall go mad in a minute," he said calmly to the farmer.

Walden Slater opened his mouth to speak and then, with a grunt that expressed both surprise and relief, he pointed to the corner in back of the stone slab. The dejected carcass of a chicken lay there in its dishevelled feathers, its crop slit open and its blood dabbled upon the floor.

"He's been divining," he said. Then he looked closely at the young doctor.

"You perk up, Doctor Dreeme," he added. "I know what I'm doing. There's no harm done to anybody . . . yet."

He bent over and fumbled about the limp carcass of the chicken and then straightened his body with a grunt of satisfaction. In his hand he held a small blood-smeared square of paper. Silently he turned and strode downstairs, Dreeme close at his heels. He did not speak until they had regained the comparative light of the library and then he sank into Jeffrey Westcott's chair by the table. The curtain from the window fluttered inward, narrowly missing the chimney of the sputtering lamp. Dreeme stood before the farmer, his eyes staring and his hands trembling.

"I reckon I'll have to explain a few things," he remarked slowly, "or you'll be fainting on me, Doctor."

"I'm not going to faint, Walden," replied the young doctor, "but I am mad to get on. I know Deborah's in grave danger and I should be with her."

Walden Slater nodded gravely.

"Westcott is playing his last card to dominate the valley," he said. "He's called an Esbat, a meeting, and he intends a sacrifice. I knew it was coming ever since I saw that goat-head in Wagner's fist. The goat-head is used as an announcement for a coming event. Wagner was on his way to somebody with the sign when he was smashed in the head and killed. That's when I started thinking. There hasn't been an Esbat in this valley since old Captain Uriah Carrier died, and my dad told me all about him."

He cleared his throat after this unexpectedly long speech. Then he renewed his distasteful task of narration.

"We don't want none of this stuff, Doctor," he declared. "The farmers want to forget what their grand-dads were. Westcott won't let us forget. He's got Uriah's black book and we're all in it. He's got some of us fooled by stirring up feelings in us that we thought had died out of us. It has died out of me. I don't take any stock in this stuff though my dad was befuddled by old Uriah and went to his Esbat."

He cleared his throat again and held up the bit of paper. In the lampglow Dreeme saw the tiny goat's head carefully drawn in blue ink and when Walden Slater slowly turned the paper he saw "Dagon—two—nigger" written in small letters. He recalled now that he had never turned over the bit of paper he had given to the coroner. He recalled, too, the antagonism of the farmers who had stood so short a distance from him when he had extracted the paper from Wagner's stiff hand.

"It seems that they meet at Dagon at two o'clock, and that Dagon is somewhere in Nigger Swamp," he said mechanically.

Walden Slater nodded his head in assent.

"That's it," he said. "Westcott sacrificed a chicken to see if the signs were propitious. Apparently he decided they were, although what a chicken's crop has to do with it is beyond me."

He stopped abruptly and turned his face toward the open window. Dreeme listened, too, and he could hear the distinct sound of footsteps going by the house. They apparently died away in the soft grass of the field that stretched from the dwelling to Briony Wood.

"They're gathering," remarked the farmer simply. He stood up and regained his lantern.

"We can't know where they've hidden Deborah," he said, "but we do know that they'll bring her to the place called Dagon. She's to be the sacrifice, Doctor."

"They wouldn't dare to kill her!" exploded Dreeme.

"There's some things worse than death," answered Walden Slater.

He moved toward the door and Dreeme followed him. Behind them the forgotten lamp perched on the edge of the table, and as the wind increased the curtain flapped ever nearer the yellow flame, a flame that sputtered but, being shielded from the worst of the gust by a protector, never went out.

The two men passed through the sitting room and out through the broken door into the storm which had now settled down into a gusty drizzle.

"And, besides," said Walden Slater slowly, "Wagner was killed, wasn't he?"

"Do you know who killed him?" asked Dreeme. "Was it Jeffrey Westcott?"

"I know that the pegs driven into his eye-sockets were whittled by a mighty dull knife," returned the farmer grimly.

They plodded on in silence after that, their heads bowed against the driving wind and rain. Occasionally they stumbled over hummocks of wet grass and once Walden Slater sprawled upon the ground, his lantern rolling from his hand and blinking out. With a grumbled curse he scrambled to his feet and picked up the extinguished lantern and examined it.

"It's busted!" he said vehemently, flinging it from him with an angry gesture. They heard it clatter against a stone wall to the side of them. After that they struggled on in the darkness across the field, the black shadow of Briony Wood in its slight elevation looming nearer and nearer against the faint glow of the stormy sky.

"If you meet anybody," said the farmer suddenly, "don't you say a damn word. Keep your head down and trudge along."

Dreeme muttered something in his throat. Mingled rain and perspiration was streaming down his face and his naked feet were cut by the sharp stones and twigs. He heard his heart beating violently in his bosom and wondered if the farmer was as tired as he. They had crossed the greater part of the field now and the ground was sloping upward before them, sloping upward to tall spectral trees that stood with intermingled branches and waited menacingly for their coming. It would be dark in those trees and there would probably be no pathway. But they would have to go on, for somewhere beyond the trees was the place called Dagon, and it was at Dagon that he would next meet Deborah. Sobbingly he climbed the slope at the heels of Walden Slater.

II

The trees reached out and took them in, circling about them in a massed formation. They were in the darkness of Briony Wood now, a darkness that was unrelieved by any light except the pale intermittent glow of the sky that filtered through the bowed branches of the trees. The unceasing storm rumbled in the leaves above them, and the incessant drip of water sounded about them as they lurched over broken branches, stones, unbared roots, and washed-out hollows. Far above the moist darkness through which they struggled Dreeme thought he could hear a faint humming, the sound of wind, perhaps, flowing along the tilted tops of the taller trees. His labored breath chimed with it. Walden Slater was lurching along doggedly beside him now, no longer ahead, but shoulder to shoulder with him except when the uneveness of the road they took caused them to stumble apart. It was good to feel his sturdy shoulder as it struck against him occasionally. It was like a tower filled with armed men who were always on guard. It was a fortress against evil and chance. The farmer was silent, conserving his strength for the difficult journey through the wood, and Dreeme, taking a lesson from him, refrained from speech, although questions were beginning to boil up in his restless mind. His intelligence was clarifying although he was still in a riot of fear over the situation in which Deborah must be. Images appeared and dissolved before his eyes. Deborah lying on the rainy ground bound and gagged. Deborah insensible in some secret retreat where George Burroughs, his sallow face aflame with malice, bowed over her and blasphemously intoned Biblical phrases that were twisted to serve the devil's purpose. Deborah sitting wide-eyed in an hypnotic trance while Jeffrey Westcott stood before her, his cloven head bared to the rain and the wind. Deborah gazing into the heavy-lidded remorseless eyes of Martha Westcott while the taciturn farmers, muttering to one another, gathered about a great dripping stone in the heart of Nigger Swamp.

The humming in the air increased steadily above the two travelers now until it seemed as though a hundred and one far-away aeroplane engines were singing their way through the darkness and rain like a swarm of huge and unbelievable mosquitoes. Dreeme's labored breath sucked in his throat as he pushed the entangling spiky vines aside and thrust his tired body forward. His bare feet were bruised and cut, but they seemed devoid of all sensation, blotches of white meat that lifted and fell with a maddening regularity. He was not sure that the humming he heard was more than the blood pounding in his ear-drums and throbbing in his temples. Yet it seemed to be more than that, to be, in fact, an ominous and steadily-increasing warning of the approach of mysterious and frightful things. It would not have surprised him to see a host of devils and witches suddenly sweep through the tree-tops screaming and laughing to one another. He could imagine them calling to one another gross phrases, turning their red-rimmed eyes downward at him, pointing with long-nailed hands and bursting into gales of infernal laughter. Then he realized that his imagination was slipping from his control and he strove to concentrate on Deborah, to save himself from his own madness through the memory of her. He pitched forward over oozy hummocks. The fierce thorns of clutching vines ripped along his legs and arms. Malicious branches lashed murderously at his face. Water sucked and gurgled about his naked feet. But he pressed forward half-blindly, hardly conscious of the direction in which he was proceeding, knowing only that Walden Slater's shoulder struck against his from time to time, and that a desperate and imperative necessity was urging them into the depths of the marshy wood. Some small beast scurried beneath his feet, and he screamed at the nervous tension of the moment. He heard laboring branches crack and groan above his head and the hollow sound where a dislodged stone rolled down an incline and landed in a huge puddle. The humming had developed into a roar about him. It was so dark that he could not see Walden Slater. He could not even hear the heavy thud of the farmer's boots. Suddenly he became conscious that a devastating delirium of fear was engulfing him and rendering him incapable of any action. "This is horrible!" he sobbed in his throat. He stopped dead in his tracks, straightened his body, and gazed upward until the faint glow of the stormy sky pierced his dulled eye-sight. It came slowly, a gradual light, a milky hue against which the silhouettes of the black branches cut sharply. Gazing steadfastly he strove to quiet the tempest that shook his mind. He thought for a moment that he could see small winking lights scurrying across the surface of that milky sky, but, forcing himself to gaze fixedly, he decided that these lights were no more than optical illusions or the small sparks that rise in tired and over-strained eyes. His heart was beating like a loud trip-hammer and he pressed one hand against it tightly. Standing so for several seconds he experienced a slowing of his nervous faculties, a sensation of again being master of himself and not the victim of an unreasonable fear that was, perhaps, self-implanted by a too imaginative mind. It was with actual surprise that he felt Walden Slater's sturdy arm about his shoulder urging him forward. Clear-headed now he resumed the laborious toil of the journey.

This is New England, he thought. This is the tired land of forgotten pioneer enterprises. This is the land of machinery and shoe factories and canned goods and ice-skates. It is everything that is material and dispiriting and "up-to-date" and unlovely. It is the land of lean farms and thin mouths, too. It is a land of humming commercial cities, of great businesses, of the New Day. But it is more than this, as well. How if all this glittering commercial civilization is no more than a huge shell, an incrustation of years, beneath which lurk the old pagan madnesses that were corollaries of the Puritan repression? How if the ancient Dionysiac urge did not perish but remained like an ominous monster in a deep cavern biding its time and waiting its day? Suppose that the May Pole of Merry Mount and the Witches' Sabaoths of Salem were to be reborn with disastrous consequences because of their long suppression? Might not the humming wind be saying, "The day is coming! The Black Man is coming! The May Pole of Merry Mount is to be reared again on the site of the factory! The witches and warlocks are to rule! The cities are to be laid waste for this huge shell of civilization is no more than a pasteboard affair and it is only the ancient furies and instincts that count in the long run!" Dreeme permitted his imagination to go to whatever lengths it pleased as he plunged through the forest with Walden Slater. He was fully aware of the fancifulness and impossibility of his thoughts, but they seemed to act as a release-valve for the feelings that boiled within him.

Walden Slater suddenly clutched his wrist in a huge gripping hand. He drew the young doctor to one side, and as he did so Dreeme became aware of the tiny bobbing jewel of light before them, a spark of yellow that disappeared behind trees only to reappear again. The farmer did not slacked his pace but kept on rapidly, but Dreeme noted that there was a tenseness in his walk. The light bobbed before them and they gained on it. It grew in dimensions and before they had traveled many rods Dreeme, by straining his eyes, perceived that it was a lantern carried by a dark figure. He grew aware at the same time that other figures were slipping noiselessly through the trees before them. He even heard the subdued mutter of a voice somewhere to the right of him. Still holding the young doctor by the wrist, Walden Slater made a detour to the left and they circled the bobbing lantern. Keeping their eyes turned toward the lantern they drew abreast of it, passed it, and then Walden Slater uttered an exclarnation as he bumped into a sluggishly moving figure in the shadow of a huge over-arching tree. "At Dagon," said a low voice. An inspiration came to Dreeme. In a calm subdued tone he answered, "For the Master." The figure fell away into the darkness of the trees and as they forged ahead Dreeme could feel Walden Slater's fingers tighten on his wrist in an approving manner. The ground was growing more marshy and their feet sank into the soft soil as they pressed forward. The young doctor suspected that they were reaching that portion of Briony Wood that degenerated into Nigger Swamp and that their objective was not so far before them now. Walden Slater appeared to sense the same thing for his pace quickened automatically. They moved rapidly now, their feet making a distinct sucking sound as they lifted them from the muddy earth. The incline turned downward and as its slope increased the two men found themselves wading through good-sized pools of water and tall scratchy reeds that tore against their legs. Their feet sank deeper in slushy mire and occasionally the sleepy croak of a frog sounded in the darkness beyond them.

Although the journey was harder now, a painful lifting of one foot after the other, Dreeme's weariness seemed to fall from him. He was like an eager hunter hot on the scent with the quarry almost in view. Any moment, he thought to himself, I may turn a corner and see a ring of dim lanterns about a huge stone and know that I am at the end of my journey and that I have seen what no other stranger in this valley has ever seen. The thought exhilarated him. So, too, did the memory that he had passed other mysterious figures in Briony Wood, for it meant that he was not late, that Deborah would be unharmed when he reached Dagon. How she was to be taken away from the group of fanatics who gathered in the swamp he did not know, but he trusted partially to the skill of the silent Walden Slater and partially to the inspiration of the moment. There would be a way, for he would make one. He was pleased to think that there was no fear in his heart now, that his brain had cleared, and that his nerves were steady. He had lost his madness in Briony Wood, and that was good. There was nothing but a clear flame of determination in him.

Walden Slater's mouth was close to his ear.

"We're not quite in the swamp yet," he said. "There's a road. We've got to find it."

He turned and started to walk rapidly at right angles to their previous direction and Dreeme followed him.

There seemed to be nothing but swampy land, and in certain sunken places the slimy water rose to their knees. The drizzling rain continued to spit about them.

"We should have followed the lantern," said Dreeme in a low voice.

"We'll find the road all right," replied Slater.

They trudged for some minutes' through the water and mud and then Walden Slater emitted a low ejaculation of satisfaction. At the same moment Dreeme stumbled upward from the sucking mud to a firm elevation. Turning again in the direction which they had previously followed the two men followed this elevation which appeared to extend in a long narrow ribbon into the darkness before them. It was the road all right, and it ended at Dagon. Some distance ahead of them they could see the bobbing lantern, and looking back Dreeme observed another lantern coming down from the higher ground upon which stood Briony Wood. There were farmers before him and behind them, and the only way in which they might hope to avoid them would mean taking off into the swamp on either side of the narrow road. Walden Slater, as though in answer to an unasked question from Dreeme, said:

"The muck is up to your waist on either side. Don't step off the road."

The trees had thinned out, although a few grotesquely-twisted forms loomed up about them. The eery glow in the sky swept across the long desolate expanse, but it was not bright enough for the young doctor to make out anything with any degree of accuracy. All that he could see were great motionless shapeless shadows, bulks that squatted on the marshy ground like prehistoric beasts. In the day-time they would probably dwindle into nothing more menacing than bushes. But now there was something sinister about them. They sat on huge haunches and watched the two men travel along the narrow lifted road that ran through the flooded land. Dreeme could almost imagine great sleepy eyelids beneath which peered motionless eyes. He was neither frightened nor moved by his thoughts. Instead of excitement the slow blood of determination ran through his cold veins. He lifted his hand and brushed the wet matted hair from his forehead and rubbed his straining eyes. He could feel how set his face was, how the lines had deepened in his cheeks, how tight his jaw was set. He could not make out Walden Slater's face in the deceiving rainy light, but he imagined that it was set like his own, reflecting a determination that would be ruthless and inescapable when the time for action came.

III

This was Nigger Swamp at last. The dark road ran like a pencil line across the level expanse that waved in the rainy wind its monotonous host of thin reeds. These reeds clacked together with a tiny rippling sound that was half-drowned in the sturdier bluster of the lessening gale. Rain still fell in a dispiriting manner, cold, large-dropped, maddening in its relentless evenness. Dreeme felt the rain no longer, for, soaked to the skin and numbed to the bone, the surface of his body had lost all sensation. Even his feet were senseless now. He followed the lurching beat of Walden Slater's boots like a man in a trance. Yet his faculties were alert. Though he experienced no physical sensation he realized that his brain was clearing and capable of swift action. It was like a live intelligence in a dead body. It was this live intelligence that noted, even before the phlegmatic Walden Slater, that the bobbing lantern ahead of them had stopped. The young doctor touched the farmer on the arm.

"Look!" he whispered. "The man ahead has stopped."

Both of them paused in their tracks and observed the stationary light with some unrest. Dreeme glanced behind him and saw that the light which was following them was steadily approaching nearer. He remembered Walden Slater's warning: "The muck is up to your waist on either side."

"What shall we do?" he whispered to Walden Slater, indicating the approaching stranger in their rear. The farmer said nothing but opened his coat a bit and loosened the revolver in his belt. He glanced first at the stationary light before them and then at the approaching light behind them. After that, he spat reflectively into the swamp at his side.

"We don't want to kick up a fuss till we locate Deborah," he said mildly.

Even as he spoke the stationary lantern before them began to return on its tracks, to approach them from the front even as the other lantern approached them from the rear. They were caught between two fires now.

"Perhaps we can hide our faces," whispered Dreeme. "Perhaps we can pass them as we passed those other fellows back in Briony Wood."

"Perhaps," said Walden Slater noncommittally.

"Shall we stand out in the swamp?" asked Dreeme suddenly.

Walden Slater shook his head.

"You'd never pull yourself out of it again," he said.

The light before them returned ten or twelve yards on its own track, and then suddenly disappeared to the right, vanishing completely from sight. Walden Slater grunted.

"They missed the cross path," he said. "It's a lucky thing for us."

He started forward, accelerating his pace as much as the hummocky road would permit, and Dreeme, suddenly relieved from the tenseness that had held him like a coiled steel spring, followed with agility. It was remarkable how refreshed he felt after that brief halt. He even forgot the lantern that was following at his heels, perhaps fifty yards behind him in the rainy gloom, a dancing midge in the deceptive air. The road dipped a bit as they proceeded forward, and soon Dreeme observed low bushes lining it, bushes that rose in height as they stumbled along over the increasing unevenness. They were entering another expanse of wooded territory, this time, without a doubt, the center of the swamp. Trees shot up out of the mist about them and the road assumed the aspect of a funnel that dwindled to nothingness before them. Walden Slater walked very slowly now inspecting the bushes at the right of the road. Soon the misty light vanished behind the climbing shrubbery and trees and the farmer cursed softly to himself.

"Whereabouts did that lantern turn in?" he inquired of the night in general. Dreeme did not attempt an answer, but went down and felt the dark ground, fumbling about for possible footprints.

"You can't find anything that way," said the farmer ungraciously. He blundered along close to the bushes, sometimes stepping through only to catch himself just in time from toppling into the sunken mire from which the soggy growths sprang. It was intensely dark now and they could perceive nothing before them. Dreeme, lifting up his hand a foot from his face, could not make it out. They were in an alley of small trees and bushes that met above them.

"The lantern came back from here," muttered Walden Slater. "I'll swear to that."

He turned on his heel and retraced his steps.

"Look!" whispered Dreeme.

The lantern that had been following them was now less than thirty yards before them. It approached slowly, its feeble spark illuminating a small circle of milky haze. Who held it or how many were in the party could not be made out. Walden Slater stopped by the side of the path and Dreeme paused beside him. The lantern approached deliberately at such a speed as to indicate that the person carrying it was walking very slowly. The stranger, or strangers, were evidently studying the right side of the road even as Walden Slater and Dreeme had studied it, searching for an ingress into the swamp, for a concealed road that would take them off at an angle from this main path.

"If they miss the road they won't miss us," murmured Dreeme.

The farmer said nothing but waited mutely for what might happen. When the lantern was within ten yards of them it paused for an instant and then disappeared. Walden Slater crept forward slowly. Dreeme followed close at his heels. Reaching the spot where the lantern had disappeared the farmer went over and fumbled at the ground. The charred trunk of a tree met his hand. He grunted and stepped by it, almost sliding as he struck a sharp incline, and then caught his balance on a narrow ribbon of hard soil. The lantern had disappeared entirely, but the farmer and Dreeme, stepping tentatively, discovered that the tiny footpath they were now on curved steadily. They walked very silently now, stepping as gently as they could along the path, a path covered with the soaked dead leaves of many seasons. Their instincts told them that they were reaching the end of their journey, that the time would soon come for any action that they might plan. Dreeme felt a momentary inclination to ask the farmer what he intended to do, but he repressed it, feeling that Slater desired silence now. Like two Indians they stole forward through the bushes and small trees, disturbing only an occasional frog that croaked dismally from the swamp about them. A musty smell of rotting vegetation was in their nostrils, of green-scummed water disturbed by violent rains, of disintegrating animal life.

After some minutes walk the underbrush thinned sufficiently to permit the pale reflection of the cloudy sky to reach them. It had practically stopped raining, the unceasing drizzle dwindling into no more than an occasional flutter of large cold drops that dashed against their faces. The few trees dripped disconsolately, however, and whenever the uneven road caused them to lurch against a bush they were covered by a tiny unpleasant downfall. Some distance ahead of them they caught unfrequent glimpses of the tiny lantern, glimpses that immediately winked out as the road turned and followed the narrow ribbon of raised territory. Something hard and cold cut against Dreeme's naked foot and he bent over and picked it up. Holding it up to the faint light he could dimly make it out. A surprised and agitated exclamation broke from him, and he turned to Walden Slater who had paused.

"Look," he said, handing the object to the farmer.

Walden Slater turned it over slowly in his large dripping hand. His long upper lip drew downward as he recognized it and handed it back without a word to Dreeme. The young doctor stared at it again. It was a brooch. A brooch upon which was the finely-cut cameo of a goat's head. Deborah's brooch. The brooch he had seen hanging on her bosom that evening before when they had walked through the quiet street of Marlborough and had told each other so much. She had passed along ahead of them, then, and was already at the place called Dagon. There could be no time to lose now. Walden Slater, who had not said a word, was walking along as rapidly as he could on the narrow uncertain road. Dreeme, close at his heels and sometimes abreast with him when the road permitted, kept pace with the farmer.

They were back among trees again. The young doctor had never realized the extent of Nigger Swamp before. He had always pictured it as a small circumscribed area of loathsome water and rotting bushes but now he understood that it covered a vast expanse of territory. It was either very large or the deceptive path they followed wound round and round it in a spiral. Perhaps they had circled Dagon. Perhaps the path was a maze that took the ignorant wanderer round and round until, by some lucky chance, the riddle was solved and he stood at the heart. As Dreeme labored onward his imagination drew into the dark void about them the first descendants of the fugitive Salem witches who had settled in this part of the world. He pictured to himself a breed of silent, mad-eyed men in steeple-crowned hats and baggy knee-breeches and homespun stockings and square-toed buckled shoes lurching along this immemorial road. On their shoulders they bore heavy bell-mouthed muskets and stands upon which to rest these muskets when they fired at enemies. Powder horns swung from their shoulders and bags of round bullets. There were women, too, sharp-faced, hawk-nosed women in white caps and dull gray dresses, hurrying along and laughing hysterically at the storm for there was no secrecy in those days, no reasons for quietude in the unspoilt wilderness, no one to watch them except the lean Indians in their breech-clouts of deer-skin, their proud fierce faces crowned by the scalp-lock and the turkey-feather peering from behind the trees in superstitious wonder. The startled deer crashed through the underbrush and the brown bears lumbered away from the flares of the torches and the old-fashioned lanterns. All this had died away, had been erased by Time, had vanished into the nothingness of dead and unwritten history.

Then, decades and decades and decades later, Uriah Carrier, by the maps in his black book, had found the lost place called Dagon and he had worked on the slumbering instincts of the people about him, appealing to the madness that slept in their subconscious memories, bringing them again to the secret stone and the place where the crumbled bones rested. He had probably promised them dominion over their days, the power of exerting their wills and destroying their enemies, the joys of the liberation of their darkest instincts. It sounded impossible enough on the face of it, like some insane fairytale that a sick imagination might bring forth, and yet it must have been a fact for here he was, a sane doctor in the twentieth century, stumbling through the rotting vegetation of an untraveled swamp in search of a madman and the fanatical minds he had released from the kindly bondage of reason. It was like a nightmare.

Walden Slater halted abruptly. The road had grown somewhat wider now and they had been walking abreast. About them the trees rose to an imposing stature and the ground to right and left of them seemed higher and firmer than that through which they had toiled for the last half-hour. Dreeme imagined that they had reached a sort of island in the middle of the swamp and his conviction was intensified when, after peering right and left, before him and behind, Walden Slater stepped from the road and began to thread a slow circuitous advance through the trees. The ground as he stepped on it seemed softer than safety might desire but the young doctor followed with alacrity. His bare feet sank to the ankles in the soft ooze but following Walden Slater's example and stepping close to the trunks of the trees he discovered that the walking was not so difficult after all. They appeared to be in a tall woodland now where the thin trees rose straight out of a soggy soil, a soil in which the rotting stumps of lightning-blasted growths and scattered boulders cluttered up and made difficult any swift passage. The boulders seemed unusual and Dreeme wondered about them. They possibly were evidence of a strata of rock, the slice of some prehistoric glacier, that thrust upward out of the marshy soil here. Walden Slater walked warily, taking care to step on no dead branches or to crash through none of the small undergrowths that sprang up between the slender trees. Dreeme followed suit.

They had walked through this woodland for a few minutes only before the young doctor observed a faint glow among the trees that faced them. He instinctively hastened his pace a little and soon was several feet in front of Walden Slater. The farmer plodded along doggedly exhibiting no excitement or unrest. Dreeme, clutching Deborah's brooch in his hand, was about to break into a stumbling run when the wiry hand of the farmer jerked his shoulder back. A trifle angry but aware of the wisdom of the rebuke the young doctor adjusted his pace to the farmer's steady progression and they moved forward toward the faint glow, a glow that brightened perceptibly as they neared it. The rain had stopped altogether, even the large infrequent drops disappearing into the mist of the night. In those few minutes while Dreeme crept forward beside the farmer a dozen and one thoughts flashed through his mind, plans of rescue, schemes of attack, possibilities of tactics to be employed. Would they rush into the group of farmers, and, while Walden Slater held them back with the menace of his revolver, would he snatch up Deborah and make away with her along the exhausting road which he had been traveling for nearly an hour? What could they hope to do against a dozen or more men who were mad? He wanted to ask Walden Slater what he thought but the farmer was so evidently bent on silence that he did not venture a word. The glow was quite bright now and it seemed to come upward from the earth, from a hollow beyond them that was masked by crowded tree-trunks. There were many lanterns in that hollow and there were many men. Deborah was there, too. Perhaps at this very moment she was a part of the unclean ceremonies that were taking place. It seemed an eternity to the young doctor while they crept slowly and silently through the last ring of trees, stepping gingerly over the protruding boulders and rotting branches and mouldering stumps. Walden Slater now carried his revolver in his hand. Leaving the last of the trees behind them and facing the yellow glow of the invisible light that formed a strange fan of color against the milky atmosphere they crept up an inclined bank toward a ring of low intertangled bushes. The subdued hum of voices reached their strained ears. Walden Slater carefully pushed aside one of the branches of the bushes against which they now rested and cautiously thrust his face forward. For a second he looked downward. Then he drew back and putting his mouth very close to Dreeme's ear said: "This is the place called Dagon."

The young doctor, his blood beating furiously, crept up to the bush, drew the branch aside, thrust his face forward, and looked downward.

Chapter Ten

I

He stared into a hollow that was filled with shifting forms, moving figures that were slices of darkness before the lanterns. Faces passed and repassed before his curious gaze, paused, bent forward, turned, leaned toward one another, disappeared, and it was some minutes before he could make them out, could recognize them as human faces that he had once viewed vacantly in the quiet lanes of Marlborough. He had not expected so much light, so much action. As his eyes adjusted themselves to the scene before them he began to perceive the spectacle as a whole, almost as a painting whose component parts might be observed and then relegated to their proper order. He sensed Walden Slater creeping into the bush beside him but he made no gesture of comprehension, merely shifting his position a trifle so that the farmer, too, might see what was going on in the hollow. For his own part, he was intent on the spectacle before him, watching eagerly for the one face of all faces and subconsciously deliberating in his mind what he should do when he did see that face. The hollow was large and level and the ground upon which these people walked was dark and firm. There was no grass, no growths of any sort. It stretched like a black carpet to the ring of bushes that hemmed it on all sides. It was a natural amphitheater, an arena formed by chance. Circling this expanse of black soil was a series of lanterns, perhaps twenty of them, placed at regular intervals and lighting up the scene as though it were a stage and they were footlights. The beams of yellow glowed upward, striking the lower portions of faces and distorting them. Chins and nostrils and the undersides of cheek bones were crazily illuminated in this unnatural light. In the center of the hollow loomed a large flat-topped rock, perhaps five feet high. It was black stone glittering now with moisture, with the rain that had fallen so steadily on it all through the day and night. There was something ominous about this stone, something unclean, and the young doctor studied it with intense loathing. Its slimy black sides were like the skin of some great horrid toad, smooth yet studded with offensive warts that caught the glow of the lanterns and flung them back again to the misty night. Dreeme wondered if it were true that crumbling bones were buried in the dark soil beneath this rock which seemed so immovable, so placed there by time in the center of this secret amphitheater. The rock appeared as old as the ages. It seemed riven immutably into the earth. Yet it was unmistakably the Devil Stone and from its moist toad-like surface the Black Man had preached his blasphemous sermons in times past, had conducted the orgiastic liturgies of the Witches' Sabaoth and the Esbat. There was no one near the stone now. It stood malevolently, a shunned phenomenon in the hollow. "Rock of Ages." Yes, this was the Rock that George Burroughs meant when he hummed monotonously the old church tune.

Dreeme's eyes drifted over the faces that moved about in the hollow. There were, perhaps, twenty people present, all men. The low hum of their subdued voices reached him distinctly. They walked about slowly, clutching their rain-coats closely to their tall bodies, their heavy boots falling heavily on the dark soil. Something feverish and repressed in their movements injected a tense note into the assemblage. They seemed uncertain of themselves, a little hysteric and desperately straining to conceal the hysteria that quickened their blood and plucked at their nerves. There was doubt here, a doubt that sickly denied itself. Sober faces gazed blankly at one another and sunken fanatical eyes glittered in the lantern glow like wet beetles. The young doctor observed one tall figure that walked round and round just within the circle of lanterns ceaselessly, pausing before no one but moved apparently by an interior restlessness that would not permit him to stop. As the man passed a short distance from where the young doctor lay hidden he recognized him as Bidwell, the farmer whose land adjoined Westcott's toward the Saccarac River. Bidwell's mouth was moving steadily as though he were talking rapidly to himself. And now as Dreeme's eyes became accustomed to the scene he recognized more faces. There was Lacy, the post-master and proprietor of the general store, a stork-like man with a carbuncular nose, and Winship, one of the selectmen, stout, worried-looking, and somewhat at a loss, and Titubit, the dark hawk-nosed farmer who was supposed to have Indian blood in his veins, and Corey, the tanned white-haired owner of Corey's Acres on the lower road. Dreeme had attended all of these men at some time or other for minor ailments and he viewed them now with a disbelieving wonder, half-suspecting that any minute the whole scene would vanish in thin air and he would wake up in bed sweating from a nightmare. Yet here they were, and others whose faces he dimly recognized but whose names he could not place, strolling nervously about the dark hollow, waiting restlessly and suspiciously for some evil thing to happen, stirred by some daemon of hereditary madness that had been wakened in their blood and brains after sleeping for years. Dreeme crouched lower in the bushes and watched them attentively. His few garments were saturated with water and the cold wind blew across his back yet his pulses were beating fast enough and the warmth of excitement shuddered along his drenched flesh. Beside him he could feel the heavy shoulders of Walden Slater.

It was all a psychological riddle, something to be unravelled at leisure and explained after the event. Some power had frightened these men out of their taciturn ruts of living into the mockery of an ancient superstition. A legend had come down with uncommon vividness through the centuries and the will of a madman had resurrected it to terrible life. Old impulses, too powerful to resist, had been set free and they were following these impulses suspiciously yet absolutely. Dreeme studied the face of Corey and wondered. White-haired, almost saintly-looking, the farmer walked slowly about in low conversation with Lacy who lifted his round uneven knob of a nose like a wolf about to howl at the moon. The fever was growing on these men now and their movements became faster and jerkier. They stared about them expectantly and as they stared their hands quivered. The yellow lanterns flung fantastic blossoms of light into the bushes, colored blossoms that glowed on the wet branches.

Dreeme caught his breath suddenly. Silently, almost stealthily, Jeffrey Westcott had appeared from behind the black stone. He stood observing the score of men with expressionless dark eyes, watching their movements as they shifted to and fro, saying nothing, waiting for them to see him. Immediately the group approached him, standing within a few feet of the Devil Stone. They gathered silently, standing in a half-circle, their backs to Dreeme and Walden Slater. Westcott observed them coldly and when they had achieved their half-circle and were motionless he climbed to the top of the black slimy stone. Standing so, five feet in the air, Dreeme could see him perfectly, a stocky figure garmented entirely in black, his cloven head bowed slightly, the yellow glow from the lanterns catching the lower part of his face—the blue shaven chin and heavy cheekbones. In his hands he held a square black book which he lifted slowly. The men before him seemed to sigh and sway back. Westcott held this book high in the air for a full minute. Then he looked up into the misty night-air intently and cried in a suppressed hoarse voice:

"Asmodeus! Asmodeus!"

The men stood fixedly, their heads thrust slightly forward as though they were listening. After an instant's silence Westcott said:

"He stands at Dagon. He enters into me."

A shudder shook his heavy frame and the black book slipped from his hand, falling to the surface of the stone with a dull slap.

Dreeme, listening as intently as the men, heard nothing but the infrequent spatter of rain-drops as the tree-tops swayed and the wind that shook them, a husky sighing wind that sounded like the hoarse breathing of a giant. He wanted to shout, "You fool! There is nothing to hear but night sounds!" The aspect of Jeffrey Westcott fascinated him, however. The farmer's face was lighted with an evil smile, his eyes glittered and danced in the lantern-light, and his heavy hands were clasped before him. A tenseness held his bulky body and he seemed to grow with this tenseness, to enlarge until Dreeme could not say whether he were six feet high or twelve. It was an illusion but an illusion so well maintained that the young doctor automatically understood how easily Westcott could sway these superstitious farmers who stood before him, a strained expectancy on their weather-beaten faces, their hands clenched, their bodies visibly quivering. It was an evil transfiguration wrought inwardly. Nothing but the most dynamic belief in one's self, in one's own powers, could cause it. The farmer was in a rapt state now, in a moving and speaking trance. He lifted his hands up to the night. In the same suppressed hoarse voice he cried:

"Enter in to us, Asmodeus! Enter in to your heritage! Were we not sold to you by the bond of blood by Salem Village two hundred and thirty years ago? In the deep forest you accepted us and made a pact with us. We forsook all other gods but you for you were the eternal will of man. Though we have slept for generations the ancient pact still holds. Under this rock lies the testimonial of the bones. The bones cry out to you, Asmodeus. We cry out to you."

A murmur like a sigh swept through the cluster of attentive men.

"By the aching of the bones, we call upon your strength," cried Westcott.

"By the aching of the bones, we call upon your strength," murmured the men.

"By the secret head of the Sacred Goat, we call upon your strength," the farmer cried again.

"By the secret head of the Sacred Goat, we call upon your strength," repeated the men.

The litany went on.

"By the Black Book that our fathers owned we call upon your strength."

"By the Black Book that our fathers owned we call upon your strength."

"By the Hidden Face in the rock we call upon your strength."

"By the Hidden Face in the rock we call upon your strength."

"By the Cloven Hoof that walks in the darkness we call upon your strength."

"By the Cloven Hoof that walks in the darkness we call upon your strength."

"By the Lost Road that our fathers followed we call upon your strength."

"By the Lost Road that our fathers followed we call upon your strength."

"O Asmodeus, give me my purpose."

"O Asmodeus, give me my purpose."

Beads of perspiration stood out on Jeffrey Westcott's forehead. His body shook violently. He cried loudly:

"Asmodeus! Janicot!"

A thin white froth appeared on his lips and his face writhed. The farmers before him were swaying from side to side excitedly and suddenly one of them, little more than a boy, screamed and fell upon the wet ground, his talon-like hands clutching at the black soil.

"Aie! Aie!" shouted the boy, his white face tossing from side to side and his eyes tightly closed. Westcott leaped from the rock and knelt for a moment by the boy. Then he lifted him up and bore him to the great stone, placing him beside the black book. The farmers surged forward, some of them moaning, all of them shaking as though in an intense ague. Their hands were outstretched and quivering.

Dreeme watched the ceremony with amazement, noting that Westcott by the power of his will, apparently, had lashed these people into a mystical fury that was close to the trance-state. They would believe whatever he had to say implicitly now for their individualities were lost and they were a mingled mob madness. The swiftness of the whole proceeding was the surprising part of it to the young doctor. Then he realized that these men had gathered here for some time, that an overpowering realization of helplessness inborn in their blood weakened their powers of resistance, and that Westcott's powerful personality had sapped their independence and reason long before this. They were a poisoned and hysterical breed.

Westcott stood beside the possessed boy, his hand upon the heaving chest of the victim. He stared about the half circle with glittering eyes, his yellow teeth—yellow as the flames of the lanterns—bared in a smile.

"He sleeps," he said, indicating the boy, "he sleeps in the arms of the Master. Dagon is filled with the Master. The ground cries out and the bones tremble."

Even as he spoke the scene darkened and a gust of wind blew so heavily that the lantern-flames behind their heavy glass protectors slanted sideways. It was like the descent of a sudden cloud, an abrupt eclipse in answer to Westcott's solemn speech. For an instant it paralyzed the watching doctor and trembling chills, icy-cold, ran up and down his spine. He felt the surge of something huge and shapeless and black and irremediably evil, a presence that was beyond description and vision filling the hollow. A soft hand seemed to tap tentatively at his face and then, without warning, sharp talons clutched at the back of his neck. For an instant he dared not move. He fought fiercely with an intense desire to scream. Then, summoning every iota of his will power, he cautiously raised his hand and thrust back the thorny branch of the bush that the gust of wind had blown against his neck. A flood of relief poured through his tired wet body and as he felt the released blood throbbing through his arteries the gust of wind died away and the lantern-flames lifted their flattened spears of yellow. He thought to himself how easily the imagination could drive the nerves before it in riotous débacle. It was fear that was the great enemy, fear of the unknown, fear of the stronger will, fear of the old wife's tales that thousands of years of self-preservation against mysterious phenomena had planted in the feeble mortal body. There was no safety in life except by the deliberate massacre of one's fears. Well, he would throttle these unworthy spasms and surmount the horror of these cruel tricks. He fastened his entire intelligence again upon the scene before him.

The inanimate boy on the Devil's Stone had ceased to breathe frantically. His bosom no longer rose and fell furiously. Instead of this he seemed to be quietly sleeping. Westcott, placing his arm beneath the boy's head, raised the body to a sitting posture and the pale unconscious face with its closed eyes gazed out blindly upon the assembled farmers. For an instant Westcott's hand rested lightly upon the boy's white forehead. Then he said:

"Are you one with the Name?"

"With the Name," answered the boy. His voice was high and clear.

"Is the Master with you?" went on Westcott.

"With me," responded the boy.

"Is he saying things?" proceeded the farmer.

"Saying things," repeated the boy.

The farmers listened avidly although they still swayed slowly from side to side and now and then one of them would whimper softly as though he were in pain.

"What do you see?" inquired Westcott. His own eyes were shut and he appeared to be undergoing a fierce mental reaction.

"See," said the boy.

There was a pause while the wind soughed softly in the trees and bushes and the infrequent spatter of great rain drops fell in the shadows.

The boy's mouth opened and closed speechlessly. He half raised one arm. His throat throbbed. Then, in the same clear tone in which he had spoken throughout, he said:

"The bones move together. The dust assembles. I see a skeleton. Flesh comes out of darkness like an army of white ants and clusters upon the bones. A body lies beneath the rock. It opens its eyes and lifts its hands. It is the body that is speaking to me."

He paused. The farmers waited expectantly. The boy's lips moved again. This time the startling voice of a deep-chested man issued from his mouth. It was like a great voice calling from a tomb and it struck upon Dreeme's ears with dismay.

"At Dagon we set the Rock for our children's children's children. We marched through deep trees and the feathered men watched our fires from the darkness beyond the rings of light. We caroused and danced through the virgin land and the Master walked before us with a smiling face. We raised our rooftrees in the valley without doors and our fires went up to an alien sky. When the moon walked on the farthest hills we traveled the long path to the Rock and danced before the Master. We beat upon cymbals and drums. We whistled and cried lewd words to the naked women who laughed in the bushes. We felt the fever of life in our veins and knew that it was well with us. We were unhumbled and proud and possessors of time. We devoured our enemies for the Master's will was our will. We set no bounds to life for all life was within our bounds. We bowed only to one law and that was the law of the Master and though the pale faced priests harried us we existed beyond them in a free land of the Master's conceiving. The Master took us up to the mountain top and showed us the riches of the world and the cities of the plain and we said 'yes' to him and all those things became our own. Our farms prospered in the valley without doors and the rain came and we saw that it was well with us. And we knew the Master to be the living god of the free will, the voice that spoke in the darkness to us and said, 'do so and so,' and we did these things and we prospered and lived long years and the sun shone upon us."

The great voice died away and the boy fell back limply upon the stone, his head resting upon the black book. Westcott lifted him quickly and bore him to a side of the circle where he placed him upon the wet ground. The farmers stood motionless now. They were like figures in a trance. They made no gestures as Westcott walked slowly back to the rock and mounted to it. His dark eyes swept over the gathering and from where Dreeme lay he thought that he could see the thin ghost of a smile flit across the farmer's determined mouth.

"You have heard," he said. "You have heard the voice from the bones, the voice of your ancestor, speaking. You have heard how good life was when the children of the Master first came into this valley. And how have you fallen away from that high estate! How have you lost that greatness when you walked like the sons of the morning! The years have come between you and the Master and you have fallen away from that source of all power. You bend weary backs over meager farms and live from hand to mouth and your heritage is just beyond you in the shadow of Time. You have but to reach out your hands and take it. Instead of this, you deny the impulses that are in your blood and avoid the final gestures that would liberate you from the entangling bonds of fear and superstition and false gods. There is no other god but the Master! He, alone, exists and he, alone, is the tower of your strength. The Master sums up all things in himself. He is the will, the invulnerable will, the will to power, the will to happiness, the will to self-realization. It is only by symbols and liturgies and ceremonies that you may induce the Master to enter into you. I bring the Master to you. I bring the key to the door, the lantern to the darkness, the will to the deed. I am the Black Man. I am the prophet possessed by the Master. I do not bring you a god that you may see, a god that you may touch. I bring you an essence, an invulnerable essence that speaks through the mouths of living people, that rises in trances, that permeates time, that joins the dead with the living, that is called evil but is yet beyond evil, a god that is strength and food and determination and skill and craft and understanding and self-realization and power. This is the god I bring you and because he has no other name you may call him what you will, Asmodeus, Janicot, Beelzebub, Satan, Lucifer, any name that stands for the opposite of the cold power that destroys the eternal will within you. He is a jealous god and he will endure no other rivals. He speaks in thunder and he walks upon the mountaintops by night. His face is hidden in darkness and his hands hover over the cities of the plain. The brightness of his face is turned only to the adept. If you desire that complete emancipation from obligations and hardships and the domination of alien things you will turn whole-heartedly to him. Your fathers did it before you and they lived in a Paradisal valley and fulfilled themselves completely. But you must cleanse yourselves of old weaknesses if you would be like your fathers. The will is buried in you but you must excavate it, must dig it out of the dross of many days and many years. To do this you must pass through rituals and ceremonies, must give yourselves wholeheartedly to the Master. Then, and not till then, will you feel the dark flower growing in you, the intense inward ecstasy that lifts you through deliriums to that plane where the Master walks and controls the events of the ages. The rituals are but the outward symbols of the interior miracles. The flesh is a weak and uncertain thing and it must be driven upward into the mystical regions by visible signs and ceremonies. It is for this that I have called you here, calling each one by the sign of the Goat's Head which your father used before you, that we may establish, or rather renew, the coven of Marlborough, the coven that was driven from Salem Village in 1692 and which has slept with all its symbols beneath this rock for so many years."

He paused and gazed about him. A few muttered words passed between the farmers, who, while Westcott was talking so persuasively, had recovered in great part from their emotional excitement. Dreeme, from his secret place of vantage, had listened with a reluctant admiration. He could understand that, given the blood impulses of these men and the dark shadow of ancestral urges and one-sided fanaticism, the speech just delivered would seem reasonable and convincing. This was what they had been fighting against half-heartedly for so many decades. The young doctor instinctively thought of all the crazy cults that permeated American life, the free love colonies, the Holy Rollers, the theosophical circles, the Rosicrucians, the Spiritualists, the esoteric societies, and he understood how easy it was to lead the secret wish into the deed. Westcott controlled these men now and he could do with them what he willed. They were ripe for a fanatical outbreak. As the young doctor observed the farmers he noted that there was no opposition whatsoever, no desire to question the truth of what Westcott was saying, no antagonistic rationalism. Even the white-haired Corey seemed to grow in stature to the farmer's words, to take into himself, as it were, the essence of will of which Westcott spoke. As for the dominating farmer he stood upon the Devil Stone with sparkling eyes, an image of self-contained power, gazing down at the men before him. Bidwell's nasal voice rose in the stillness.

"What must we do?" he asked.

Westcott shut his eyes. He appeared to be communing with invisible powers. Then he picked up the black book and held it against his breast. He said:

"We must throw all our strength into a sacrifice. Into this sacrifice we must wish all our weaknesses and when the ceremony is accomplished we shall be cleansed and bound together by an awful and secret knowledge."

He paused and glanced about him as the men gazed fearfully at one another. Then he said:

"We must abolish fear. We must destroy the conscience. We may only do this by a terrible sacrifice."

He shut his eyes and turned his face upward to the night.

"Asmodeus!" he cried. "Is this well?"

Suddenly from the recumbent body of the boy which lay near the circle of lanterns came the deep voice that they had heard before.

"A sacrifice!" he cried. "A sacrifice!"

At the same instant the bushes opposite Dreeme's haven of concealment parted and the Reverend George Burroughs, tall, sallow, serious, stepped into the light of the lanterns. He walked slowly toward the rock, his eyes expressionless wells of darkness. Dreeme's pulses beat faster at the sight of him for he understood that the presence of the preacher meant also the presence of Deborah. Beside him he felt Walden Slater cautiously move. The farmer seemed to be extricating something from beneath his coat. Burroughs paused by the rock, his long yellow hand resting lightly on the toad-like surface. He gazed about him calmly. Dreeme, as far away as he was, could sense the impalpable atmosphere of malevolence that emanated from the preacher. It was a still icy restrained power confident of itself and supremely indifferent. For the first time the young doctor saw the preacher as he was, a creature of vindictive strength and sly calculation, a quiet creeping madness that permeated Marlborough. If Jeffrey Westcott was the self-appointed god of this impossible fanaticism then George Burroughs was the high priest, the militant Satanist, the tactician who hid behind a veil of holiness. The man's sallow horse-like countenance dominated the assembly although he had not spoken a word. Even the repressed hysteria of Jeffrey Westcott faded before this still horrible strength that poised lightly by the Devil's Stone and with a single glance read the minds of the perturbed and chaotic farmers before him. Dreeme crouched lower in his place of concealment. Beside him he could feel the tense form of Walden Slater coiled like a heavy steel spring, ready to dart forth at the slightest gesture. There was strength in Walden Slater and it seemed to seep mercifully into the cold body of the young doctor. Burroughs opened his wide mouth and his neighing voice broke the shifting silence. He said:

"In the beginning there was nothing. But the Will moved on the face of the flickering gases and the Will established the earth and the vegetation on the face of the earth and the beasts and men who walked upon the face of the earth. And there were two gods. And one was the god of that weakness called good and the other was the god of that strength called evil. But the god of goodness was an invisible god who lived in a mist. The god of evil made the world and all the things that are in the world. He fashioned all our pleasures and placed the seed of his eternal Will within us. It is that god who calls us to the place called Dagon that we may worship him and enter into our heritage."

He paused and stared before him. For an instant Dreeme thought that the piercing black eyes of the preacher threaded the heavy leaves of the bush behind which the young doctor lay and he tightened his muscles, preparing to spring forward at the first word. Burroughs made no gesture, however. His eyes reverted to the farmers before him. He was patently searching for new words, for further demonstration of his Manichean doctrine of an evil god controlling an evil world. Apparently he found the words for his neighing voice rose again in the stillness.

"We have been chosen out of all the people in this land for we are the children of our fathers. I am the child of my fathers and if you will read the withered records you will find that my name is not unknown among the disciples who followed the Master. I have lived and died many times. I have walked through many centuries. I have listened to the Voice in many lands and the Voice has told me many things. I carry the wisdom of the decades within me. I have told you these things before, in your houses, in the fields, in the dark places of the forest. You have listened to me. You are here. To-gether we shall discipline our wills until they become a part of the major Will that controls all things. We shall persecute our enemies in the darkness. We shall achieve our ends, our desires, through the malefic intensity of our wills. We shall dance at the full of the moon and sink into divine trances where we shall discover all things. The Past and the Future will become like open books to us. To reach this desirable plane we must murder the pale sick consciences, inheritances of the god of mist, that murmur weakly within us. We shall cleanse ourselves by charms and sacrifices."

His voice changed to a deeper tone and he gazed significantly at the absorbed farmers.

"The one sin in our decalogue is weakness," he said. "There was a man amongst us who was weak. He was shaken by qualms. Through his stupid brain crept the faint messages of conscience. He listened to a woman and became her willing tool. He drew into our secret circle a stranger, an obtuse fool from the outer world whose curiosity was like that of a gossiping woman. What became of that man?"

He glanced savagely about him.

"The will of the Master came into me," he cried, "and I struck him down by the river. With my own hands I drove the pegs into the eyes that had seen too much!"

Dreeme heard Walden Slater's suddenly indrawn breath.

"And the obtuse fool!" neighed Burroughs. "What about the obtuse fool?"

"Let him leave the valley," said Jeffrey Westcott suddenly. "Let him leave the valley and forget us."

"Too late!" cried Burroughs, still facing the farmers and paying no attention to Westcott. "He must not leave the valley. He must be buried in the valley."

Dreeme's mouth was a sharply drawn line. They would have to catch their bird first.

"The will of the Master is ruthless," declared the preacher, stretching out a long skinny hand toward the silent group of farmers. The men mumbled and muttered among themselves. Dreeme could see that they were still crazed, that they were like men in a trance half-knowing what they were doing but without the power of asserting themselves. Both Westcott and Burroughs had these victims semi-mesmerized. They had ceased to be rational men but were fanatics oblivious of consequences and moved by a common spirit.

The insensible boy lying near the circle of lanterns moaned. He lifted a hand weakly and it fell with a wet thud to the dark trampled soil.

"Sacrifice!" he cried. "Sacrifice!"

The glittering-eyed farmers surged about the rock. They lifted up their hands to the night and bayed like lost hounds. Bidwell began to shake rapidly and then to perform an awkward dance before the Devil Stone. His eyes were closed. Suddenly Lacy lifted his snout up and laughed, a long high-pitched mad laugh that sounded like a scream. The white-haired Corey was clapping his hands together rhythmically. Neither Westcott nor Burroughs moved. They stood by the rock watching the insane farmers and once Dreeme thought he caught a significant glance that passed between the two men. It was impossible to tell how sincere these two leaders were, how much faith they placed in the crazy doctrine they enunciated. Dreeme was certain that Westcott was driven by his theory of the omnipotent will, that it had unhinged him, that one half of his brain was diseased, but Burroughs was different. He might just be a great charlatan, a born criminal who saw a way of controlling the community by urging it into crime. Ostensibly he was a minister of the gospel but inwardly he was a ferocious beast, a furious figure all the more to be feared because of his saintly mask so well worn in public. There was a blood-lust in him but whether or not this blood-lust was propped up by the knowledge that he was a direct descendant of the Salem witches was a mystery. Perhaps one would never know. As Dreeme watched the swaying madness of the farmers he recalled how, for two years, he had sat at a common table with the Reverend George Burroughs and given him no more attention than he had the back of the chair against which he had leaned. It was amazing, something that either gave proof of the preacher's skill at self-concealment or his own stupidity as an observer. However, it was too late now to wonder at these things or to berate one's self for failing to read character as it loomed before one's nose. As Dreeme watched the gyrations of the farmers his glance traveled beyond them to the line of bushes opposite him, drawn, as it were, by some invisible power and there, hanging bodiless on the wet green leaves, he saw the white face of Martha Westcott peering into the circle. He was not surprised to see her, indeed, he had expected her to put in an appearance sooner or later. Just what her status was among these men, however, he could not say. He did not believe that either Westcott or Burroughs trusted her too far or permitted her to go any great distance beyond their scrutiny. Her appearance seemed to be a signal for Burroughs walked rapidly toward her and disappeared into the bushes with her. Dreeme's attention now concentrated upon that spot in the bushes for he was sure that behind it was the woman he loved, the woman for whom he would fight until the last drop of blood in his body had been spilled. The farmers, too, were watching this spot in the bushes through which Burroughs had disappeared. But they were watching with a mad laughing expectancy, their tanned hands stretched out, their faces twisted and their eyes glittering.

The bushes parted and Martha Westcott walked through them very slowly. Her eyes were shut and she seemed to be in a trance. Holding her arms straight before her she held in her hands a long thin-bladed knife. Gazing neither to right nor left she proceeded straight to the Devil Stone and stood by it holding the knife out-stretched. Jeffrey Westcott took the shining blade from her and placed it upon the rock. An awful silence had fallen upon the hollow. The rain-drops had ceased and even the wind, that had soughed so hoarsely through the leaves, had died away. The farmers stood like wax-figures, their faces frozen into twisted smiles, their arms stiffly outheld. Dreeme felt the flesh crawling upon his body. He stared fixedly at Martha Westcott, noting how like some strange priestess she stood in her long black garment, her white insensitive face an oval of clear luster in the light of the lanterns, her heavy eyelids partially lowered over the great wide eyes, her archaic mouth a mystic hieroglyph. She was like a being from another world, a spectre from some pagan land. Though her smooth white shoulder was garmented in black he could sense the blue goat's head burning upon it, shining through the close fabric, the goat's head that made her one with these maniacs who gathered in the darkness of Nigger Swamp. Conflicting thoughts rushed through the young doctor's head. This woman had desired him. This evil goddess had come to him in the middle of the night and she had shaken his will. If they were both in another world perhaps . . . He swiftly put the thought from him. No! No! He must not weaken. He must not think of her in any way except as an ominous reality that would steal his soul from him.

The bushes parted again and Burroughs strode forward swiftly carrying in his arms a limp form. Dreeme recognized the preacher's burden as soon as he appeared with it and sprang up from the ground. It was Deborah. She hung limply from the long black arm of Burroughs, like some fragile white bird that had been shot down but not killed. Even as Dreeme sprang to his feet Walden Slater's resistless arm, the muscular arm of a giant, dragged him down again and held him in the shadow of the bush with a clutch like iron. "Wait!" the farmer whispered. "Wait!" Burroughs advanced rapidly to the Devil Stone and laid Deborah's body upon it. The head of the girl fell sideways and Dreeme could see her thin face and the blue circles of her closed eyes. Her bosom was rising softly and regularly. She appeared to be in a calm sleep. Burroughs, his black eyes fixed on the recumbent figure of the girl, reached for the long knife and took it up. He climbed slowly to the top of the Devil Stone and stood towering above the assemblage. He opened his mouth to speak. He raised the knife. It glittered wanly in the light of the flickering lanterns.

"Asmo . . ." he began.

A thunderous report over Dreeme's head pitched him forward. In the single instant when he sprang down the bank he saw the preacher's eyes wide with amazement and the dark gush of blood out of his neck. Then the Reverend George Burroughs fell forward as a log falls, the knife clattering from his hand upon the Devil Stone, and landed with a heavy thud upon the dark soil. His skull crashed against an iron lantern with the sound of a bursting cocoanut. Dreeme, already in the circle, leaped over the body and rushed toward the rock. Behind him he heard Walden Slater kicking the lanterns over as he stumbled forward, the smoking revolver in his hand. The amazed farmers had scattered in all directions and as Dreeme gathered Deborah up in his arms he caught a moment's glimpse of Westcott, the black book clutched to his breast, darting through the bushes. The farmer was heading straight into Nigger Swamp. All of this was observed automatically for the young doctor's sole concern was for the girl who had lain so helplessly upon the Devil Stone. As he staggered along with her he gazed anxiously into her face and listened to her breathing. She stirred a trifle and moaned and a second later one thin arm slid over his shoulder blindly. He understood that she was slowly coming out of an hypnotic sleep. He wanted to shout, to laugh, to burst into tears. He clutched her all the tighter to him in his delirium of joy and hurried forward striving to find the narrow ribbon of road that would lead him back to the Westcott farm and the highway to Marlborough. He had forgotten the maniac farmers, Westcott and Burroughs, Martha Westcott, even Walden Slater. It was not until he had plunged one leg up to the knee in the slime of the marsh and knew that he was off the road that he reconsidered his predicament and knew that only Slater could guide him through the swamp. He turned and looked directly into the farmer's face. There was a light of victory in Walden Slater's countenance and his eyes glistened. In his hand he still held the revolver.

"Here," said the farmer. He reached down a burly arm and hauled both Dreeme and the girl back to the road. Then, without a word, he took Deborah from the young doctor's arms and stepped ahead. They circled the hollow partially without gazing through the bushes and soon struck the path by which they had come. Then, at a dog-trot, the sturdy farmer started back to town with Dreeme at his heels.

"What . . . happened?" inquired the young doctor breathlessly and bewilderedly.

"Judgment Day," replied Walden Slater. His voice was grim.

Behind them they could hear confused voices.

"Will there . . . be more . . . fighting?" panted Dreeme.

Walden Slater cleared his throat.

"Nope," he said.

He coughed loudly and spat into the darkness.

"Nothing to fight about," he added. "Nothing to make those fool farmers mad now. It's all over."

They went on in silence after that. It was not until they had left the swamp, climbed the open stretch into Briony Wood, and were once more among the trees that Walden Slater spoke again.

"Westcott got away," he said significantly. His voice was the voice of a trial judge. He was the law personified. Dreeme understood him perfectly.

"You've got five shells left," he said.

"We'll stop at the Westcott farm," replied the farmer.

Chapter Eleven

I

The twisting path through Briony Wood had never been traveled at such a speedy pace before. Walden Slater, carrying Deborah in his arms much as he might carry a small baby, maintained his dog-trot over the hummocky path, through puddles, across deceptive roots. As Dreeme, close behind him, running, too, in his bare feet, observed the square back of the farmer, a back against which the water-soaked shirt clung tightly and so revealed the contours of the great sliding back-muscles much as a skin might, a feeling of wonder and intense indebtedness crept over him. He had never known Walden Slater but now he knew him, knew him for a determined and relentless machine bent on justice. He had seen him in previous years bowed by the killing toil of his stony acres, eating gluttonously at table, sagging in his creaking rocker on the back porch, always silent, always (now that he came to think of it) self-contained. The young doctor's mind swept back over the past few days. Walden Slater eating cabbage. Walden Slater rocking in the darkness. Walden Slater finding words with difficulty, announcing that Deborah might stay with him as long as she pleased. Dreeme knew now that this statement was a secret challenge to Westcott and Burroughs. Walden Slater whittling on the back porch, asking the preacher for a knife. The knife was dull. How easily he had achieved this bit of detective acumen. Walden Slater thinking, reaching conclusions in that slow dogged mind that was, after all, so far from stupidity. Walden Slater watching night after night, keeping guard under the bright moon. Walden Slater like an enormous hound on the scent. Walden Slater rising like justice with the smoking gun in his hand. The figure of the farmer grew to colossal dimensions in the young doctor's estimation.

All this while they were hurrying through Briony Wood, hurrying through trees that were no longer malevolent spectres of a diseased fancy but merely slender birches and pines. Though the branches whipped across his face, though he stumbled into muddy hollows, though sharp thorns tore at his soiled and soaking garments, Dreeme no longer experienced that instinctive fear that had haunted him so short a time before. His body was emptied of fright. It was almost emptied of exertion as well for a growing hollowness within him, a tightening at the pit of his stomach, a painful numbness in his legs informed him that he was approaching the end of his endurance. Still, an implacable nervous energy pushed him forward, a febrile comprehension of one more important thing to be done. He knew what it was but he did not permit his mind to dwell upon it too fiercely. After all, what had he to do with the peculiar ideas of justice in the valley? He had seen what could be accomplished by established authority during the day following the murder of Wagner. Nothing. Absolutely nothing. There had been evasion, then, a deliberate slowness, a maddening deflection of proper proceedings. But this time it would be different. Justice would secure its own and would even the balance. He hurried on at the heels of Walden Slater serious but determined. He could see the loose hair of Deborah resting against the stout shoulder of the farmer and the sight of it filled him with a vast pity. It would be justice accomplished for her sake so far as he was concerned. She, the innocent victim, would be furiously avenged. Walden Slater might have the future of the whole valley in his thoughts, its complete release from an evil domination, but the safety of Deborah was enough for him to think about. There was only one way in which to fight madness.

They were at the height of Briony Wood now and the soughing wind was a cold lance against their faces. It was remarkable how swiftly they had proceeded on their return journey. The way to Dagon had seemed much longer. As they pressed forward the heavens seemed to split apart like two halves of a dark shell and out of the break sprang the moon like a great white seed. A milky light flooded the black shining leaves and the tall thin tree-trunks. It was like a miracle, a glittering phenomenon that translated the dripping environment into a place of mingled silver and tossed diamonds. There had been a moon like this when he had held Deborah's slight figure close against him and understood that she was an absolute part of his life. He had walked home that night from Humphrey Lathrop's cottage and phantoms had walked on either side of him. One of them had said: "I had a very good lawyer, Mr. Stopes." He had forgotten what the other phantom said. It did not exist any longer. It had been a world of glittering jewelry. It was marvelous, the way in which the earth changed. It was the slave of imagination, the willing Genie that brought whatsoever the dreamer desired. Though he was surrounded by trees and following a path that permitted no view of the country on either side he yet experienced the sensation that he was on a sort of Mount of Vision, that everything was being made clear to him here without words, that the answers to all he had been asking were in the sparkling moonlight and among the dark wet green leaves of the trees. He felt immeasurably grown in spiritual dimensions, enlarged so that he might contain all the love and wonder that abounded in the world. The uneven stones cut his feet but he was oblivious of them. Malicious branches lashed across his face like small whips but he laughed to himself as he thrust them aside. It was all right now.

The path turned and slanted downward and he understood that they were on the final stretch that led into Jeffrey Westcott's land. The name sprang back into his intelligence ominously and his lips tightened at the thought. There was still justice to be accomplished. Glancing back, he wondered vaguely what had become of the score of farmers who had gathered about the Devil Stone in that hollow which he should never see again. What justice could there be for those deluded men? He strove to remember what had actually happened but all he could recollect was the report of a gun, the log-like fall of Burroughs, and his own mad rush when he had snatched Deborah up from the stone and darted into the bushes with her. A vague idea of scattered running forms lingered in the back of his consciousness but he could not verify it by any reasoning. Had those men fled into the swamp or were they now slowly returning along the path which Walden Slater and he had followed? Were they, even now, lurking among the trees to the rearward of him, watching him with fanatic eyes, planning among themselves some secret onslaught? He could not tell and he did not care. He knew that the head of the serpent had been crushed in the Reverend George Burroughs and that the heart of the serpent would be stilled when justice was accomplished on Jeffrey Westcott. After that, the blind body could do what it desired. He understood that the frenzied farmers had been controlled by a malicious power of will and that when that will was destroyed there would be, as Walden Slater had said, "Nothing to fight about." Comforted by this thought, he plodded on, Walden Slater's dog-trot having dwindled to a fast walk on the downward grade.

The last stretch of woods passed swiftly and as the path turned and they faced the thinning trees Dreeme became aware of a reddish glow that lit up the heavens before him. It was not the light of the moon for that great white miracle hung directly above his head in the wide cleft of the split storm-cloud. It was something else, something that glowed upward from the ground, and as they burst through the final fringe of bushes into Westcott's back meadow, he saw that the mysterious farm-house was a mass of high leaping flames. At the same instant Walden Slater started forward in a run and the young doctor, accelerating his pace, followed closely at his heels. As he ran his mind automatically snapped back to a lighted lamp with a protector and a flying end of curtain that ever blew closer and closer to that lamp. Had they put that lamp out? He knew that they had done nothing of the sort, that, in their hurry, they had left it burning just as they had left the window open regardless of the wind that puffed the curtain inward. His first thought was one of relief that the farmhouse, a hive of malevolence, was burning up with its books, its sacrilegious altar, and its memories. The lair of the serpent was destroyed. Then he remembered the purpose that brought them back here. Where would Jeffrey Westcott be? Would he hide in the swamp while his years of evil knowledge went up in thick smoke and spurting flame? Walden Slater shifted Deborah from one shoulder to the other and ran all the faster.

II

A few men and women were gathered about the Westcott farm-house, gazing helplessly at the flame that thrust sudden tongues of fierce yellow through the shattered windows. Mrs. Slater, among them, moved, a small fluttering-eyed plump woman, back and forth, gesticulating but saying nothing. Her mouth opened and shut, a round black hole in the light of conflagration, but no sounds issued forth. In the first place, she could find nobody with whom to converse. There was Lucinda, sitting awkwardly in Humphrey Lathrop's old buggy, holding the somewhat startled horse tight-reined, as she watched the burning house, but Lucinda was speechless. She had nothing to say and she conveyed this to Mrs. Slater by a cold vinegary downward stare whenever the plump little woman wandered near the buggy. She was there to observe and then to report to Humphrey Lathrop who sat at home, a helpless mountain, waiting eagerly for news. As Dreeme and Walden Slater circled the house and came out on the Leeminster Road below it Mrs. Slater ran toward them.

"Where in the land's sake . . ." she began.

Walden Slater silenced her with a look.

He brushed by her speechless and she followed in his wake, a small fluttering-eyed creature. Behind them came Dreeme, unshaven, mud-splashed, soaked, barefooted. The farmer walked directly to Humphrey Lathrop's buggy.

"Get out, Lucinda," he said.

Lucinda turned her thin face down at him in wrathful amazement. She opened her mouth to retort and then she saw the senseless form of Deborah. Without a word she climbed from the buggy and, turning, lifted a rug to draw over Deborah as the farmer deposited her in the seat.

"I'll drive her down to Humphrey's," said Lathrop's housekeeper.

"Will she be safe?" interposed Dreeme hastily. He had visions of men leaping out from the side of the road. "Perhaps I'd . . ."

"She'll be safe," snapped Lucinda.

Without another word she climbed back into the buggy, picked up the reins, clucked to the horse, and the revolving wheels grated on the road. Dreeme stood watching the retreating carriage dubiously until he felt Walden Slater touch him on the arm. He turned with the farmer and they walked up the road toward the burning house.

"What time?" said Slater laconically to the group of watchers.

"'Bout two-thirty," answered one of the men.

"What time is it now?" questioned the farmer.

"'Bout three," the man returned.

Dreeme turned with Slater and watched the fire.

The flames, darting out of the windows, licked upward against the walls and the white paint sweated and bubbled in the fierce heat. A low roaring like the roaring in a wood-furnace reached the ears of the watchers. It was obviously too late to do anything. The entire interior of the farmhouse was burning. Dreeme could imagine the books in the library blackening in the smoke, their pages flaming along the edges and then spurting up furiously as the tomes tumbled forward to the floor. Small fiends screamed in the heat of those books. The wax figures were melting, running into mere blobs, then vanishing as the fire ate them up. The table at which Westcott had studied night after night was festooned with a dazzling magic. Even the window through which Martha Westcott had gazed was ringed with a bright frame of splendor. Low crashes reached the ears of the helpless watchers as objects within the cauldron of the building fell before the buffets of victorious flame. The wind blew; the flames darted up to heaven; a bellying scarlet-hued balloon of heavy smoke seemed attached to the house by ropes of yellow flame. It tugged at the dwelling, strove to lift it upward with an enormous strength. The house groaned and cracked. The rumbling of destruction continued within the white blistered walls.

It seemed as though any minute the house would be torn from its foundations and lifted high in the air leaving beneath it a flickering-tongued bonfire, a bonfire gigantic in size and unbearable in heat. The long ell of the kitchen was a mass of ochre flame now, a dancing madness against the darkness of the sky. Showers of sparks shot upward, dipped, and veered downward again like fire-works. With a rumbling crash the roof of the kitchen fell in and the detonation of the collapse was like a discharge of cannon in Dreeme's ears. These old houses burned quickly. Time had seasoned the wood for destruction, dried it out, honeycombed it with the tiny tunnels of wood-borers so that the bright spirit of destruction might dart along it. It was all going now, chairs, tables, wax flowers beneath glass, family portraits. The spirit of things was turning all this into a heap of smoking débris, of blackened jagged beams and heaps of fuming ashes. Dreeme stood in the glare of the flame beside Walden Slater and his face burned with the heat. His few garments smoked and dried. His skin seemed crawling and parched. He felt as though he were watching the fires of Tophet. He glanced about him at the group of sober-faced observers and suddenly caught his breath in his throat. Leaning sideways he struck his hand against Walden Slater's arm and when the farmer turned his slow eyes toward him he indicated an eddying knot of men some distance from the conflagration. The farmer studied them with narrowed lids but said nothing. Then, with the utmost calm, he resumed his attention of the burning house. He seemed to be watching the second-floor windows, windows through which wisps of curling smoke projected like lost snakes. Dreeme was faintly astonished at his lack of interest in the men toward whom he had directed Walden Slater's attention. For his own part, he continued to keep a watch on them, observing them sideways through the corners of his eyes.

These men were not so far away but what he could recognize them. They were muddy and distracted in demeanor, uncertain of themselves, self-conscious of their presence in the light of the burning building. They clung together as though for common strength. In the center of the small group Dreeme could see the lanky figure of Bidwell and beside him was the white-haired Corey. Threading the clustered group, talking first to one man and then to another, was Lacy, his carbuncular nose glowing in the fierce light of the flames. How they had emerged on the road, whether they had followed along the narrow path from Nigger Swamp or found some secret passage directly across the sunken marsh were mysteries to Dreeme. He did not care greatly how they had reached this spot. The main thing was that they were here, that they dared show themselves in public. He wondered if others in that mad group had followed Lathrop's buggy to town and this conjecture aroused an angry fear in him. He stared boldly at the group and scowled. These men were equally aware of him and Walden Slater for they persisted in glancing toward them as they continued their nervous conversation. Once Bidwell gesticulated openly toward the young doctor. They were strong men, broad-shouldered, browned by changing seasons, hard-sinewed and tight-lipped. Still Dreeme felt no fear, nothing but a righteous fury. A loud crash before him diverted his attention to the farm-house. The right wall of the kitchen had fallen in. When, after observing the shower of flame and sparks, he resumed his observation of the self-conscious knot of men the white-haired Corey was walking slowly toward him. The grave old man continued his approach until he was within a yard of Dreeme and then he turned and surveyed the fire. The young doctor, trembling at the nearness of this man whom he had seen so shortly before in the grasp of a mystic delirium, said nothing although a flood of recriminatory words rose in his throat and quivered on his lips. He thought it peculiar that Walden Slater made no gesture of recognition, that he stood so easily with his attention apparently confined to the blazing building before him. Corey moved a single step sideways toward Dreeme and still keeping his eyes directed before him began to speak. He said:

"Doctor Dreeme, after a great madness comes a great sanity."

Walden Slater, beside the young doctor, was listening, too, although his expressionless face did not shift from its steadfast inspection of the burning farm-house. Dreeme made no answer to Corey. The old farmer spoke again. He said:

"You have evidently seen what you have seen. You can never see it again."

He extended one hand as though he were discussing the fire. At a distance the little knot of farmers observed them fixedly. Corey said:

"There are no explanations. The chain is broken. I am an old man, Doctor Dreeme, and I know what I am talking about. I am speaking for a score of men who were lost and who, through a great shock, have found themselves. I cannot tell you what dominated us but the domination has ceased. The valley is cleansed. We are cleansed. We ask for silence."

There was something behind his words that impressed Dreeme. He opened his mouth to speak but Walden Slater forestalled him. The farmer said:

"We lost our tongues in Nigger Swamp."

Corey observed the fire fiercely.

"What's done is done," added Slater mildly.

"Let what's done rot with the body by the stone," said Corey softly.

After a moment he withdrew quietly and a second later Dreeme saw him back among the little knot of perturbed men. There was a brief conversation and then calm blank faces resumed their observation of the flame-wreathed Westcott farm-house.

"What does this mean?" inquired Dreeme of Walden Slater.

The farmer shifted his feet.

"It means what it means," he said. "Let that be enough for you, Doctor."

Dreeme wondered if it meant no retribution for these men who were willing to connive at the destruction of a human being. He opened his mouth to say something to this effect when the farmer snatched at him. At the same time an exclamation of mingled surprise and horror rose from the group of people in the road. Dreeme turned hastily toward the burning house.

In one of the upper windows through which the thin snakes of curling smoke had crept stood a man. There was flame in that window now and he was silhouetted against the bright flare. He seemed just about to leap for one foot was on the sill of the window and one heavy arm was raised against the side of the house. Dreeme saw the fierce light play over a cloven skull and lowered forehead. He saw, in the man's other hand, a black book clutched tightly. All this he saw in an instant for even as he looked the window-sill seemed to cave inward to crumbling fire and the figure, black against the light, fell backward, one hand snatching desperately at the air. The next instant a great puff of flame surged through the vacant window. There was nothing there, nothing but a roaring cauldron that devoured its own. The destroyed building seemed to emit a great sigh of relief, a hoarse gasp that soared upward and spread out over Marlborough. Dreeme imagined that sigh of relief permeating the air as far as Leeminster, sweeping through the moonlit heavens and driving the intangible mists of mystery before it, cleansing the valley of an old horror. He even pictured a calmness and relief on the attentive and wide-eyed faces that watched, as he did, this instantaneous tragedy. There seemed to be nothing left to say, nothing to do but watch or go home. Walden Slater, after his first instinctive grasp at the young doctor, had said nothing. He stood with his great shoulders bowed, his long lip dangling loose, his coat gaping and, through its opening, the revolver glistening. Dreeme suddenly felt exhausted, a complete exhaustion that was flesh-weariness and great relief mingled.

III

Humphrey Lathrop put his tea-cup down and wiped his huge pursing lips. He nodded slowly.

"Yes, sir," he said, "Walden's right. Walden's a great fellow. He knows where justice is due."

The bright sunlight of the early afternoon plucked at the curtains. A refreshed and neatly shaved Dreeme sat before the ancient oracle, toying with his cup of tea.

"Perhaps you'd like apple-jack, Daniel?" The old doctor was solicitous. Dreeme shook his head slowly.

"No," he said. "I don't understand it all."

"You never will," replied Humphrey Lathrop. "You are too young to understand anything."

He said it pleasantly.

"And why shouldn't the farmers get off scot-free?" asked Lathrop, pursuing the thread of the conversation. "They haven't done anything." Dreeme opened his eyes very wide.

"No, they haven't," persisted the old doctor. "Corey was right. Corey is a good man. They're all good men."

Dreeme sat looking at him in amazement. Humphrey Lathrop chuckled wheezily, leaned over, and prodded the young doctor.

"Use your head, Daniel," he said. "Use your head even if you have lost it."

He wheezed again merrily at that.

"Do you hold a sick man accountable for what he does when he's out of his head?" asked the old doctor.

Dreeme shook his head negatively.

"All right," said Humphrey Lathrop conclusively. That seemed to settle it for the old doctor looked in his empty tea-cup, wheezed mournfully, and then chuckled.

"I never felt so young in eighty years," he remarked blandly to the room in general.

Dreeme had to smile at that.

"Now, *say!*" exclaimed Lathrop. He pounded vigorously with his cane. An instant later Lucinda's vinegary visage thrust itself through the door.

"The apple-jack bottle and two glasses," ordered the old doctor. Lucinda's visage wrinkled into an absurd map. She started to withdraw her head when Lathrop shook his huge cane.

"Y'd better make it three glasses," he declared, winking in a knowing manner at Dreeme.

"I'll bring four," announced Lucinda in nasal tones. "I believe a teeny mite 'ud do me good."

She withdrew the wrinkled map of her visage after strangely contorting it. Lathrop stared after her with his mouth open.

"I believe the old fool was laughing," he said in a husky whisper. Then he chuckled. He beamed. His three chins shook waggishly. He added:

"Well, well, well!"

It seemed a period to Dreeme's adventures. Suddenly Lathrop's crinkling face sobered. He leaned forward and said to Dreeme hastily:

"I heard this morning from young Barnson. He'd been over to Leeminster. He saw a tall dark woman come into town. She had no luggage. She engaged a buggy to take her over to Pittsfield. She . . . ."

Dreeme raised his hand.

"She's gone," he said. "And that's that."

"That's that," agreed the old doctor cheerfully.

The door was pushed open and Lucinda stalked in balancing a tray on which reposed a bottle and four tumblers. Dreeme did not see her. He had risen to his feet and was gazing past her at the slight figure that came smilingly at her heels.

The girl's eyes were like wet violets, a soaked blue so deep as to be astonishing.

Afterword: Gorman and Lovecraft

I am sure I am not the only person to have been intrigued when, many years ago, I first read H. P. Lovecraft's comment in *Supernatural Horror in Literature* about Herbert Gorman's *The Place Called Dagon,* "which relates the dark history of a western Massachusetts backwater where the descendants of refugees from the Salem witchcraft still keep alive the morbid and degenerate horrors of the Black Sabbat." Now I knew that Lovecraft himself had written a story early in his career called "Dagon"; and in my youthful naïveté and ignorance I wildly conjectured that Gorman might have been a friend of Lovecraft who had written this novel as a tribute to his mentor. Perhaps Gorman was the first "Cthulhu Mythos" writer!

It did not take me long to ascertain that this was impossible, and that Gorman almost certainly knew nothing of Lovecraft's existence. Still, that plot description sounded uncannily Lovecraftian, and I sought out this rare book with fervency. Finally locating it, I read the book at last and came to the conclusion that the novel may well have influenced Lovecraft, specifically in "The Dunwich Horror" (1928), "The Shadow over Innsmouth" (1931) and "The Dreams in the Witch House" (1932). But this is by no means the most important thing about *The Place Called Dagon;* the fact of the matter is that it is a thoroughly entertaining and substantial horror novel.

It is clear, as Larry Creasy has elucidated in his introduction, that Gorman drew upon his Massachusetts upbringing for *The Place Called Dagon.* In this novel he evokes—as powerfully as any writer aside from Hawthorne and Lovecraft—the hoary antiquity of New England and the long, dark shadow cast by the region's Puritan heritage. The tale is set in Leominster (which, for some reason, Gorman spells Leeminster) and Marlborough, small towns northeast of Gorman's native Springfield. Is it merely coincidence that Lovecraft—who read the novel in April 1928—used this approximate location as the setting of his imaginary town of Dunwich in "The Dunwich Horror," written that August? Curiously enough, Lovecraft's initial impressions of the novel were not entirely favourable; he wrote to August Derleth (2 April 1928): "I have also read Gorman's 'Place Called Dagon'—which is rather puerile & poorly written; but which held my interest because of the authentic New England colour & certain isolated bits of weird atmosphere whose merit is undeniable. I advise you to read it." To be sure, Lovecraft's impressions of "Dunwich" were largely formed by his visit that summer to the home of Edith Miniter in Wilbraham, but the very idea of using a central Massachusetts locale may have come from Gorman.

Although much of the action of *The Place Called Dagon* is seen through the eyes, ears, and voice of Daniel Dreeme, a young doctor who takes up his practice there, Dreeme is not in fact the central figure in the novel. This role is shared by two individuals, Doctor Humphrey Lathrop, a huge and ancient man who chose Dreeme as his successor upon his retirement, and Jeffrey Westcott, a learned and sinister figure who has entered the area for purposes of his own. Lathrop appears to be the fount of all knowledge in the region; and in this sense he bears a certain resemblance to Zadok Allen in "The Shadow over Innsmouth." Like Lathrop, Zadok is an aged toper who knows the ancient secrets of Innsmouth but will reveal them only when his tongue is sufficiently loosened by draughts of bootleg whiskey (Lathrop's preferred tipple is apple-jack). Westcott, on the other hand, appears to be a significant model for the figure of Wilbur Whateley in "The Dunwich Horror"—a man seeking to bring back the "old gods" by means of incantations out of a hoary tome of occult lore. The frequent mentions of the Black Man of the witches' sabbath recalls the similar use Lovecraft made of the term in "The Dreams in the Witch House," although his Black Man was the more redoubtable figure of Nyarlathotep.

The Place Called Dagon—along with such other distinctive works as Francis Brett Young's *Cold Harbour* (1925), Leonard Cline's *The Dark Chamber* (1927), or R. E. Spencer's *The Lady Who Came to Stay* (1931)—could only have been written, and published, at a time when there was no such thing as a "horror genre." All these novels were issued by mainstream publishers, and all these works were written by writers who by no means specialised in horror or published in pulp magazines, but who simply happened in this one instance to be attracted to a supernatural or weird scenario. I suppose something of the sort has always gone on, and perhaps in some senses still goes on today, as mainstream writers write the occasional horror novel in order (as Lovecraft piquantly put it) to "discharge from their minds certain phantasmal shapes which would otherwise haunt them." It is too early to say whether the novels of Peter Ackroyd or Michael Cadnum will ever have quite the charm of the works I have just mentioned. Perhaps they may in fifty years. In the meantime, Gorman's *The Place Called Dagon* remains a book that, until now, the ardent weird bibliophile has had to scour used bookstores or rare-book catalogues to secure. It is very much a lost classic of our little realm.

It is not at all surprising that Lovecraft found the novel compelling. Its ruminations on the dour Puritans, strikingly similar to what he had written in "The Picture in the House" (1920); the mention of "old gods" who lurk behind the surface events; the occult books mentioned throughout the text, some of which are the very ones that Lovecraft cites in his stories; and even Westcott's brief mention of a journey overseas to pursue his eccentric research, exactly analogous to that of Charles Dexter Ward—all these and other elements in *The Place Called Dagon* may have made Lovecraft think of it as a novel he himself could have written. Indeed, one wonders whether his reluctance to submit *The Case of Charles Dexter Ward*— which remained unpublished until after his death—was in some small part due to his suspicion that it might be thought too similar to *The Place Called Dagon*. Whatever the case, Gorman's novel is of consuming interest to the Lovecraft devotee; but it deserves recognition not merely because Lovecraft appreciated it.

   The Place Called Dagon is only one of the many "lost" works of weird fiction that deserve resurrection. If it has gained a new life, it is largely thanks to H. P. Lovecraft's diligence in scouring the obscure corners of the already obscure realm of supernatural fiction and recording his appreciation in letters and essays. Lovecraft knew that he was working within a limited but well-defined literary tradition, and he felt it his duty to read both the past and the present masters of his field before undertaking his own ventures. But it was more than a duty; it was an active pleasure for him to stumble across some forgotten minor classic of the weird and to sample its reserves of wonder and terror long after it had faded into oblivion. We ourselves now have increasing opportunities to duplicate that pleasure, as one by one these lost gems are unearthed to shine for a new generation.

—S. T. JOSHI

Breinigsville, PA USA
24 December 2009
229731BV00001B/6/P